Róisín Campbell

An Irishwoman in Gilded Age New York

Joseph P. Garland

Author of
A Studio on Bleecker Street
and *A Maid's Life*

DermodyHouse.com

The characters and events portrayed in this book are fictitious. Any similarity to real persons, living or dead, is coincidental and not intended by the author except that several characters are historical figures. Sister Helen Bowdin was a London nurse who was the first director of the Bellevue School of Nursing, and Mr. William Osborn and Dr. W. Gill Wylie were New Yorkers who were instrumental in establishing that school. Also, Cardinal John McCloskey was the archbishop of the Archdiocese of New York from 1864 to 1885; he became America's first cardinal in early 1875, which is at the very end of this story.

ISBN: 978-1-7355923-0-5 (paperback)

The Cover; *The Blue Feather* (1917), by the American William J. Edmondson (1868–1966). The model is Caroline Mytinger. Kindly made available by the Open Access policy of the Cleveland Museum of Art.
https://www.clevelandart.org/art/1917.400

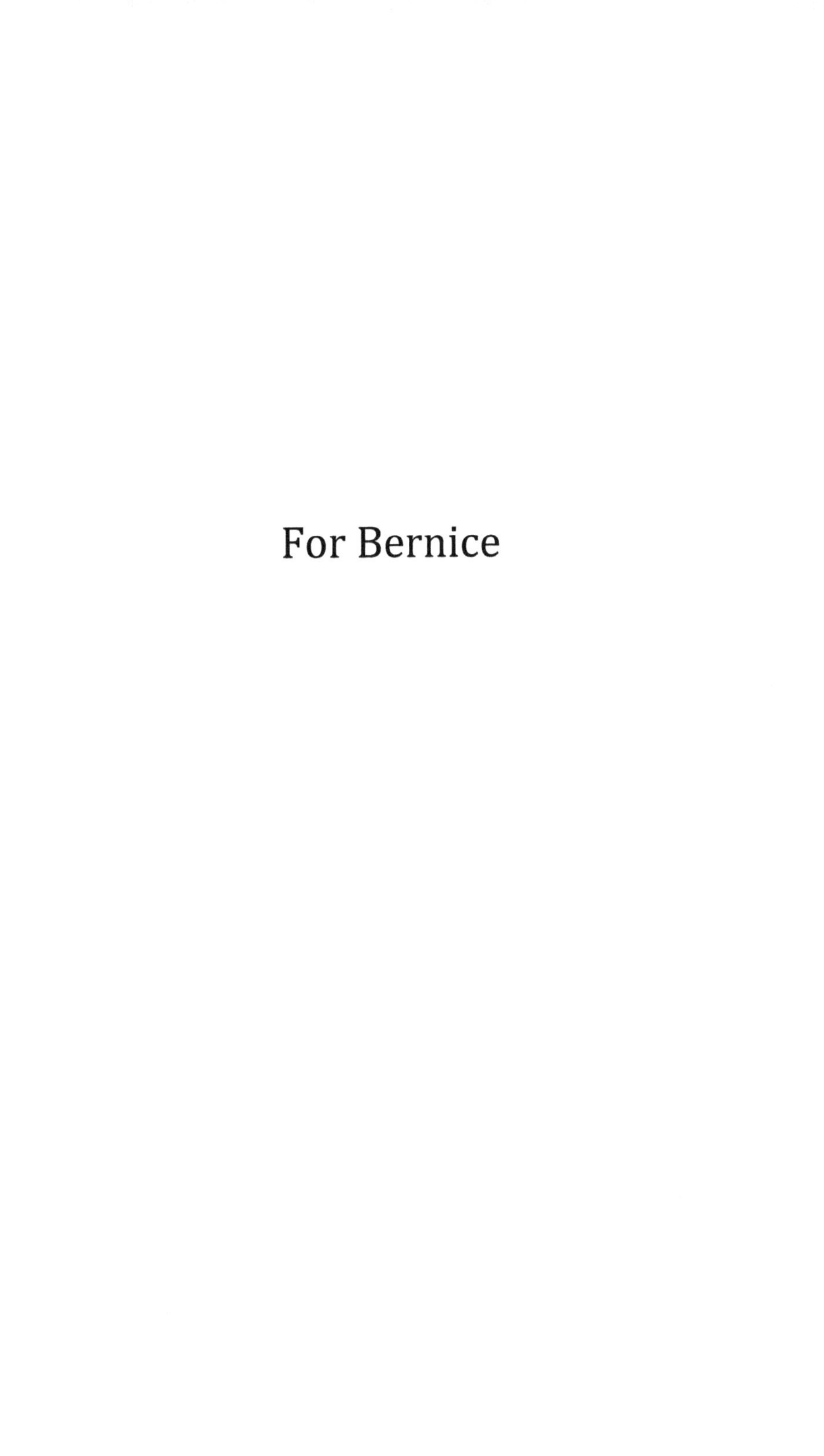

For Bernice

1.

"**Y**our beauty will be your curse."

Róisín Campbell was eighteen. She could take no credit for how she looked. Yet she did not deserve to be punished for it. Now, though, she was being dismissed because of her "beauty."

The woman who said this to Róisín, the woman who was dismissing her, was Abigail Geherty. She was the mistress in the house where Róisín was a maid. Róisín did nothing to warrant dismissal. She was conscientious. She obeyed orders. She did it all well.

"You are a clever girl and I know you work hard. But I am afraid that Mrs. Collins"—Mrs. Collins was the dour housekeeper—"says you are at times a bit forward with my sons and their friends."

"Ma'am. I admit to being friendly, but I have never—"

"It may not have been intentional, Róisín, but the effect is the same. Men are enough trouble at any time but with…someone as pretty as you, it is too far. I am sorry."

It was not her sons and their friends that concerned Mrs. Geherty, although her eldest daughter, Mary, was vocal in her dislike for the servant. No. It was her husband, Charles. He seemed to have taken a particular liking to this young farmgirl who had been in America for just under twelve months, the last ten in the employ of the Geherty House. She did nothing improper and it is doubtful that she exchanged more than a few dozen words with Charles Geherty. Still, his wife was well within her rights in doing what she was doing.

Róisín expected she would be dismissed when she was told by Mrs. Collins before the family was up that "Mistress wants to see you in her study." She had just finished her breakfast and wore her uniform of a black frock and white apron with a cap pinned across her rusty-red hair, which she kept in a bun. The other staff watched her follow Mrs. Collins out. They liked her well enough, but this was not their battle.

Róisín and Mrs. Collins climbed the servants' stairs to the second floor and walked down a broad hallway. Mrs. Collins knocked on the third door on the left and opened it when Mrs. Geherty bade them enter.

The study was painted in a pastel blue with complementing yellow wainscoting, and a vase graced a table in one corner, brimming with flowers (shortly to be replaced by freshly-cut ones) whose fragrance colored the room. Mrs. Geherty's desk was in the Louis XIV style, and with the room facing the rear, the sound through the open windows was that of morning birds going about their business in and above the rear gardens of the Gehertys and of their neighbors. There were flowers in the room's fireplace instead of wood and screens in the windows, it being early summer in 1871.

The pair stood before the desk where Mrs. Geherty sat in a wrapper dress. She asked Róisín to take a seat and asked Mrs. Collins to leave.

The maid sat as her mistress toyed with a piece of paper on the otherwise empty desk before looking up. Róisín's back was stiff, in the manner drilled into her, though she'd never sat before Mrs. Geherty. She recalled being in this room with her only once before, on the day she was retained.

Today, though, Mrs. Geherty displayed none of the light-heartedness of that other morning. After remarking on Róisín's beauty, she said, "I am truly sorry, Róisín. You are a good girl. But you must find another position. I will provide you with a testimonial, and you will surely find something."

The girl nodded and then returned her eyes to the hands clenching and unclenching in her lap. Had she been told the day before that this would happen she would not have believed it. While Mrs. Collins's command in the kitchen helped to prepare her, Mrs. Geherty's words felt like a slap, however gently she delivered them.

Róisín's mistress lifted the paper. "Here are families that you shall not approach." She handed it to Róisín, who reached across the desk for it. On it were the names of Irish-American families with whom the Gehertys socialized, all with mistresses about the age of Mrs. Geherty and masters about the age—in their late forties—of Mr. Geherty.

"I understand, Ma'am. Thank you."

"You may leave," Mrs. Geherty said as she sat back in her chair. Róisín again nodded and rose before heading to the door. She held the list tightly in her left hand. When she reached the door, the girl turned and with her head lowered, she curtsied. Mrs. Geherty stood and approached. "I think and I pray that you will do well." Róisín shook the hand that was unexpectedly extended to her. She gave a slight bow and another awkward curtsey.

"Thank you, Mrs. Geherty. I hope so."

The now-dismissed servant walked through the door and climbed to her room to gather her belongings. It was a small room on the top floor, beneath the sloped roof. There was a tiny window with a small, yellowed lace curtain providing slight shade. The room's size was a blessing; Róisín had it to herself. The bed was old and lumpy, but it was flat, and she was provided with enough blankets when it was cold. It was not cold now, though, and the summer air was finding its way through the city. She was in part relieved not to have to suffer in the heat of August in a small room with a small window on the top floor.

Róisín owned only a few things—three frocks and two pairs of shoes, three bonnets, plus an assortment of undergarments and stockings. There were the photos of her parents and siblings. A Claddagh ring. Letters from home, chiefly from her mother. The necklace given to her by the family on St. Stephen's Day. Her books, some, including the Gaelic Bible, she'd carried from Ireland and others she bought since her arrival. She had neither the money nor the inclination to buy things since coming to New York, except for her books. She sent some of what she made home and kept the rest inside a sock. It was not much, but it would keep her going till she found another position and another place to live. She lay these few things in the satchel she carried from Ireland.

She sat on the bed and ran a hand across the rough blanket. After a minute or two of looking around, she rose. Her door was open, but Róisín heard a knock. Mrs. Collins was making sure she was gathering what was hers so she would be gone before lunch. And not gathering what was not hers.

"Come on, now. We don't have the whole day."

"May I take—?"

"You take what's yours. And leave the rest. Now let's get you out of here. The mistress wants you gone."

There was an embroidered seat cushion she fancied, but as it was not hers it would remain. After a final look around, she put the satchel over her right shoulder. Mrs. Collins stepped aside to let her pass and stayed close behind her in the hallway.

"And don't think of going through the front door," she said as they went down the servants' stairs.

As Róisín reached the basement floor, her escort took something from the table. An envelope.

"Here's the testimonial—probably better than you deserve if you ask me—and two weeks' pay—which is better than you deserve, as we all know. Now go on."

Biddy, the chambermaid with whom she was closest, was tending to something, and she looked out to watch

Róisín leave by the side entrance, giving a slight wave, which Róisín returned with a nod. No one else came to see her go or did anything, and an hour later she sat in a dark tavern named The Thistle near where she'd spent her first night in America.

2.

It was just about a year earlier and Róisín Campbell's final day in Hospital, the farming town on the eastern edge of County Limerick where she was born. She did not know what time it was when she shot up from what had been a deep sleep. All was quiet except for the rhythmic breathing of her sleeping sister, Sophie. It was dark, too dark to see anything, and thus her hearing seemed heightened. And she understood that she would never again hear what she heard at that moment. Her sister would never be dreaming beside her. The slight Limerick wind she would wake to in the night would never whistle through her room.

It was that realization, the concept of *never again*, that finally chilled her. She long knew the day would come. It was a Wednesday in June of 1870. Her eyes were open, but it made no difference in the pitch black. Still, it gave her the illusion that she was seeing something, and the something she *imagined* she was seeing was burning into her memory. From the ceiling to the bedroom to the farmhouse itself. Moving from room to room, imagining she was running her fingers along the walls and the windowsills and the tops of the old, dark furniture she took for granted. The kitchen with its pots dangling. The outhouse discreetly in the rear corner of the yard, sometimes too far and sometimes not far enough from the back door.

Soon—she could not know how soon—her daddy and her brothers Liam and Aidan would be heading into the fields with the dog to drive the cows to the barn for milking. Her mamma would start making a small breakfast while she and Sophie tried to stay in bed as long as they could. Róisín had three older sisters and another older brother, but the oldest sister, Ciara, was married with a baby girl on the Owens farm about a mile to the north and the other two sisters were off in Liverpool, working as maids. John, the second son, was in Liverpool too, working on the docks. The night before, her mamma gave Róisín the letters the three in England wrote to her, and each told of how there was a good, or good enough, life away from the farm. That she should not be afraid though she was going far, far away.

Her mamma also handed her the letter from her sister's son Jimmy, who worked on the New York docks. In it, Jimmy said he would see to Róisín when she arrived and that he hoped he could help her get placed at the home of an admirable Irish-American family once she received training.

Hours after reading those letters, she was looking at the dark ceiling and trying to memorize every part of the house that was her home since she was born there just over eighteen years before, and she could not control her sobs. She refused to cry before about this. She knew that she would have to leave. She was strong till that moment. The farm, because of where it was, was prosperous with its dairy products, especially its butter, finding its way to England's booming industrial north. It did not suffer as the small parcels in the west and northwest did during the Famine, but even so, it could only support one boy. The rest had to leave. So Liam would stay and he would marry the eldest daughter of a nearby farm—much as Ciara married Gerry Owens—and Aidan and Sophie would follow her or their other siblings to England or America when they, too, turned eighteen.

Róisín fell back asleep, and it took several shakes from Sophie to awaken her.

"Get up, you fool. Today's no day to sleep in." Sophie was a troubling sort and far too unsettled in Róisín's mind, even for a fifteen-year-old. Still, Róisín would miss her.

Things were somber when she reached the kitchen, and her mamma insisted that Róisín do nothing but be waited upon. She told her mamma when she saw the men finished with their milking, and Mrs. Campbell got the tea ready. Everyone was quiet as they had their eggs and toast and tea, and they were somber as they went about doing chores. For those in the house, the ticking of the clock above the mantel in the front room seemed to get louder with each minute, approaching the moment when Róisín would have to leave to be in Knocklong to catch a train that would begin her journey to New York.

Liam carried Róisín's satchel to the parlor. She'd packed it the night before with her mamma, and it contained the clothes they bought two weeks earlier in Limerick City supplemented by family mementos, her siblings' and Cousin Jimmy's letters, and three of her beloved books. Her daddy made a point of buying one for her when he went to the city. She was a good, bright student, and she read alone when she could in quiet times and appreciated that her parents did all they could to encourage it, hoping it would give her an advantage in her new life.

Finally, Róisín's mamma went to her room and she sat on the bed with her child, holding her hands, and Róisín put her head on her mamma's shoulder as the others had done before her, and her mamma said everything would be grand. Not long after that, Liam rushed in.

"Daddy says...you must get going," and he hurried down the stairs, followed a long minute later by the two women, who went to the drive at the front of the house as Liam put Róisín's satchel in the back of the single-horse trap her pa had brought around. Mamma handed her a large package containing food to have until she reached Queenstown, where she would board a boat to New York. Aidan and Sophie were joined by Ciara, holding her baby and beside her husband, as well as some of Róisín's friends. One by one they hugged and kissed her—except for little Meghan Owens, who received Róisín's lips on her forehead—until she reached her mamma, and that dear woman clutched her tightly and made her daughter promise to be a source of the family's pride.

Finally, Róisín joined her daddy in the trap for the six-mile journey south to Knocklong. There she would catch a train that would ultimately take her through Cork City and to the port of Queenstown where she would spend the night in a hotel. It was a pleasant day, and Róisín sought to imprint it on her memory as she looked back one final time just as the trap started a turn that would forever leave the farm behind. With a wave, it was gone.

Her father was his usual taciturn self for the early portion of the ride, and Róisín's head leaned against his shoulder. Neighbors on farms along the way stood at their stone walls to wave their own goodbyes and shout their own encouragements as had become a ritual, and they stopped at the church, where the teacher, Mr. Sullivan, reached up to her to hug her goodbye and the parish priest, Father Crowe, handed her the book, a Bible in Gaelic, he gave each who left. After the Campbells received his blessing, they continued south, and Róisín took her last look at the town and could just see the church's steeple until it, too, was all gone.

As they neared Knocklong, her daddy spoke in a way he never had before.

"Your mamma and I will miss you, that's for sure. You understand why it must be?"

"Yes, daddy."

"From Jimmy, we hear good things about New York. And some bad things, too. You are a good girl. I know you will do good."

"I will, daddy."

"Lots of people who are not like us, though. Some very poor. They are God's creatures and do not forget that. You will also see people who think themselves superior to you. Like the English do. Remember you are a good, Irish girl."

"I will, daddy."

"And be sure to write to your mamma regular. Some of the ones in Liverpool are not so good. But you are in America. Write when you can."

"Yes, daddy."

They arrived at the station shortly after nine. Róisín's daddy handed her a bag with money. This was for the train and the boat and the hotel in Queenstown plus enough, according to Jimmy, to tide her over until she could cash the modest bank draft her daddy got for her in Limerick City, which was safely stowed in her satchel. He also reserved a cabin for her on the boat so she would not be in steerage. While sailing ships still plied the route to New York and were cheaper, they were also far less predictable or comfortable, and the Campbells could afford passage on the *City of Paris* steamship. It was among the fastest that made the crossing.

Father and daughter found a place for the trap, and after Róisín bought her ticket, they went to the platform. When the train pulled in some ten minutes later, the two hugged. She put her head out the window and waved as she looked upon her father, waving back, for the last time.

As the train neared Cork some hours later, Róisín was amazed at how crowded and congested everything seemed. She was in Limerick City a few times. It was nothing compared to this. But she was in Cork only briefly as she switched to the train to Queenstown. She had the name of a small hotel near the quay. At the desk, she was asked what boat she was on and when it was departing. Róisín shared a room with another girl, from County Sligo. She'd arrived at the hotel the day before, and the two went to the dining room. It was full of girls and boys near Róisín's age and some older men and women and some families with wee ones. All were waiting to go to America, and Róisín was at a table with seven others.

"You think Cork is big, lasses?" It was addressed to the table by an older man. "I hear tell that 'tis tiny compared to New York." He slurped his soup, and his wife said, "And the hurrying. Our son be there, and he says they never stop. But he says it'd be a good life for us." They looked to be from a farm, and Róisín could not place their accent, and she missed some of their words.

After the meal, Róisín went out with her roommate and several others for the air of their last night. They were mostly quiet, paired arm-in-arm till dusk appeared. Róisín had never seen the water before, though some of the girls from the west had. The group strolled to the quay, where they saw the *City of Paris* on which they would all sail to America, and they watched the darkness cover it and the sea. They returned to the travelers' hotel, going to their rooms to sleep at home one last time.

3.

The *City of Paris* had both cabins and steerage. Róisín could afford a small cabin in second class, though the others she walked with that night in Queenstown were deep belowdecks in steerage. She tried not to become too attached to such girls. They were the ones in desperate straits, and she wanted nothing to do with them.

She would find work as a domestic servant, she hoped, preferably in a mansion of one of the wealthy Irish families she heard about at home. Cousin Jimmy spoke in his letter of a connection to a grand house with a good master and a kind mistress and that he expected that she could maybe work there.

Róisín was not so foolish as to believe a well-bred and handsome gentleman would carry her away, notwithstanding how often it happened in the romances she read and re-read. She knew they were fantasies, and that no man of a good family would marry a farmgirl, no matter how handsome he might think her. To such a family, she would be little better than the poor from the west of Ireland who could barely speak let alone read English. She knew there would be many a man in a good family who would seek to take advantage of her, promising her all manner of things to seduce her and that such a man would be her ruination. There were many such rakes in her books too.

Róisín had her share of attempted liaisons with the idiot boys around her farm and in the village. Older ones especially, making her silly promises, promises even they did not believe.

Still, she feared she would end up in the squalor she read about in other, more serious books set in London and Manchester and prayed that that would not be her fate, and she took comfort in the letters her mamma received from her sisters in Liverpool about their hard but tolerable lives in service. During mass on the fourth day out, she could not help but feel some sympathy and more pity for the girls and boys, most about her age, from steerage. Yellow and thin, they were.

Róisín's fate would be different. *She* would find a position in a fine home—her cousin practically promised which one in his letter—and she would be clean and presentable and fed. She would have a kindly mistress who would speak to her and treat her properly and recognize her grace and intelligence. Perhaps she'd be allowed to read some of the books that cluttered the grand library she was certain the master would keep.

She was relieved that she was not one of those she pitied. These thoughts hardened on board, when she had much time to think of what lay ahead. She encountered the occasional first-class passenger-of-means aiming to establish himself in America. Indeed, on the evening of the third day, a young dandy who wore a diamond pin in his cravat approached her as he strolled after dinner. He called himself Michael Henry from Cork City and assured her that he would soon make his fortune in American railroads or trade. He was a handsome man, though not tall, with a well-trimmed beard and an easy smile. He could not be more than five or six years older than her. He presented her with his card and urged her to contact him at his New York banker's office. He would, he said, be happy to spend some time with her as they both became accustomed to the new world. Perhaps a dinner?

He was, in fact, a creature of such absurdity, an absurdity of which he was well aware, that he must have learned how to behave from one of Róisín's novels. But Róisín was pleasant. From then, each evening (save the sixth when an Atlantic storm kept everyone from the decks) the pair strolled together often, and Róisín found it the highlight of her day.

On the morning of the ninth day, she crowded the deck railing with the other passengers as the steamer headed into New York harbor. The crowd was too large for her to find Mr. Henry. She was amazed by the buildings in Cork, but this was miles different, the towers lining the waterfront as far as she could see. The water itself was chock-a-block with ships and boats and ferries going hither and yon, again and again avoiding collisions that to Róisín's farmgirl eyes seemed inevitable.

The *City of Paris* arrived on schedule. As she docked, doctors came on board to examine the passengers. Róisín was permitted to disembark ahead of those in steerage. She was herded through New York's processing center on the southern tip of Manhattan, and when that was done, she was in America. She wondered, but only for a moment, whether she would ever again encounter the girls she walked with in Queenstown the night before they left Ireland.

When through with the processing, she was pleased that Mr. Henry had not forsaken her. He stood on the sidewalk, reminding her that he looked forward to meeting her again, reminding her of his banker's name and New York address. He offered to have a cab take her where she was going, but after asking for directions found that she had but a few blocks to walk. He doffed his hat to her and kissed her hand before signaling a cab to collect him. She waited until he and his trunk were in the cab and watched him give a final wave as he headed north.

Róisín again pulled out Jimmy's letter with its direction for how to find him. It was, as she said, not far. She carried her satchel north and to the right, or east, side of Manhattan. Even this small corner of the City was a mass of rushing. Of strangers seamlessly navigating their way through the crowds, pushing and jostling with no ill-intent in their hurry to get somewhere other than where they were. The streets and sidewalks were paved, though not in gold, and the former had a patina of manure as well as civil servants with shovels and cans who did what they could to make them passable and tolerable to those walking or riding by.

Soon she caught sight of a large structure along the docks. As she neared it, she saw crowds of men congregated. She fought her way through, though news of her presence quickly spread, and a path opened before her. She entered the building. It was a large hall with a dais on one end, on which a cluster of men in suits and ties sat. It was to them that she was directed. When she reached the dais, a portly man in an ill-fitted suit looked down on her.

"Might I help you, lass?" It was a strong brogue, distinct from what Róisín was used to.

It was evident that she was just arrived, carrying as she was her satchel and wearing clothes that showed the effects of her journey.

"Aye. I am looking for Jimmy Regan. He is my cousin."

The man looked to the side.

"Anyone know this Jimmy Regan?"

A short man came to the front.

"I do." He pulled out a book and after scanning several pages pronounced that Jimmy Regan was working on Pier Six, with the *Ajax*.

The portly gentlemen looked down.

"I'll send someone to fetch him. He be expecting you, yeah?"

"I do hope so," Róisín said.

"While he's being got, have a seat," and he directed the men watching to make room and had someone hand a chair down from the dais. Someone else ran to get a glass of water and handed it to her when she sat, her satchel to the side, and the water was quickly drunk.

Róisín, the object of attention from the entire hall, sat amazed at what was happening to her. Her ship was crowded, with far more people than she imagined ever seeing. Then suddenly she slowly disembarked and went through an immigration station with papers checked and stamped by a uniformed man who did so with a flourish and a "Welcome to America, miss" before being set out into the vastness of New York.

It was warm, and she was sweating, fearing her odor would be detected by the men around her. But the varying smells of the hall, the sweat most of all, had long since disappeared into the atmosphere of the place. Instead, as Róisín slowly began to cool down, staring at the door where she expected her cousin to appear, she was viewed as an object of curiosity by most of the men, who gradually lost interest and drifted away.

She had not seen Jimmy in years and did not know if she would recognize him. Each time the door opened, she looked, hoping for a flash of recognition, always disappointed. Till, finally, a man came rushing in, his hat in hand, dodging the men loitering. He was a tall, thin man with curly brown hair. When he saw her, he waved and grinned.

"Cousin Róisín Campbell, as I live and breathe."

She stood before he reached her, and he banged into her, harder than either expected. Now the attentions of the others returned, but the two were unaware of it.

Jimmy looked up at the boss.

"Tommy. This here is my cousin Róisín. She is from County Limerick. A real farmgirl. Do you think we can teach her to live in the big city?"

Tommy, the boss, looked down.

"Lass. Just donna listen to what he or anyone of us says and you'll do just grand."

With that, Róisín handed her empty glass up and shook Tommy's hand, thanking him for his kindness, and a moment later she was back on the streets of the metropolis, her cousin carrying her satchel over his shoulder and leading her to where things would begin.

As they walked, Jimmy was speaking his mile a minute, but little of it was reaching Róisín's brain. All she saw were the buildings and the people and the wagons and carriages with their horses and all she heard were the sounds of what she saw echoing against the buildings and all she smelled were the odors of a grand metropolis in action.

Róisín began to make sense of the apparent chaos in the streets. There were avenues and there were streets. Some went uptown and some went across and some were cut at strange angles to others. She picked up that Jimmy was taking her to a boarding house run by a Mrs. Flanagan. On the boat, Róisín heard of all the tenements that flooded with people desperate to flee Ireland and find food and work. Things were not as bad as they were during the Famine years, but they were still harsh for those with little schooling and less hope at home.

As she walked with Jimmy, she saw poverty she had not imagined. The sounds and sights and smells were nothing but chaos, particularly with the rising heat and the blaring sun. But after several minutes they were clear of it, and the streets resumed a more orderly shape.

"You need to keep out of this part as much as you can," Jimmy said. "They say they was once quite grand but now, now these people got less than nothing, and if you have anything going in, you won't have it going out. So just keep away."

Róisín could only nod as she tightened her grip on his arm.

Once clear of that neighborhood, the sun and the smells were no longer stifling. About halfway down one of the blocks, Jimmy said, "Here is Mrs. Flanagan's. I told her all about you, so much as I know. It is a very respectable place. The rent ain't high, and you can stay here till you go to the nuns and then you be living in-house, like the one I talked about in me letter."

Mrs. Flanagan's looked much like the other houses on the block. It was brick with three windows on the front of each floor. There was no gap with the buildings to the left and right of it. A stoop of some twelve steps rose from the sidewalk to the left side of the building, and there were two large windows to the right. It had four stories.

The door itself was large and black. A brass "145" was above a large, plain knocker. Jimmy, though, simply opened the door, calling out for Mrs. Flanagan as they crossed in. From the rear of the first floor, Róisín heard a sing-songy, "Coming, coming," and a woman, Mrs. Flanagan it was, appeared. She was a wide woman and a little short. Her gray hair was in a bun, and she wiped her hands on an apron as she approached the pair.

"Mrs. Flanagan. 'Tis my cousin, Róisín Campbell." Turning to Róisín, he said, "Your landlady, Mrs. Flanagan."

Róisín extended her hand, but Mrs. Flanagan was too quick, and her arms were around the girl's waist.

Jimmy told Róisín as they walked that the landlady was a widow. Her husband died in an accident on the docks, and she somehow managed to have enough to acquire the boarding house. Jimmy said how that happened was something of a mystery, but that all agreed it was best left as one.

Mrs. Flanagan directed her into the sitting-room. The room had two windows looking out onto the street and since they faced south and the sun was high, the room was very warm, even with the windows open. It had a high ceiling and a fireplace and was populated by several mismatched armchairs and a threadbare couch and small tables dispersed about.

Before they sat, Róisín asked Mrs. Flanagan where she might relieve herself and was surprised—pleasantly—when she was led to a small room in a back corner of the ground floor. There was a toilet, and Mrs. Flanagan explained how it worked. After Róisín was done, she joined Mrs. Flanagan in the kitchens as a kettle was set to boil. Her host said that many parts of New York, though not yet the tenements Róisín walked through with Jimmy, had central plumbing. She carried the teapot, and Róisín carried a small tray with two cups and saucers and the women sat in the front sitting-room.

"Your cousin had to get back to work, but he brought your bag to your room. We'll lead you there shortly, but we thought you should have tea first so we can learn something about you."

Róisín nodded, and sat on the couch, as Mrs. Flanagan indicated. Her host sat on the other end, balancing the cup and saucer in her lap. It was a brief conversation, what with Róisín being very tired from the voyage and from all she heard and saw since arriving.

Mrs. Flanagan led Róisín up three flights of stairs. On the top floor, there were two doors, each leading to a bedroom. Both doors were open, and Mrs. Flanagan led Róisín to the one that was to the rear of the house. It was very neat, with two large beds and two dressers and a single closet. The beds were to the right, their headboards against the wall. Each had two pillows, and Róisín would be sharing one.

"As the newest girl, you have this side," Mrs. Flanagan said as she put her hand on the right side of the bed away from the window. "You will not get quite the breeze that the girls closer to the window will. But this is how things are."

"Does it get very warm?"

"Good God, child. At this time of year, it can be sweltering. And the bugs. We shan't mention the bugs."

This was of scant comfort to Róisín, and her landlady left her alone for a nap. She did not know how long she slept. It was still light outside when she was awakened by a woman who was about her size.

"Mrs. Flanagan told me you be here. I be Mary Bette Flynn from County Mayo and I work as a seamstress," and she extended her hand, and Róisín shook it.

She saw that Mary Bette Flynn from County Mayo was a peasant. Mayo was one of the places hardest hit by the Famine, and its children were still coming to America, hoping to send money home so a relative could follow. Her skin was a little yellower than was Róisín's, suggesting she was still recovering from her Irish diet.

But Mary Bette was a sweet girl.

"Do you know what the time is?" asked Róisín.

"It must be going on eight," was the answer. "Mrs. Flanagan said she kept some supper for you, but you had better come down for it."

With that, Mary Bette was gone, and Róisín heard her bounding down the flights of steps. Mrs. Flanagan did have some supper ready, and Róisín did not realize how hungry she was until it was placed in front of her on the large, dark dining table, where Mary Bette extracted her history while she ate.

For the next three nights, Róisín shared Mary Bette's bed as two girls shared the other. It was brutally warm, well beyond anything Róisín knew, and they slept naked and with the window open, thankful for the window screens that Mrs. Flanagan had installed several months before. On the second night, after Róisín spent much of the day wandering the streets, she woke and found Mary Bette's arm around her. She relished the touch and soon drifted back asleep. It was repeated on Róisín's third and final night at Mrs. Flanagan's, though this time promptly after they were in the bed and when they were both awake, though pretending not to be, each aware of the other's heat, sweat, and smell. To Róisín it was a too-brief pleasure as she was quickly asleep and awoke on the opposite side of the bed from Mary Bette.

On her fourth day, though, it was time for Róisín to leave Mrs. Flanagan and Mary Bette so she could begin to train to become a domestic servant in America.

4.

Róisín, of course, had no inkling of what a domestic did in a great house let alone how to do it. Jimmy arranged for her to attend the House of Mercy, a clearinghouse for Irish girls newly in the city. The House itself was a bulky building on East Houston Street. Róisín appeared there on her first Monday in America. With a letter of introduction her cousin procured thanks to a chain of relationships he developed, which he gave to her when he met her after mass on her first Sunday in America, she sat in a large hall across a table from a novitiate. Her satchel with her belongings from home was in the entry hall, and she was told they would be in her room when she finished the preliminaries. She was asked where she came from and when she arrived. If she could read and write and whether she was Catholic. She gave her Cousin Jimmy's address and where he worked. The novitiate was efficient and gave Róisín a paper and sent her to a row of chairs along a wall.

At the end of the row was a second novitiate. Each girl sat and moved one seat over as one of them was processed. When Róisín reached the young sister, she handed the paper given to her and was directed behind a screen. There, an older sister wearing gloves and an apron told her to disrobe. "Come on, now, love. We haven't all day, you know" spurring Róisín to remove her frock. Somewhat roughly, but somewhat gently, the sister ran her hands over Róisín's body, having her turn around and then back again to face her.

"I see you are not from the west." After Róisín said she was from Limerick, the sister said, "Aye, and I see you can read and write. You shall do well, Miss Campbell, I think." The sister signed the paper and directed Róisín to a door she had not noticed. When she was through it, Róisín met yet another sister, this one holding a measuring tape, which she efficiently used to take the measure of the girl. She stepped into a room lined with black frocks and removed two.

"Here you go. Try them on," nodding to the small room behind Róisín, "and we'll get you the right size."

This sister was repeating the process with another girl when Róisín returned and when that girl was off to try on an outfit herself, the sister said to Róisín, "That fits you very well. You will get three of these and three aprons as well as undergarments. Then go down to the next door and pick yourself a pair of shoes that fit. I warn you, make sure they are not tight or you will be in torture for I won't have you come back here for another pair."

After collecting the frock that did not fit, the sister went into the room and brought two more of the proper size. She handed them to Róisín and ran her hand across Róisín's arm.

"Do not be afraid, dear. You will be fine. After you get your shoes, head to the end of the hall and they will take care of you."

With that, Róisín went to try on several shoes before finding a comfortable pair, and with her new uniforms and her own frock over her right arm and the shoes in her left hand, she went down the hall, to a large room to the left. Perhaps twenty-five girls around Róisín's age were mingling. Most of the accents were unfamiliar and some spoke Gaelic. None was particularly stout. Several appeared to know one another, whether from home or from New York she could not say.

Six rows of eight chairs faced a small dais on which four chairs sat on either side of a lectern. In front of that was a table with two chairs facing the six rows. Róisín sat some halfway back and in the middle. After several more girls came in, carrying their frocks, aprons, undergarments (beneath the other things), and shoes, there was a bang. A sister led several others up to the dais, and two sat at the table.

"Girls, please be seated," a sister she had not seen before barked, and the room quieted.

And so began Róisín's tenure at the House of Mercy.

During the first week, she and the other forty or so girls rotated through various skills. They wore identical black frocks that reached nearly to the floor and frilled white aprons that went several inches above the frock's hem. Their shoes were simple and black, and each girl had a white cap. Initially, the sisters were vigorous in teaching personal hygiene. This was chiefly so the girls would learn how to care for themselves, especially in the cluttered environment of Manhattan. More, it was so they understood the needs of those who they would serve, in the likely event they went into service.

Most were from farms in the west and northwest of Ireland, the area hardest hit in the Famine. Others came from Dublin or Cork or other towns. They slept together in one of two large rooms, each with cots running along both sides. At times, Róisín heard crying or praying from those who lay nearest her. It was at meals that she felt more an outsider than otherwise, as the sort of natural chatter she heard when she went into the hall on the first day continued to her exclusion.

The others were pleasant enough to her, at least after the first week, but also wary. In fairness, Róisín did not make a major effort to befriend the others. She was overwhelmed by the change in her life and frightened of where she would go. In Limerick, she mostly kept to herself and was used to and even comfortable in the solitary life. So, at night at the House of Mercy, she wrote her letters and volunteered to write letters for illiterate girls. They, too, dictated their own fears, speaking in low tones as Róisín took down what they said. But they looked at Róisín as a scrivener, simply transcribing what she heard with no emotional connection.

During the day, the group spent much time perfecting their sewing and cleaning of garments, though most were adept from their time at home. Whether working as a seamstress or in a house, sewing and the care of garments was essential, especially for a domestic servant in her early days of service. She would spend far less time in the presence of her mistress and the family than she would mending and cleaning and polishing.

After two weeks, a selection occurred. The girls were divided into those who would be employed in service and those not deemed up to the task, who would likely become pieceworkers in a factory, spending their days sewing.

Girls going into service were further divided, with those who displayed kitchen skills being taught the fundamentals of various cooking styles. Becoming a cook was among the most sought-after positions for a newly-arrived Irishwoman, but Róisín was not picked for that. Nor was she sent off to sew. She was among the fifteen designated to work upstairs in a great house.

Once placed into service, domestics remained at their houses six evenings a week. On their free night, many came to the House of Mercy for prayers or to mingle socially, and in her final week there, Róisín and the others of her group destined to work in houses were allowed to join them in what became a rite of passage, learning secrets and dangers of domestic life from girls who passed through the House of Mercy not long before them.

Róisín envied the ease with which the other girls fell in together as she largely remained to the side of the noisy groups of threes and fours and fives, a mixture of her group and those recently sent to work, with Róisín picking up little bits of conversation.

5.

Before Róisín reached New York, her Cousin Jimmy approached a dock boss, asking whether he could help in getting his cousin a job. The boss put him in touch with a jobber of leather goods and the jobber promised to look into it. Several days later, Jimmy received a letter from Charles Geherty. The letter said that the Geherty family could well need a servant and would be happy to consider someone who was capable. It was this letter that Róisín took when she interviewed at the House of Mercy, and now she carried it with her as she stood on a side street well north of Mrs. Flanagan's in front of number 37. Its number was painted in black on the two columns on either side of the front door. The building was white with five stories. It had a pair of large windows on the ground floor on either side of a large ebony front door with a brass knocker. Each of the upper floors had windows of decreasing size as one went up.

She knocked, and a butler promptly opened the front door and after looking her up-and-down he advised her that in future she was only to use the servants' entrance, and he nodded to his left. Róisín apologized, saying it would not happen again, and the butler said it had better not.

"I am here to meet Mrs. Collins," Róisín told the butler. Mrs. Collins, she was told at the House of Mercy, was the housekeeper of the Geherty House and would be the person to whom Róisín reported were she to get the position. The butler, who Róisín would learn was Mr. Mason, opened the door wider for Róisín to enter and then upon closing it instructed her to follow him.

She barely glanced at the two large rooms on either side of the foyer as he led her straight back, to the left of the grand staircase, which rose along the side and turned left to the second-floor landing. Shortly before they reached a window overlooking the back garden, Mr. Mason opened a door and stepped down a flight of steps. Róisín followed. At the bottom, there was a series of doors on the left side of a hallway with the large kitchen open to the right. Cook and a scullery maid looked to see who was going to see Mrs. Collins, but Mr. Mason ignored them and knocked on the third and final door, and upon hearing a "come in," he opened it.

"The girl you mentioned has arrived, Mrs. Collins."

"Thank you, Mr. Mason. Please sit down." This last was directed to Róisín and before she sat, Mason closed the door and vanished.

"How long have you been in New York?"

"Just under five weeks."

"Five weeks? And I understand that before that you worked on a farm. County Limerick was it?"

"'Twas, ma'am. The eastern edge of County Limerick."

Mrs. Collins looked at her crossly.

"Why on God's green earth do you think you can work as a domestic servant in a proper house? Doing *anything*?"

"Well, Mrs. Collins. I spent four weeks at the House of Mercy, learning skills. I am told I am a clever girl and always have been. Before leaving home, I performed numerous chores around the—"

"Around the farmhouse? What is that to us? Around a farmhouse, indeed. Do you know anything about folding linen and helping a lady dress? Would you know anything about assisting at a ball? Accompanying a young lady on a shopping trip on Broadway? No. No. I do not think this is possible. I cannot teach you to do all you have to do as a maid in a house like this one. It is too much."

Róisín sat immobile. This was her chance. If she could not get this position with someone familiar, at least indirectly, with Jimmy, there was no hope.

"Still. My instructions are to present you to my mistress, and I do not challenge the instructions of my betters. If you are employed here, it is something you had better remember. Mrs. Geherty is here and is waiting to see you. I will tell her what I think, which is that you have no business in this house. I prefer a girl with some experience in a house before she comes here. But it is for her to decide and, as I told you, I follow the instructions of my betters."

With that, Mrs. Collins rose. As she did, she turned to check her image in a small mirror on the wall by her desk, pushing some hairs away from her forehead.

Mrs. Collins was not an unattractive woman. She had the trace of an accent that Róisín recognized from the boat. It was common among the poorer girls. From the northwest, most likely. Mrs. Collins was the right age to be a Famine child, coming to America in a coffin ship at the end of the 1840s. The crossing would have been hard and existence harder, and she would have begun at the lowest rung at whatever house would have her. She was "Mrs. Collins," but that did not mean she was ever married. A life of service suggested otherwise. It was, Róisín thought, likely a term of respect earned as she moved up through a house.

Mrs. Collins knew Mrs. Geherty would solicit her opinion, and she would be honest. But a house is a complicated being and sometimes going by one's instincts could work out. Sometimes not.

Róisín rose to follow Mrs. Collins from the office. Before they reached the hall to the first foyer, Mrs. Collins continued up the servants' staircase for another flight. The stairs continued up, but she opened a door to a wide hallway, and Róisín followed. This hallway had two doors to the left and another at the end. A pair of doors, likely opening to the drawing-room, was to the right.

Mrs. Collins led Róisín past the front staircase, to the second door on the left, and knocked. After a moment, they heard an "Enter." Mrs. Collins gave Róisín a cross look and opened the door. The pair stood in front of Mrs. Geherty's ornate desk.

"Good morning, Mrs. Geherty. This is the girl you inquired about. Tell Mrs. Geherty your name, child."

"Róisín Campbell."

"'Roe-SHEEN.' Did I pronounce it correctly?"

"Exactly right, Mrs. Geherty."

"Tell Mrs. Geherty where you are from," Mrs. Collins demanded.

"From County Limerick, Mrs. Geherty."

"And tell Mrs. Geherty where you lived before you came to America."

"I lived on my father's dairy farm, Mrs. Geherty."

Mrs. Geherty, who listened politely, said, "Yes, I understand that. How long have you been in this country, Róisín?"

"I came over five weeks ago, Mrs. Geherty."

"And you were at the House of Mercy?"

"Yes, Mrs. Geherty," Mrs. Collins repeated.

"And, Róisín, do you have any experience working as a domestic servant in a house? Any at all?"

"Again, ma'am, what I learned at the House of Mercy and doing all sorts of chores in my house in Ireland."

"I see. What makes you believe you could work in this house?"

"It is the very question I asked her, Mrs. Geherty."

"Thank you, Mrs. Collins. I will let her answer."

Mrs. Collins was angry at Róisín for the reprimand.

"Yes, Mrs. Geherty. Mrs. Collins did ask me that, and as I told her, and all I can tell you, is that I will work hard and I think I will be able to do it."

"Well, you are certainly presentable enough."

Róisín was embarrassed. She lived in the country and while she imagined people found her looks pleasant, she could not imagine they thought her more than that.

"Ah," Mrs. Geherty replied. "You should look at yourself in that mirror Mrs. Collins is so fond of in her office."

Mrs. Collins's anger grew. Mrs. Geherty ignored it.

"You can read English?"

"Yes, Mrs. Geherty."

"And write? You can write as well?"

"Yes, Mrs. Geherty."

Mrs. Geherty looked at Mrs. Collins.

"Oh, Mrs. Collins. Do not look so forlorn. Consider yourself as having warned me about her glaring deficiencies. And I will try to avoid burdening you with teaching her how to do things. But I do like her. It will make my husband happy to be of some service to that friend of his, who apparently is related to her."

"My cousin, ma'am. He works on the docks."

"Yes, yes." She turned back to Mrs. Collins. "If she does not work out, I bear full responsibility."

She turned back to Róisín.

"Do you understand, Róisín? I am going against my housekeeper's advice and have taken responsibility for doing so. If you fail, Mrs. Collins will never allow me to live it down."

Mrs. Collins could not resist a slight smile at this, much as she disdained the slightest levity with those above her and especially those below, even when alone with her mistress.

Mrs. Geherty turned again to the housekeeper.

"So, Mrs. Collins. Take her from me. Show her to her room. Teach her what needs to be taught her. But Róisín Campbell," she turned again to the girl. "I may make light of it in this room. But do not believe for a moment that I will tolerate any willfulness on your part. I have faith that you will work hard and will learn to work well. But this is a house. We, each of us, have positions in it. These positions are well-defined. Do not cross them. Is that understood?"

Róisín was a little taken aback by the changed tone. But that did not constitute. She nodded and thanked Mrs. Geherty. She was being hired and Mrs. Collins was to show her to her room.

With her position at the Gehertys secured, Róisín returned to the House of Mercy for the several days remaining before she went into service. The other girls, except two or three (though they, too, would get jobs soon enough), also found positions, and a large dinner was held for the group on their final Saturday.

On Sunday, after mass and a slight dinner, they went their separate ways. That afternoon, Róisín arrived at her new home and ate supper with the staff after the family was finished their own supper. At six the next morning, she was awakened when a footman who minutes earlier heard the call of his alarm clock banged on her door, and those of the others in the staff's quarters, much as one of her brothers did in Hospital.

She did not sleep well in her little room. The entire world of the house was unfamiliar to her and she tossed and turned, wondering how she would ever manage to understand the first thing about being in it. The Geherty House, she knew, was part of a larger world of Irish houses which were part of a larger world of fashionable houses. And the world of fashionable houses was all that mattered in the end to the Geherty family. And because the world of fashionable houses was all that mattered in the end to the Geherty family, Róisín had two responsibilities.

First, she was to do her part to ensure that the house was in proper condition should a fashionable guest come through the door. Second, she was to do her part to ensure that Miss Mary Geherty was properly attired when she went through the door of another fashionable house.

Róisín was familiar with starting work at an early hour. At six-thirty, she was in the basement kitchen with the ten or twelve other members of staff. They were split among those who worked in the kitchen, those who worked in the house, and a coachman and a footman who cared for the house's horses and carriages. The house, Róisín would learn, had six horses stabled several blocks away, where a carriage and a gig were also kept.

Róisín was assigned to Mrs. Collins. As Monday's cold breakfast was being eaten, she was the object of curiosity and humor. All of the others were Irish. They either came directly or their parents had been part of the Famine emigration. When everyone was done, Mrs. Collins directed Róisín to her office. Biddy O'Casey followed them in. Biddy was perhaps six years older than Róisín. She was short and wide, and her flowing brown hair had a hint of red. As with the others at the table, her skin was fair.

"Biddy O'Casey takes care of Miss Geherty. There may be times when she needs assistance in this, so you must learn how to aid Miss Geherty in whatever she does. Biddy will show you. But every day, you will see to it that the house is immaculate. It is not winter so you will not need to set the fires unless I instruct you to. Is that understood?"

"Yes, Mrs. Collins."

"I assume you know how to set fires but if not, I will have Biddy show you. Is that understood?"

"Yes, Mrs. Collins."

"The girl who did your job left because of…unforeseen circumstances, so Biddy O'Casey has very kindly agreed to show you how to do what you are to do. Thank her."

Róisín gave a slight curtsey then turned and detected the slightest tinge of a smirk on Biddy O'Casey's face. "Thank you, Miss O'Casey."

"You are very welcome, I'm sure," was the reply, spoken with a clear Connaught accent that was only slightly hardened by her time in New York.

Mrs. Collins looked crossly at Biddy O'Casey, and the smirk was gone.

"If you have any questions, direct them to me or to Biddy O'Casey. Do not, under any circumstances, speak to a member of the family or to a guest without being spoken to first. Is that understood?"

"Yes, Mrs. Collins."

She sat. "I do hope Mrs. Geherty is correct and that you do provide passable service to the family. I truly do. You are both dismissed."

With that, the pair left. When they reached the stairs and were out of earshot, Biddy O'Casey said, "Don't be worried about sourpuss there. She hates everyone. Wanted to get married, we hear, and ended up in this place. The family? Well, other than Mrs. Geherty, they are no better and no worse than any other family, I guess. Mrs. Geherty is a saint, I tell you. Smart as a whip. She'll treat you square."

When they reached the ground floor, Róisín's days in service began. As they did, Biddy informed Róisín about the other family members. "Mr. Geherty, of course. We don't see much of him during the day. The two sons are Charlie—Charles, Jr.—and Michael. They're pretty much alike, but Master Michael ain't as short with us as is his brother. Miss Elizabeth is much like her mother and not much like her sister. We don't know when she'll be back from Europe. You will meet Mary—Miss Geherty—shortly. I'll let you judge for yourself."

6.

Róisín and Biddy went through the house. On the first floor, they opened the drapes and ensured that each room was tidy. In the dining room, they saw Mr. Mason. He was less dour and did not seem quite so tall to Róisín as he had when he opened the door and chided her for knocking on it.

"Biddy. I trust that you are instructing the new girl as to her duties?"

"Yes, Mr. Mason."

"Very good. She seems very raw." He turned to the new girl. "You have not been in such a house, have you Róisín?"

"No, sir."

"Yes. It is our responsibility to maintain this house as it is meant to be maintained. That allows the Geherty family to be as it is meant to be. Is that understood?"

"Yes, Mr. Mason."

"Good. I am sure that Mrs. Collins has explained this to you."

"Yes, Mr. Mason. That she has."

"Very good. Carry on, girls."

Mr. Mason continued to do what he had been doing when the girls walked in, which was ensuring that the table settings were proper and that the places for breakfast were ready for those who elected to come down instead of having it brought up.

As the girls walked up the steps to the second floor—neither knowing why it was the "second" floor in America and the "first" in Ireland—and the grand drawing-room at the front of the house used for entertaining and before- and after-dinner gatherings, Biddy told Róisín that while Mr. Geherty came down on most week mornings before eight and would leave the house at the stroke of nine by the grandfather clock in the foyer, the sons and the women rarely came down before ten unless they had a particular appointment.

"If they do not come down until so late, why must we be up so early?" Róisín asked.

"You will find that Mrs. Collins has much to prevent us from having idle hands, I can assure you."

The two were in the kitchen polishing silver when Mrs. Geherty's bell—among two rows of them high up on a kitchen wall—rang, signaling that the mistress was ready to rise. While those who came to the dining room for breakfast handled it themselves, Mrs. Geherty and Mary—Miss Geherty—usually chose to eat in their rooms. Cook prepared a tray for the former, and Mrs. Collins took it.

It was not long before Miss Geherty's bell rang. Cook soon had a tray ready for her as well. In addition to a napkin and silverware, it had a coffee pot, cup and saucer, a cruet with milk and a bowl with sugar, several slices of well-done toast in a caddy, and bits of butter on a small plate.

Biddy looked at Róisín. Seeing that Mrs. Collins had not returned, Biddy said, "This is the most important thing you may ever do in this house. You will meet Miss Geherty. Miss Mary Geherty. She has good days, and she has bad days. She is...well, you will see what she is. Never, ever not call her 'Miss Geherty' when you are with her. You cannot say it too often, I assure you."

With that, Cook shook her head amiably at the girl's remarks and Róisín picked up the tray. She followed Biddy up the servants' stairs, the silverware clattering as she did, to the third floor where the family's bedrooms were.

Biddy knocked on the door and opened it without waiting for a response. Miss Geherty had opened the curtains and sat up in her bed as Róisín set down the tray. Biddy poured coffee into a cup and handed it and its saucer to her mistress. Miss Geherty lifted the cup, took a sip, and returned it to the saucer.

"So, you are the new girl."

"Yes, Miss Geherty."

"My, you are pretty."

Róisín looked down.

"Have you nothing to say to that? What is your name?"

"I am Róisín Campbell, Miss Geherty."

"Róisín Campbell. And where are you from, Róisín Campbell?"

"County Limerick, Miss Geherty."

"County Limerick? I don't know that I have ever met someone from County Limerick. Can you recite a limerick for me?"

Róisín was embarrassed.

"Perhaps another time, then. Are you a farmgirl?" She took a sip of her coffee.

"Yes, Miss Geherty."

"Did you grow poh-tay-toes?"

"No, Miss Geherty."

Mary looked at her crossly.

"Well, Róisín, what is it that you did farm?"

"We are a dairy farm, Miss Geherty."

"Can you read?"

"Yes, Miss Geherty."

"How did you come to read, Róisín Campbell?"

"I was taught at the local school, Miss Geherty."

"Biddy here can read only tolerably. Ain't that right, Biddy?" Miss Geherty did not deign to look at Biddy when she said this. Her eyes were trained on Róisín, whose eyes were trained on the floor.

"Yes, Miss Geherty," Biddy said.

"Have you ever read a book, Róisín Campbell?"

Róisín looked up. She knew enough to know she was being patronized but also knew enough to not pay it any mind and lowered her head again.

"Yes, Miss Geherty."

"I will say that you are a failure at being able to converse with someone, farmgirl. I will not ask you what you have read and whether they had pictures. The two of you may go now. Biddy, I will need you in thirty minutes. Do not bother bringing the pretty girl with you."

"Yes, Miss Geherty," Biddy said. The two servants backed up, curtsied, and left the room.

As they were approaching the kitchen, Biddy told Róisín, "She does not like you. She hates even the thought of not being the most beautiful woman in the house."

"What do you mean?"

"Róisín, you may be a country girl, like me, but sure you know how pretty you are?"

Róisín was embarrassed, as she was when Mrs. Geherty said it. That Miss Geherty thought so frightened her. She needed to have Miss Geherty like her, but what if she did not by the accident of her face? From what she could tell, Miss Geherty was not unattractive. She seemed tall and very thin, with no bosom. Her hair was dark, almost black, and her skin was fair, with traces of freckles drifting across her face. In this regard, she very much resembled her mother in build and, save for the freckles, in her face.

Mary Geherty hated those freckles. And she hated the paucity of her bosom. She knew it did not matter in the getting of a husband; that would be a financial transaction between her family and another. But she was fully aware that the women she needed to like her scorned and perhaps mocked her freckles and her scant breasts. She was glad of her parents' money. She hated the lack of physical beauty she saw in her looking glass and she blamed her parents for that.

Later, when Miss Geherty went out for the day, Biddy brought Róisín to a group of rooms at the back of the house on the fourth floor. Here were the rooms in which the Gehertys' clothing was kept.

The largest room had but one window. To the right were various items of men's clothing with perhaps two dozen pairs of shoes in shelving by the floor. To the front, Biddy said, was Mrs. Geherty's clothing. It nearly filled the wall, with a small collection of Miss Elizabeth's beside it. But the balance of the room, with far more outfits than were Mrs. Geherty's and Miss Elizabeth's, contained, Biddy said, Miss Geherty's things. The sight left Róisín speechless. Every woman in her village, and beyond, could have two or perhaps three of the gowns and dresses and there would be plenty left over for all the women in the next village.

"One must never wear the same dress twice," Biddy said, her smirk directed in a different direction from earlier. "Miss Geherty goes out up to four or five times in a week, though not so much in the winter. Sometimes twice in a day. Mrs. Geherty, on the other hand, is a homebody to her daughter. She goes out no more than twice in a week, usually with Mr. Geherty."

Miss Geherty had done Europe, though unlike Miss Elizabeth, who was ensconced in a type of school in Switzerland, she had done the tour of London and Milan and Venice and especially Paris with her mother. And unlike her mother, her experience—the clothing in Paris and the well-defined hierarchy of London—took. She learned the place of those who served her and how they were to be treated and since such treatment was fully in accord with Mary Geherty's natural inclinations, she happily applied them upon her return to New York.

Looking at the room, Biddy led Róisín closer. "She will not wear a dress again, yet she keeps each like a trophy. She spends much of her day at fittings. Though she sometimes gets something at Arnold Constable or Lord & Taylor."

"How can they afford them?"

"Beats me. Mr. Geherty did very well in the War, I hear. He seems to be doing well since then, too."

Biddy explained that she was at the house for four years and that she was at another house for the prior two. She came to New York six years before Róisín and she was taught to be a domestic servant at the House of Mercy.

"I should have had nothing if it wasn't for the good sisters. I'm happy enough in service. I can send money home. A brother has already come to New York since me. He works on the docks. I hope a sister will come, too."

Biddy was continuing the tradition begun in the Famine years of being the first in a farm family to come to America and provide the means for brothers and sisters to follow. Róisín was fortunate in that her family was not poverty-stricken as was Biddy's or, she understood, the others who worked in the Geherty House.

With Biddy's blessing, Róisín ran her hands across the hung garments. Velvet dresses, walking dresses, and ball dresses. Many well out-of-style from what the fashionable woman in New York was currently wearing, though not when they were worn.

There were white llama jackets, overskirts of lace, and traveling dresses in black silk for when Miss Geherty traveled to Stockbridge in western Massachusetts where, Biddy explained, the family kept a house.

"But," she informed, "they have never been invited to Newport or Saratoga and they never will be. Thank goodness for that. Then she would need dresses for croquet-playing and going to horse-races and yacht-races and receptions and parties and who knows what else."

Róisín was incapable of calculating the cost of this collection. Each of the houses on the street, in this neighborhood—and in better neighborhoods—had rooms just like this, she expected. Where women who thought they were not pretty enough in the eyes of other women who did not think *they* were pretty enough kept their outfits. Not that they would ever venture into such a room. They would, as Miss Geherty did, receive the delivery of a newly-made dress and have it placed in the room. They would direct a maid, as Miss Geherty did with Biddy, to collect the dress on the afternoon of the evening on which it was to be worn.

The maid would assist in the dressing, beginning with the undergarments and ending with the delicate robing of her better. A selection of jewels—Biddy had yet to show Róisín the house's jewels—would be brought, and the lady would select those appropriate for the occasion, and the necklaces would be draped and the rings would be placed and the earrings would be hooked and the mistress would carefully walk down the steps in the front staircase to the practiced admiring glances of the men in the house to be led to the carriage that would take her to a party or dance or ball where the women would smile and nod and assess the inadequacies of all the women they had not seen since the day before and would not see again until the day after, with the same ritual repeated again and again, *ad infinitum.*

Róisín understood the absurdity of this at once, but so did Biddy and all the others in service at the Geherty House. But it was and always would be.

7.

The Gehertys themselves were not far removed from Ireland. Charles Geherty, the family's current patriarch, was the grandson of Sam Geherty. Sam was the third son in a family that operated a dry goods store in Galway. He had enough of a stake from his father to open a small store in New York. It sold mostly gloves and other leather items.

His son Michael did well by it. Michael, though, died suddenly in 1859, and Charles was left to carry on. And carry on he did. Through connections, he obtained a contract with the U.S. Army to provide leather goods in the build-up after the start of the Civil War. It was a lucrative trade, even after the payment of the bribes necessary to keep it. Charles bought the house in 1866 from an English family whose patriarch did even better in providing blankets to the Union Army and was moving to more opulent quarters further uptown.

Róisín learned most of this from the gossip that helped pass the time downstairs during meals and the endless drudgery of keeping things cleaned and polished.

Although Charles Geherty was indifferent to who was hired to serve the household, as a courtesy he wrote the letter Jimmy sent to Róisín. Charles's wife, Abigail, was partial to Irish girls. Her mother's mother was from Dublin, and her father was a lawyer. She was by no means a catch in terms of her pedigree, even to a second-generation immigrant from Ireland, but caught the eye of one of them, Charles, at a church event and had just enough New York gentility that Charles's father and mother bent to his insistence and blessed the marriage.

That was over twenty-five years earlier. Charles and Abigail retained affection for one another but in his constant efforts to outdo his father's success and her efforts at rising through the ranks of the Irish elite, they spent little time in each other's presence except on Sundays, when they took a carriage or strolled to the ten o'clock mass at St. Stephen's and had dinner with those children who were in town.

Of the children, Róisín had few dealings with the sons, except insofar as they happened upon her while she was doing her duties. At those times, they seemed to encourage each other to make those duties difficult to fulfill. When they realized it was not feigned but genuine distaste that she exhibited, their obnoxiousness eased and they became less difficult.

Róisín had the misfortune of having regular dealings with Mary Gehery, and her judgment of the superior woman was not flattering and did not improve over time. Mary was perhaps four years her senior and was looking to become, and was shortly expected to become, engaged.

Róisín did not meet Elizabeth, the final member of the family, who was off to Europe shortly after coming out in the spring of 1870. During their various conversations, Biddy said Elizabeth resented the attention Mary insisted on receiving. Mary, she said, engaged in petty behavior against her younger sister (as Charlie did with Michael, truth be told), always aware of the necessity of not doing anything of that sort while their mother was around. Mrs. Geherty was far too observant not to notice, Biddy said, and she chided Mary about it frequently. This had the unintended effect of increasing the ferocity of Mary's conduct to Elizabeth.

"I dunno if it be that or her nature, but Elizabeth is always a bit on the quiet side. Reads books and the like and is free to take whatever books she likes from the master's library. Only one ever in there other than the master, as a matter of fact. Miss Elizabeth didn't have many friends while she was here. Maybe she'll be different when she gets back and Mary is off married. I won't prejudice you, but good riddance when that happens, I say." After a beat, she continued, "But you mustn't say I said that."

Married off? Róisín soon understood from the kitchen tutorials that the daughters were fated to marry one from a select group of families. Mary, the oldest girl—Charlie was older—would be the more sought-after bride and Elizabeth would be relegated to some less-favored son of a business colleague of her father's.

"'Tis said," one of the footman once said, "she's the much better prize that Miss Geherty," which seemed to be the consensus.

"Aye," agreed Mr. Geherty's valet. "Whoever gets Miss Geherty is welcome to her," which also seemed to be the consensus.

Her interest piqued, Róisín wondered about the absence of photographs of this younger daughter, but Biddy said while Mrs. Geherty planned on having a portrait done of her when she came out, like the one made of Mary when she did, Miss Elizabeth never got around to it before departing for Europe.

As for Mary and the alliance into which she would surely enter, that happened some months after Róisín began at the Geherty House. Mr. and Mrs. Geherty engineered an engagement with the McNabbs. Their son, Peter, was the scion of this fine, Catholic family, and it was recognized that the marriage was a step up for Mary Geherty. He was several years older than his fiancée and had, as they say, seen much of the world. The family's money came from land-speculation in the Midwest and, unlike with the Gehertys', it predated the War.

The McNabbs were among the "New Rich" or Shoddyites, though they would bristle at that term's use to describe them. Their money was a bit older than was the Gehertys', and it was more secure. Still, neither family was invited to Mrs. Astor's parties, although, in fairness, nor were the Vanderbilts.

Peter McNabb, the oldest son, was neither brighter nor dimmer than Mary's brothers, and they little traveled in the same circles. Peter McNabb found Mary Geherty tolerably pretty, and she found him tolerably handsome. Neither had expectations of a spouse being more than that. They were confident in his virility and her fertility and so when their parents pushed them together, they agreed to the match.

The Geherty sons, Charlie and Michael, approved of Peter. More important, both Mr. and Mrs. Geherty thought him a good match for their eldest daughter. And the Misters got along well with one another and were members of some of the same clubs and while the Missuses were not as chummy as their husbands, they got along tolerably well.

Elizabeth's views would be irrelevant, of course, but she would not have had any anyway, since she never met Peter, only learning of his existence when Mrs. Geherty wrote to her with word of the engagement, and when she heard she hoped that Peter McNabb would rein in the more unattractive of her sister's qualities and knew at the least that he would take her from the house.

Thus, some six months after Róisín started, the Gehertys held a party for about thirty at which Mary's engagement to Peter McNabb was announced. Though it was not Róisín's first experience with such a gathering, she remained nervous as she carried a tray with hors d'oeuvres among the guests before and assisted the other members of staff at dinner and continued to do so until Mr. Mason instructed her to see that the ladies' bedrooms were in order and then to retire for the night.

By then, Róisín was settled into her routine. She was often in the kitchen when not required upstairs, and sat with Biddy polishing, polishing, polishing. On some nights, her time was spent sewing or helping with the cleaning of the family's laundry and learning all about New York society. She suffered through her first New York winter and received a small gift—a necklace—on the day after Christmas, St. Stephen's Day.

Róisín made it a point of writing every two weeks to her mamma and heard of the happenings of the others in her family in her mamma's regular letters to her. She could buy books at a store on the avenue—she would never think of asking to borrow a volume from Mr. Geherty's library— and sat with them and a candle in her small room when the family was settled. Though she went to the House of Mercy on a night off early in her tenure at the Gehertys, as was the case when she trained there, she was not from the worlds of the other girls and did not return.

The staff did not have to attend mass with the Gehertys, and she and Biddy usually went together. There was a small public park not far from the house and when the weather was fair, they walked around its path arm-in-arm and nodding to the other domestics before returning to another week of service.

8.

If Róisín had a singular pleasure in New York in the months after she arrived, it was her walks with Michael Henry. She wrote to him upon obtaining the position with the Gehertys and he promptly wrote back to express his happiness for her and hoping that they might renew their acquaintance. Far from objecting, she arranged to meet him on the very next Sunday after mass. He confessed to not being a church-going man but stood on the sidewalk across from the church's door waiting for her. Róisín was thrilled to see him and dragged Biddy across to meet the dapper man. On cue, he doffed his hat to the pair and kissed the top of Biddy's hand.

After this introductory flourish of the sort she often witnessed but had never before participated in, Biddy left the two to go for their walk. Immediately upon beginning their stroll, Róisín realized how much she missed him, and it was as if they were again alone on the deck of the *City of Paris* when he put his arm through hers.

She wore her only public dress, which was quite plain, and he reveled in his dapper best as he led her to a fine restaurant on the avenue for dinner, and it was the most lavish meal Róisín ever had. It ended too soon, she thought, only to find herself enjoying walking with him over to the river even more.

So, it became their routine on many Sundays. Sometimes they even took a hansom up to Central Park to enjoy promenading arm-in-arm through the Mall. She could, and did, speak to him as she had with no one else, and he did the same with her. They agreed at their very first meeting on the deck of the *City of Paris* that they would be the greatest of friends but nothing more, and it served them both and would eventually become crucial for Róisín's life in the city.

But that was for later. While at the Gehertys', it was enough that she had someone she could share her life and thoughts with, simple as they then were.

9.

Róisín was in contact with Mr. Geherty only in group settings. With one exception. On a cold Saturday evening in February some seven months after she began at the Geherty House, Róisín was doing rounds, ensuring that the fires on the ground floor were doused before the house shut for the night. She thought the Gehertys were out, and fires were roaring in their bedrooms in anticipation of their return.

She entered Mr. Geherty's library. The room was dark, and the fire was flagging. As she began to dampen it, she heard a voice.

"'Tis Róisín, isn't it?"

She turned and barely saw Mr. Geherty in the dim light. When she did, she jumped up and curtsied.

"Yes, Mr. Geherty."

He had a snifter in his hand, which he twirled gently.

"'Mr. Geherty.' 'Mr. Geherty.' You make me feel so old."

He took a sip of his brandy as she stood frozen.

"This is your first house, so I hear. Yes?"

"Yes, Mr....sir."

"Does my house impress you?" He spread his arms as he said this, and Róisín could just see the roiling brandy in the fire's light.

"It is a magnificent house, sir."

"'Magnificent,' you say? It is a hut. A mere hovel compared to the others. Do you know that we are not invited to any of the real houses? My money is not good enough for some of them. Did you know that?"

Róisín did not know anything outside the Geherty House. It was, to her, "magnificent." She could not imagine something more so that was not owned by the princes of Europe.

"It is a wonderful house, sir. 'Tis all I understand."

He put his glass down.

"Please sit, miss—"

"Campbell, sir. Róisín Campbell."

"Miss Campbell."

Róisín stiffly perched herself on the front end of a leather chair that faced the desk, and he leaned back in his chair.

"Miss Campbell, I love my wife more than anything. She is the most wonderful woman in the world. 'Magnificent,' to use your word. I do not know that she knows that. She is magnificent and far better than I deserve."

Róisín now sat frozen. He was speaking to her but not *to* her, his words slurring one into the next.

"I am not made of money," he said as he pounded his fist on the desk, before quietly repeating the words.

"I am sorry. Carry on. Sometimes I feel sorry for myself."

He lifted his glass and stared into it as he gave a final twirl before draining it in a single gulp. He placed the empty snifter on the desk and took some papers and placed them in a drawer. He got up and headed to the open door.

"I am sorry. Carry on," and he was gone. Róisín was still on the chair and she rose to finish her dampening of the fire and then lifted the snifter and brought it to the kitchen to be cleaned.

Róisín did "carry on" that evening and for several months, her initial nervousness long gone. Until that morning when Mrs. Collins told her that the mistress wished to see her, and she found herself carrying all her belongings and trying to compose herself at a small table towards the rear of The Thistle.

10.

The Geherty House had once, before it was the Geherty House, been on one of the most fashionable streets. But the "most fashionable" was constantly moving north so that Irish and newish money, such as the Gehertys', moved into houses vacated by English and Dutch families that moved on. And further uptown.

One of those English families was that of Bradford Reynolds III. Its money came from some eighteenth-century slave-trading and was enhanced significantly by some Civil War profiteering. But the source of the money was never an issue with the "most fashionable." It was the fact of the money and at least one, preferably two, prior generations of ladies and gentlemen. New York did not have much time for the landed gentry since there was so little land, though the buying and selling of it in recent years created more than a few new fortunes (and, as fortunes waned, more than a few bankruptcies among the overextended). Nor were there official titles, though there were well-understood unofficial ones. The older the money was, the better, of course. But it was the fact of the money that was best of all. Unless one were old Dutch.

The Reynolds House was several blocks north and a universe from the Gehertys'. The family consisted of Mr. Reynolds, the third Bradford Reynolds to be the president of Bradford Reynolds & Sons; Mrs. Hyacinth Reynolds, the matriarch; Bradford IV, the heir; Alfred, the spare; and Marilyn Anne, a sweet woman of nineteen. The family was among the top of the class that was not quite the top of New York's class.

The testimonial from Mrs. Geherty was enough to get Róisín an interview with the Reynolds' housekeeper, who took a sufficient liking to offer her a lower maid position on a trial basis. This was only three weeks after the Geherty dismissal. She moved from Mrs. Flanagan's, her home after leaving the Gehertys, to another small room, though with a larger window than at the Gehertys', in the rafters.

Mrs. Reynolds, a portrait of impeccable deportment, gave brusque approval to the appointment when Róisín was presented to her. Róisín was tasked with helping to keep the bedrooms in order along with the normal cleaning, mending, and polishing. This would not be too strenuous since the family was only the master and mistress and the two sons and one daughter.

The elder son, Bradford IV, was fat. It was his defining characteristic. That and being engaged to a plain woman of good stock whose name Róisín could not recall even if someone happened to mention it to her. The wedding was to be in autumn and then he would be out of the house. While "IV" was in the house, she rarely encountered him except when he gathered with other members of the family.

The second son, Alfred, was large but not so fat as his brother. And he was far more adept with ladies than was "IV." His betrothal would come soon enough. Till then, he was happy to enjoy the freedom of a single man with neither children nor responsibilities.

The daughter was not fat. Marilyn Anne Reynolds had her mother's fine looks. Not thin, but well built. She was occupied with finding her husband after completing finishing school. She could afford, though, to be particular, and her mother's sentimental streak allowed her the luxury of seeking something other than a business arrangement. Within limits, of course. Miss Reynolds was more attractive than not and had some, but not all, of the haughtiness of her brothers. Her great faults were a sweetness of character and a weakness of will. Róisín spent more time with her than she did with any of the other Reynoldses, and they got along, Róisín thought, quite well.

Róisín enjoyed the routine of her new house and liked Miss Reynolds. When she was there for about seven months, the Reynoldses held a small ball with dancing and such in the large, second-floor drawing-room and an oasis for conversation in the sitting-room on the ground floor. This meant significantly greater duties in the days beforehand. While various outsiders would be brought in, the bulk of the work would be by the house staff. All went well, and the ball itself began smoothly on a Saturday night in late January. Among Róisín's tasks was seeing to the cleanliness of the water closet used by the women guests.

Given the frequency of events at the house, the Reynolds had, as had many other families, installed two water closets on the second floor down either hall from the drawing-room, and on this evening one was designated for the men's use and the other for the women's. They were not the full bathrooms for the family on the third floor. Instead, each contained a small commode clad in wood with a cistern for flushing and a sink to be used for washing up. The rooms were tiled because of the moisture. There were water closets in the basement and on the fourth floor for the staff, but they were not nearly as elaborate as were the ones for the guests nor, of course, as were those on the third floor used by the family.

Most guests were meticulous in the toilet, but some were not, and Róisín at times fought her way through the smells of their discharges. She was nearly done with one such incident when there was a knock on the door.

"I shall be but a moment," she called and hastened to finish cleaning. When she opened the door, she found herself facing Mary Geherty. Both were taken aback.

Mary—Mrs. McNabb, as she had become—was with two other women, friends obviously, planning to use the toilet.

"What have we here?" Mrs. McNabb said when she recovered from the shock of the meeting. "Cleaning toilets?" She turned to her friends. "I only wish I had a chamber pot for this one, which would suit since she came from a poor Irish farm."

Róisín fought the urge to lash out or cry, aware of the other women's chuckles.

"Is not that right, Irish girl?"

Róisín curtsied. "Yes, Miss Geherty."

"You recall my name. Too bad I never bothered to learn yours. And it is 'Mrs. McNabb' now. As even a simpleton like you knows."

With that, she went through and closed the toilet's door. Róisín, head down, sidled over to the side to make herself as inconspicuous as she could. The waiting women spoke quietly, occasionally laughing as Róisín tried to ignore them. Finally, the door opened, and Mrs. McNabb emerged.

"I have done what I came to do, whatever your name is."

"Róisín, Mrs. McNabb." Róisín bowed her head.

"Yes. Róisín. Róisín Campbell. Now you must do what you are paid to do." With that, she laughed and told her friends she would see them downstairs, "Once you are finished with this one."

When Róisín entered the toilet, she saw that Mary had made no effort to clean the chamber after herself. She had seen enough of her at the Gehertys to know that she was careful in her toilet. But neither of them were in the Geherty House, and Róisín choked on the smell. Others were worse, but it was difficult anyway.

Both of the other women left the toilet in a horrid state when they were done, the second laughing as she emerged. "You may have your work cut out for you for the next lady," and then she headed down the stairs, adjusting the bustle of her gown as she descended.

Róisín was relieved simply for being rid of Mary and her friends. No matter how vile things were with other ladies, it was nothing compared to what she had to do when the three finished their toilets. But do it she did. As the evening wound down, there was a final rush, and no one dawdled. Róisín thought the last one was gone and that she was almost finished when she saw Miss Reynolds come up the stairs, lifting the front of her gown to do it quickly. Mary McNabb was close behind.

"Is it true?" Miss Reynolds asked Róisín.

"I am sorry, Miss Reynolds. I don't know what—"

"That you were discharged from the Geherty House for inappropriate behavior?"

"I was at the Geherty House and, yes, I was discharged. But I did nothing inappropriate."

"Liar." Mrs. McNabb was around Marilyn and pointing a finger in Róisín's face.

"Do you deny trying to seduce my brothers and their friends?"

"Of course, I deny it."

"And my father. My dear father. Do you deny trying to seduce him?"

"Of course."

"Trying to have him make you his...mistress? As if my father would be so unfaithful to my mother."

"You know none of that is true."

"Yet you were discharged. Admit it!"

"Yes. Your mother dismissed me."

"And you did nothing wrong, that there were no grounds for your dismissal?"

"Yes. There were no grounds. Even your mother said—"

"Do not blame my mother."

Miss Reynolds stood troubled at the scene unfolding before her. Several ladies intending to use the toilet stopped on the stairs, although they did not remove themselves. Far too interesting.

Miss Reynolds liked Róisín. She truly did. She was too quick in her reaction to Mrs. McNabb's accusation and wished she spent more time considering it before she rushed up the stairs. Now a crowd watched. Even were what was said about Róisín not true—and Miss Reynolds suspected it was not—its truth no longer mattered.

"I do not blame your mother. I only say that your mother gave me a testimonial."

"But did she not tell you not to apply for a position with any of the families that she knew."

"Well, yes, but—"

"And you insist that you did nothing wrong."

"I do."

Mrs. McNabb looked to Miss Reynolds.

"I must say. As you can see, this creature is a liar and a seducer. She took advantage of my mother's goodwill. Collins, our housekeeper, told my mother not to hire her." Her head nodded in Róisín's direction. "Collins warned her and," Mary looked back at Róisín, "she betrayed that trust!"

With that, Mrs. McNabb started down the stairs, scattering the women who stood to listen like tenpins.

Miss Reynolds watched her go down and then turned to Róisín.

"I do like you, Róisín, but—" She nodded at the crowd of women staring, "you will have to be dismissed."

"But Miss—"

The other lowered her voice. "I am sorry, but it must be done." She turned and walked where Mrs. McNabb had gone moments before, through the stares of the others.

Róisín continued to clean the toilet until the last woman was finished, and then instead of going downstairs to report to the maid, she went up the servants' stairs to her space. She heard the clamor from the kitchen as she did, and when she got to her room she sat on the bed. Dismissal by the Reynolds meant she would never work in service again. Never.

She prepared her things and did not go downstairs in the morning. She left her door open, and at about seven fifteen the housekeeper appeared at it.

"Róisín. The mistress has instructed me to tell you that you are dismissed from this house."

There was an envelope in her right hand, and she handed it to Róisín.

"There be two weeks' pay. You shall not get a testimonial. You are to be gone within the hour." She lowered her voice and reached a hand to Róisín's wrist. "I am sorry. It cannot be helped."

She turned and left.

Róisín did not need an hour, or half of one, to leave. There were those at the house with whom she had grown close, but they were gone to her now. More, she was gone to them. It was a cold day, with a hint of snow later in the morning. Róisín took her satchel with her few things and headed south, hoping that Mrs. Flanagan would be home when she arrived. Had she looked up, she might have seen Miss Reynolds watching her leave. But she did not look up.

11.

Mrs. Flanagan again had space for Róisín, who had enough money to buy one fancy outfit, which she would need in her search for work.

Having been dismissed a second time, and from a somewhat prominent family at that, Róisín would not get another position in a respectable house. But what she learned in those two positions would be of use in one of the few alternative places for a woman to work: the department store. While most of those who sold were men, some elected to use the softer touch a woman could provide.

Several recently moved north from their original downtown locations to Broadway in the high-teens and low-twenties. These were stores with numerous departments chiefly catering to ladies, who could loiter and wander and buy things they could afford but had no need for. The stores became an alternative to the cloistered lives many ladies led, and the women spent hours wandering from department to department, catered to by men and an increasing number of women who were very much servants to the ladies' whims and caprices.

So, dressed in that one presentable dress, Róisín took the trolley north. She entered the largest and most famous store, Arnold Constable. She inquired whether she might speak to someone about being employed. A salesgirl directed her to a matronly woman called Alice Taylor who sat behind a large desk in a small office in the rear of the second floor.

Mrs. Taylor looked Róisín over quickly but carefully. She asked Róisín when she had come to America and where she worked. When told that it was two years ago and that she worked as a maid at the Geherty House and the Reynolds House but that she was dismissed from each position through no fault of her own, Mrs. Taylor said, "I am sure that is the case, my dear. But I do not believe that you are the sort of salesgirl we can use. I wish you well."

With that, Mrs. Taylor returned to whatever she was doing before Róisín entered, and Róisín retraced her steps to the street, the morning's drizzle having turned to rain. Even with an umbrella, the hem of her dress was damp as she entered Lord & Taylor a block away. A skeptical doorman directed her to a flight of stairs on the left side which led to a hall that led to a small office at the rear of the second floor. There sat a Mrs. Charlotte Houlihan. Mrs. Houlihan was in her forties but retained her beauty. Her red hair marked her as a fellow Irishwoman even before her slight brogue proved it.

When Róisín admitted that she was rejected at Constable's, Mrs. Houlihan laughed. "Of course, you were, dearie. You are too off-the-boat for the likes of Alice Taylor. Hide you in the back, she would, even if she employed you. Afraid of offending customers."

Mrs. Houlihan stood.

"Come with me, my dear." They walked down a hall. As they did, the noise from the store grew, echoed by the towering ceiling covered in stained glass. After skirting several areas of shoppers and salesgirls, they reached a railing that overlooked the main floor. It looked much like a ballroom of the sort Róisín had seen while working for the Gehertys or the Reynolds but broken up into well-defined sections and rectangles of display cases. It reminded Róisín of paintings she'd seen in picture books of Wellington's squares at Waterloo, with the customers like the French cavalry passing through the gaps.

It was difficult for Róisín to make out what Mrs. Houlihan said in the bluster from below, but she realized that she was being told to follow her back into the relative quiet of where the goods were sold on the second floor. En route, she was startled by a rattling noise.

"Oh that. That is Mr. Otis's fancy new elevator. It's a miraculous thing it is."

Róisín had heard of but never seen such a contraption, and Lord & Taylor was becoming famous for its one, which she someday hoped to ride. But first, she had to return to Mrs. Houlihan's office. The older woman leaned towards the girl after they sat.

"I take it that you have seen nothing like this."

"No, ma'am. It is, well, amazing, and I must say frightening."

"You will get used to it. It was new once even to an old hen like me," and Mrs. Houlihan laughed at her joke.

"Tell me, Miss Campbell, what did you learn at the house of the famous Bradford Reynolds the Third?"

"Well, ma'am. Both Mrs. Reynolds and Miss Marilyn Reynolds, her only daughter, went out often so there were always a lot of dresses they wore. I worked on Miss Reynolds almost every day, and she at times asked me my opinion concerning what to wear. And with her jewels. And her undergarments."

"As I thought. Come with me."

Róisín was embarrassed by the condition of her dress as she was led down the broad staircase to the main floor and passed counters selling various gloves and jewelry and perfumes.

"Tell me, Miss Campbell. You are accustomed to serving one lady at a leisurely pace. As you can see, this is far different. How would you fare?"

Róisín studied the various counters as the women—ladies—were pushing and shoving like the men on the docks she first encountered on arriving in New York. She also saw the calmness of the clerks. Politely but assertively controlling the customers. Always subservient, yet always in charge.

"I should like to learn."

Mrs. Houlihan laughed. "They are not so different from the cows on your farm, you see. They comply with a confident handler, and all my girls are confident handlers."

Róisín could not disagree.

"Come," the older woman said, "Follow me back. In time you will understand the dance we orchestrate here."

As the pair walked up to Mrs. Houlihan's office, Mrs. Houlihan put an arm through Róisín's.

"I think you shall do well here. I shall find you a good teacher on the floor and you will prove yourself and we shall both be happy."

Mrs. Houlihan was as good as her word. She found a good teacher for Róisín, someone five or so years older who was at the store for three years already. Róisín moved from Mrs. Flanagan's to a flat near Sixth Avenue, which she shared with another salesgirl. It was a building occupied almost exclusively by girls from the department stores and reminded Róisín of her days at the House of Mercy.

As happened at the Geherty and the Reynolds Houses, she was given a uniform—three long, black dresses with white lace trim at the collar and wrists, the cost of which were taken from her wages. Róisín quickly fell into her routine and provided a more than competent level of service, this time working at a glove counter with two other girls in a square to the left and back of Lord & Taylor's main entrance.

<h1 style="text-align:center">12.</h1>

"Ah," Mrs. Houlihan said when she reached the counter. "Miss Campbell. You may go home for the day. You will be paid for the time off. I will see you tomorrow."

"Tomorrow?" Mary cried. "Do you mean to say that Lord & Taylor will still employ her?"

By this point, Róisín had moved away, with a nod to Mrs. Houlihan, the slightest of one to Mrs. Geherty, once she recognized her, and nothing for Mary McNabb, who she immediately recognized.

Mrs. Houlihan turned to Mary's mother.

"Might I have a word, Mrs.—"

"Geherty. Mrs. Geherty."

"Mrs. Geherty. Of course. Please excuse me for not recognizing you. And Miss Geherty."

"Mrs. McNabb."

"I am sorry. Mrs. McNabb. Please let us have some tea."

Mrs. Houlihan herded the two to the small tearoom at the rear of the main floor. She nodded to one of the servers, and they sat at a round table. Almost as soon as they settled in, the server brought a tray with cups and saucers and a teapot and set about pouring the three teas.

"Thank you, my dear," Mrs. Houlihan told her.

Addressing herself to Mrs. Geherty, Mrs. Houlihan said, "I am rather fond of Miss Campbell. She and I come from the same part of Ireland, you know. Although I came here well before she did."

Mrs. Geherty smiled at the remark. Mary—Mrs. McNabb—held her scowl.

"I believe she is a good worker and have no reason to doubt her honesty and her morals. She told me that she was dismissed from two houses. She mentioned one by name but not the other. May I assume that she worked in your house?"

"Yes, you may. We employed her soon after she arrived in New York."

"And why was she dismissed?"

Mrs. Geherty hesitated while Mrs. Houlihan took a sip of her tea, and her daughter filled the vacuum.

"She had a very loose eye and was trying to ingratiate herself with the men in the house. I did my best to deter her, but she was insistent, and it was necessary that she be removed from the house."

Mrs. Geherty looked at her daughter and then back at her host.

"Mrs. Houlihan. It is a matter of some delicacy. Suffice it to say that I at least was unaware that Róisín did anything improper in my house. I merely thought it best for all concerned that she find another position, which I understand she did with Hyacinth Reynolds."

"Yes. That was the house she named to me. She was, however, vague as to why she was removed from there."

"I can tell you about that," Mrs. McNabb said. "I saw her working at the Reynolds House at a ball where I was a guest. I did no more than simply inform Marilyn Anne Reynolds that her family employed someone of loose morals and would do well to be rid of her as soon as possible." She finished with a self-satisfied grin.

Her mother looked at her.

"Mary. Do you know of anything that Róisín did to even suggest that she had loose morals? Anything?"

"Well, nothing specific. But I saw how she behaved when Charlie and Michael were in a room with her. Or father."

"What on earth do you mean, 'how she behaved'?"

"Mother, there was nothing specific. I just got a bad feeling about her and them and other gentlemen who visited. Especially Peter. It is what I told Mrs. Collins."

Mrs. Geherty turned back to Mrs. Houlihan.

"Peter is Mr. McNabb. Mrs. Collins is our housekeeper. I assure you, Róisín did nothing to warrant what my daughter says about her. Her dismissal had nothing to do with her. That is all I can say, but I assure you that that is the case."

She looked at her daughter.

"Is that clear?"

"Yes, Mother."

Mrs. Houlihan, who was sipping her tea slowly during the exchange, smiled.

"I am glad to hear it. As I say. I do like her, and she is a good worker. But Mrs. McNabb, I thank you for bringing it to my attention. Now if you will excuse me, I do have to tend to some other matters."

She left the other two to finish their teas.

When Róisín got to work the next morning, Mrs. Houlihan asked to see her in her office.

"Mrs. Geherty vouched for you. I never doubted it. That daughter of hers, though. She seemed very, very angry. Tell me. Was she married when you worked at the Geherty House?"

"No, ma'am. But she became engaged. To a Peter McNabb."

"Well, she is Mrs. McNabb now. What can you tell me about Mr. McNabb?"

"Well, I had very little dealings with gentlemen in the house, even Master Geherty and Michael. Or Mr. Geherty. But when the ladies were out of a room, they and their guests would sometimes become...inappropriate. Mr. McNabb was, I think, no worse than the others. He was not an attractive man and a little too proud of his father's money. But, as I say, I had few dealings with him or any other male guests."

"Well. I can see the source of Mrs. McNabb's hostility to you. Let us hope that you never cross paths in the future. As I say, Mrs. Geherty vouched for you. She told her daughter that there was nothing untoward or dishonest or immoral about you. Let us hope that the message took. If not, let us hope you never see Mrs. McNabb again. If you see her come into the store, please excuse yourself from the floor. If anyone asks, have them speak to me."

With that, Róisín left her employer and headed for another day behind the glove counter. Her life returned to normal after her brush with near dismissal. Her commission income steadily increased in her time there as she was well-liked by both the women with whom she worked and the women who came to buy their gloves. And she never saw Mrs. McNabb in the store again.

13.

On Sundays, her day off, Róisín at times walked to the church near Mrs. Flanagan's for mass, and she often spoke to her former landlady about how she was faring at the store.

She was doing so on a Sunday about three months after the unpleasantness with Mrs. McNabb, and there was a slight morning rain. As she neared Immaculate Conception, she heard a neighing horse and then a crash as a two-seat gig slipped across the avenue, smashing against a light post. The horse seemed fine if shaken, but a man and a woman were caught in the gig, which was nearly on its side. Róisín had seen her share of horse collisions and the patching up of injured men in Limerick. She and a gentleman ran, and they reached it at the same moment along with several passing laborers heading to church. One opened the door and passed the two occupants to the wet street, on which they were gently laid. There was blood everywhere. The man was barely conscious, the woman barely aware.

Someone said there was a clinic of some sort near, and laborers carried them to it with Róisín following. The couple looked out of place in the neighborhood. Both were of the sort Róisín saw time and again at the Geherty and Reynolds Houses. After a block or so, they were directed to a storefront on a side street. Róisín had never noticed it before. It was closed, being Sunday, but someone ran up the stairs, and a few minutes later a man and a woman who looked to be preparing for mass themselves came down, the latter with keys, and the front door was opened and the man directed that the two injured be taken to an examination room in the back.

It was clear that the gentleman was by far the more damaged, evidenced by his screams. The lady seemed more in shock than anything, and Róisín led her to a small chair at the side as the man was placed, still screaming and gasping for air, on a table. Róisín took to examining the woman and saw no signs of physical injury. Instead, the blood appeared to be that of her companion. Róisín wrapped her arm around her and ran it up and down her upper arm, leaning her head towards her so she could whisper that it would be alright.

With the gentleman on the table, the man from upstairs, who Róisín realized was a doctor, called for the Samaritans who brought him in to leave except for one or two who were needed to hold the victim. The woman with the doctor was plainly a nurse, and she immediately took to cutting the ruined clothing from the gentleman's upper body. For a moment, the doctor turned to Róisín and the lady, and Róisín said that she did not appear to be injured.

"Fine. Try to keep her calm. I will be with her presently." Her time in New York had taught her that his was a Dubliner's accent. The doctor returned to the gentleman, and Róisín continued her ministrations. As the lady recovered her senses, she turned to Róisín in a panic.

"He is not my husband. No one must know. I will tell you who he is. You must send for someone for him. But no one must know."

She looked to be around Mrs. McNabb's age, and the gentleman was about the same. A Sunday morning liaison gone wrong. Róisín did not know the lady but knew she was relying on her. As the doctor and nurse worked on the screaming gentleman, she promised the lady that no one else need know.

"Are you hurt?" she asked.

The lady was diverted in examining herself.

"I am sore, but I believe that is all."

Róisín saw a screen and moved it so it blocked the view from the others. The lady wore a brown daydress, which had a frilled vest mimicking a corset atop it. Fortunately, the vest and the dress itself had buttons on the front and when the lady agreed to Róisín's request to touch her, she unbuttoned the two pieces and spread them to expose the lady's shoulders and upper undergarments, which Róisín lifted. She found spots that were sensitive to her fingers along the left side. Róisín asked if she could look, and again the lady permitted it, and Róisín found several bruises forming where the tenderness was.

"I will have the doctor look, but I do not believe you have any serious injuries. Just bruises. I will see about taking you home directly. But you must tell me who the gentleman is, and we should find a boy to tell his family."

The lady identified him and said where he lived. Róisín went around the screen and asked the doctor whether the gentleman would be sent to a hospital. He bridled at the interruption but eased when Róisín said his family must know where to find him.

"Yes. He will go to the German Hospital. I will send a boy to get an ambulance. He can tell his family. What about the woman?"

Róisín said that she did not seem seriously injured and that the blood was the man's.

"I should like to take her home."

The doctor and nurse looked at her.

"They are not husband and wife?" the nurse asked. Róisín shook her head. It was enough, and it was dropped.

The doctor said, "I will look on her in a moment, and if she is alright, you may take her home. Do you know her?"

"No, sir. I happened by her on the way to mass."

The doctor gave the gentleman a morphine injection for the pain, and it calmed him. He sent one of the men helping to restrain him to fetch a boy, and when he returned with one, the lady gave the boy the gentleman's address and the doctor told him to hurry to fetch an ambulance and in a moment the boy, a ten-cent piece in hand, was gone. With the nurse tending to the gentleman, the doctor repeated Róisín's examination of the lady, concluding by looking into her eyes.

"Aye. You do not appear to be harmed. If you have any discomfort or severe pain, you must immediately have your physician call on you." After the lady nodded, the doctor looked to Róisín. "Please take her home."

After helping the lady dress in the ruined dress and vest, she and the patient walked around the screen to the table on which her companion was trying to make himself tolerably comfortable. The lady said goodbye to him, though it seemed unlikely that he heard her. While she did, the doctor asked Róisín to write down her name and where she could be reached, which she did. The two women went out to the sidewalk, and they drew much attention from passersby. They were able to clean up the blood on their faces and hands. But their dresses were ruined.

The lady hailed a hansom cab on the avenue. The cabbie looked at the blood and was tempted to ride off, but the lady said she would make it worth his while and she reached into her purse, which someone brought to her from the crash, and showed him a one-dollar bill. Once they were seated and the cab was moving north, the anonymous lady shook slightly and leaned lightly against Róisín. She became talkative in the silence. She admitted being married but said she enjoyed innocent (she insisted) liaisons with men who were on the outer edges of her circle of friends.

"I do like this one. But he can be a fool. Like today. He decided to show me how adept he was at driving a gig. And you saw the results. He went much too fast in the wet and tried to turn and, well, we soared through the air. He deserves all the pain that his pigheadedness is putting him through."

"But do you not care about his condition?" Róisín asked.

"Of course, I care. But he is not a real friend. Just someone to break up the boredom of my life and the proper friends I have and the events I must attend. You are lucky to have a job. It gives you something to do."

Róisín was silent.

"But you are from Ireland, are you not?"

"Indeed, ma'am. I have been here only a few years."

Róisín was not interested in sharing her life with this woman, and thankfully this woman was not interested in Róisín sharing it with her. She immediately returned to the drudgery of her existence and how revolting she found the whole thing and her husband and his family.

Róisín was relieved when the cab reached the house. The two got out after the lady handed the dollar bill to the cabbie, instructing him to take Róisín home. Róisín got back in, but not before noticing the house. It was large, as Róisín expected, and not far from the Reynolds House. Róisín thought it likely that Marilyn Reynolds was among her circle of friends and was relieved not to have said anything that might inform this woman of her former position.

The lady began to walk towards it but stopped. She returned to the cab, reaching into her purse as she did.

"I have caused the ruination of your dress," she said, and she handed a five-dollar bill to Róisín, insisting that she take it to purchase a new one. She turned again and walked up the steps to the front door and into the house without looking back, and the cabbie took Róisín home.

She climbed the stairs to her apartment and used the sink in the bathroom in the hall to clean herself as well as she could before changing into something presentable. Her roommate and the others on the floor were out, and with little food, she left and got a sandwich at a shop on the corner and carried it to a small park near her apartment.

She was exhausted from the morning's ordeal, and the Lord would have to forgive her for missing mass.

It was early afternoon, and she found an empty bench in a corner. The rain had ended, and the sun had dried the bench. Róisín brought one of her lighter novels, called *Clifden Dreams*, from her flat and sat. It was a familiar love story about a member of the Protestant Ascendancy and the Catholic servant girl he secretly adores. Soon Róisín was oblivious to the noises around her as she found herself on an estate in the west of Ireland with a breathtaking view of the Atlantic battering the rocky coastline.

It was disconcerting when Róisín was shaken awake by a governess asking if she was alright.

"Oh, I am sorry. I must have dozed off."

"Do not be sorry. I was just seeing to you."

The woman was slightly older than Róisín. Her dress established her as being something other than a domestic, and she said she was a governess, originally from Dublin. She became learned enough in Ireland to secure a position in an Irish-American house, the name of which Róisín vaguely recalled from her time at the Gehertys'. She sat, briefly, giving her name as Deidre O'Sullivan and explaining that her position was lonely and awkward, being neither staff nor family.

The two chatted comfortably. But Deidre said she had to leave and that she hoped to see her new friend again and with a handshake she was gone. After she was, Róisín wondered if that were a life she might enjoy. Perhaps she had enough knowledge to obtain such a position where she could instruct a child. Perhaps it was something that she would like to do. She kept *Clifden Dreams* closed as she watched the others, especially the children, in the park and let her mind wander in this pleasant until it was time for her to return to her flat.

Monday and Tuesday at the store were like the others. She bought a new dress during her lunch break on the latter. On occasion Róisín scanned the floor, wondering if the lady from the accident would happen by but she did not. When she was back at her apartment on Tuesday, she found a note slipped into the frame of her door.

Miss Campbell,

You provided valuable assistance on Sunday in my clinic. Mostly, you did not faint at the sight of blood and proved dexterous with your hands and were gentle with the lady. I should very much like to speak to you on the question of whether you might be interested in working in my clinic in the future.

I am there every morning save Sunday, and I would be pleased to meet you at your convenience.

Your humble servant,
Callum Doyle, MD

Róisín stared at it. The evening was warm, and the window was open wide, and the street noise was loud in her room. *"You did not faint at the sight of blood and proved dexterous with your hands and were gentle with the lady."* She would, of course, go to him, at least to learn what he thought she could do for him and how much she would be paid to do it.

She enjoyed Lord & Taylor and was in no hurry to leave it. She was not paid very much, but enough to share her apartment and buy her books. She went to entertainments at times and could even remit money to Limerick as her commissions increased. She made friends with several of the girls with whom she worked, especially her roommate, and sometimes went to eat with them after work. She made friends, too, at her church.

She admired Mrs. Houlihan. She was a Famine girl who arrived in New York in 1850 and found work as a seamstress when she came from the western part of County Limerick, near the Shannon, which was hurt much more in the Famine than was the east where Róisín was soon to be born. She married someone named Houlihan shortly after they arrived, but he was killed in an accident on the dock. In this, she was much like Mrs. Flanagan (whom Róisín visited every month or so after mass).

Mrs. Houlihan had managed to get a low-level job at Constable's when it was downtown. She worked hard and got a job at Lord & Taylor when it opened a new store on Broadway, before its move to Twentieth Street. There she caught the eye of one of the sons of the original Lord for her diligence and knowledge of merchandise and, more important, of customers. She was appointed an assistant manager, the most senior woman at the company, in 1868 and succeeded the manager two years later.

She proved her worth, and Lord & Taylor became one of the premier department stores in New York. Yet for all of her work, Mrs. Houlihan knew she was less respected than the lowest boy hired for the loading dock. Though Mr. Lord made a point of treating her well, his influence only went so far, and she was forever an outsider.

So, when Róisín spoke to her on Wednesday about what Dr. Doyle asked her, she encouraged the younger woman. She was in a man's world and ultimately a world in which a woman's role was either to have children and make a pleasant home for her husband and to be waited upon when out or to be the person who tended to those children and helped make the home pleasant and to wait upon her betters.

14.

Mrs. Houlihan gave Róisín leave to meet with Dr. Doyle on Saturday.

When she entered the clinic, it had been open for some time though it was still early. The nurse, who recognized Róisín and said her name was Margaret Evans, rose from the desk and greeted her. She was quite a handsome woman, seeming to be near Róisín's mamma's age and also with the slight hint of a Dubliner's lilt.

"He is all talking about you since Sunday. I can tell you that we can use the help. He asked me, and I told him I would be pleased to work with you, and I would be. It is not easy work, mind you. But it is good work, the Lord's work in its way. I will lead you in."

Róisín said she could not stay long as she had to get to work.

"I will interrupt him," Nurse Evans said.

While she went to the examination room, Róisín surveyed those in the waiting room. It was not full. Those who spoke did so with a brogue, and Róisín assumed the rest, too, were Irish.

A moment later, a woman came through the door followed by Nurse Evans. The nurse instructed Róisín to go see the doctor. This drew an audible groan some several of those waiting, which drew a rebuke from Nurse Evans about Dr. Doyle seeing 'em when Dr. Doyle was ready to see 'em.

In the back, the doctor stood beside one of the examination tables. There were two chairs, and he directed her to them, and they both sat. He got to the point directly.

"As I said in my note, I do not think you will embarrass either of us should you assist me. I will be unlikely to be able to pay you what you earn wherever it is you work, but you would find the work rewarding and I will be able to provide you with living quarters on the second floor.

"We survive on donations from the community and are hopeful of getting some support from the city. I need someone like you. How were you able to handle yourself so well?"

"Sir. I was reared on a dairy farm in County Limerick."

"How old are you?"

"I am just past twenty and I arrived in this country when I was a little past eighteen."

"Where have you worked?"

"Well, sir. And I must get to Lord & Taylor. But first, I worked as a domestic servant."

"Why did you stop being in service."

"Well, sir. It seems that in my first position the mistress was concerned that I might...be leading the master into temptation."

"Did he partake of the apple?" the doctor asked severely.

"No, sir. I am no fool. But as a result, no Irish house would hire me. I got a job in an English house but...but the daughter in the first house took a dislike for me, sir. She made all sorts of accusations about me to my new mistress."

"And the new mistress believed her notwithstanding your protests, and you were again on the street?"

"I don't know that she believed her, but I think she had no choice in the matter after what the other woman said in front of a crowd."

"Very well. Think about what I said. I am looking to hire someone so do not spend too much time thinking. I would very much like for you to work here. Given your manner with that lady, I think you would be very good with the patients."

With that, the audience was over. He smiled for the first time, and rose and extended his hand to her as she got up.

They stepped into the waiting room, and the doctor asked Nurse Evans to show her the room she would have.

"She will show it to you. I do hope you agree. And now, alas," he shrugged, "there is always another patient."

After Nurse Evans showed an elderly Irishman in, she fetched a set of keys from a drawer. She led Róisín to the sidewalk and then the door on the west side of the building. It led directly to a flight of steps. Upon going through, she turned up the gaslight to show the way and did the same as they reached the second floor. There they entered the hallway, at the end of which, Nurse Evans said, there was a bathroom with a toilet, sink, and tub. She opened the first door on the right. The room faced the front and had two large windows. It was about the size of Róisín's flat. It had a small stove, cabinets, and a sink to the left. One bed (which Róisín found not too lumpy), several chairs, a desk, a dresser, and a closet with several hangers filled it out with a small table and a pair of gas sconces along one wall. More than anything, it was clean.

"I've the room next to this. A charwoman comes in once a week to clean. She is nosy but better than most, and she does a good job."

After leaving the room, Róisín thanked the nurse and rushed to catch a trolley to her store. She reported to Mrs. Houlihan that things had gone well and that she was thinking about it.

It happened that Róisín was to stroll with Mr. Henry and one of his friends after mass the next day. They walked to Broadway and headed north towards the window displays of the closed department stores, including Lord & Taylor. As they went, Róisín told them of the clinic and the story of the gentleman, the lady, and the overturned gig, and the resulting interaction with Doctor Doyle and Nurse Evans. She explained about the note and the meeting with the doctor. She described the flat she would have.

Mr. Henry and his friend debated the question with Róisín. Finally, Mr. Henry asked her whether she could afford to work for the doctor. She said that with the flat she could. She added that perhaps she could become a nurse herself, though she had not truly thought of that prospect until she sat with the lady at the clinic. The three stopped abruptly, and Mr. Henry looked at the girl.

"You, my dear, will make an excellent nurse, and should I ever be so foolish as to be shattered in a gig accident I hope that I will be placed in your care. It is something I think you should do," and his friend echoed the sentiments, and the three resumed their walk, and Róisín thought how much she loved her dear Mr. Henry.

She sat with Mrs. Houlihan the next morning. The older woman said Róisín would be a fool not to jump at the chance.

"I have been here for a while and, God willing, will be here for a while longer. But you're young. I think you would do well as a nurse and be more satisfied than you are here. I fear you will become very bored were you to stay."

15.

With doubts removed but nerves intact, and aided by Mr. Henry, Róisín moved her meager belongings into the flat above the clinic on the next Sunday. She had her own room again, far larger than the tiny ones at the Gehertys and Reynoldses, and part of her was sorry to be leaving her roommate and the other salesgirls with whom she lived while at Lord & Taylor, especially after the farewell dinner they had, with Mrs. Houlihan's financial contribution, on Saturday after work.

But move she did, and her work at the clinic was to begin the next morning. It was just over two weeks after the accident. The clinic chiefly provided care to portions of the Irish tenements, the sickness-infected, unsanitary buildings that housed significant parts of the recently-arrived Irish.

The facility itself was in a row of identical buildings. Each had some type of business on its ground floor with wide windows out onto the sidewalk. The large space on the ground floor was divided across so there was a waiting area in front and an examination and support rooms behind a wall that divided the space. The examination room, which Róisín saw on the day of the accident, was large and had two examination tables, separated by a screen. A pair of windows opened up to the small yard in the rear and looked out to the identical building one block to the north. There were several cabinets in which various tools and curatives were stored. To the right was a large storage room and next to it a room that was used for the temporary storage of corpses.

The building had three floors above the clinic itself, and each had two apartments. As she saw, they were reached via a staircase entered through a door on the sidewalk. New York had few hospitals since the well-to-do received care at their homes (and new members of that class came into the world in their homes), but more were being built. The closest one to the clinic was the German Hospital and Dispensary on East Third Street. Dr. Doyle had an arrangement with it. People on the lower east side of Manhattan were encouraged to seek care first at the clinic. If they were found to require hospitalization, they would be sent to the hospital.

On that first Monday, Nurse Evans was pleased to see Róisín. She had long been pestering Dr. Doyle to bring in another set of hands, and she saw on the day of the accident that Róisín's were steady.

But she warned Róisín as they waited for the clinic to open on that first day. She should not expect every day to be like the one with the accident. Although there were frequent cases of broken bones from work or riding accidents, most days involved mundane aches and pains suffered by those in the neighborhood. Diseases and addictions, too. So Róisín found it to be. She spent much of her days cleaning the backroom or the front room and interviewing patients about whatever was bothering them. On occasion, she was called in to provide an extra set of hands with a patient, and Dr. Doyle did what he could to tell her what he was doing so she could ultimately become a nurse.

Initially, Róisín wondered what she had gotten herself into. Since arriving in New York, she worked as a servant for those superior to her. Such superiority, or inferiority if one chose to look at it in that way, existed in her Irish county but was not so blatant. Her first experience at the clinic was along those lines, caring for a lady and gentlemen injured in an accident.

Now she realized the clinic catered to the poor and the poorer, not far different from the girls in Queenstown or at the House of Mercy from whom she felt apart. They were so sick and dirty and stupid. Perhaps Mrs. Houlihan would take her back.

It all changed about three weeks after she began, when Róisín saw someone die. She was a young woman. Not much older than Róisín. Perhaps not sick but surely dirty and stupid. This woman believed she could make it across the avenue before a carriage passed, but she miscalculated and may have slipped on manure and while the driver tried to stop, it was too late and she was knocked unconscious by the horse. They rushed her to the clinic. She was brought to the examination table in the back, still breathing. But, as Róisín and Dr. Doyle watched, her breath stopped, and she was gone.

She was not a pretty woman and wore the clothing of a washerwoman. Who knows where she was going in such a hurry. Why she would run in front of the carriage. It did not matter. She was dead. She wore a cheap wedding band, and someone brought the small bag she carried to the clinic. Dr. Doyle covered her face with a cloth and opened the bag. He found a paper with her name and address in a primitive scrawl. He sighed. It was several blocks away, in one of the tenements. She was dead though the hoof had not broken the skin and there was no blood. Her brain was crushed. The doctor and Nurse Evans moved the body to the small room used for the purpose while Róisín watched.

Though there was a waiting room full of patients, Dr. Doyle quietly walked out. He carried the dead woman's bag. While he was gone, Nurse Evans sent a boy to contact Bellevue, the city's morgue, so the body could be removed, and then she stood with Róisín on the sidewalk and with her hands on Róisín's lower arms spoke to her and promised her that they were doing good work, necessary work.

Dr. Doyle returned perhaps half an hour later. He remained taciturn as he went into the examination room, bidding that Róisín come with him and paying no mind to the patients waiting.

"I am sorry that you had to see that. But it is necessary. We see many, too many, people die. Suddenly they are gone. She woke up this morning and will never wake up again. I left word for her husband to come here. Someone at her tenement sent a boy for him. He will likely be here shortly. We must be prepared for that."

Róisín could only nod and then walked to the front. She had seen animals die many times. But it was so different with a person. Alive. Then dead. Doctor Doyle and Nurse Evans had seen countless deaths, and it seemed that neither lost sight of the finality of it.

As she reached the door, Dr. Doyle instructed her to send in the next patient in the now crowded waiting area, and after she did Nurse Evans came to her again, dreading when the husband would arrive. But there were patients to see, and the two women turned to the living.

At times, the clinic was overwhelmed, particularly when a fever ran rampant through the tenements and patients had to be kept away. Such a fever occurred not long after Róisín began. Fortunately, it proved painful but generally not fatal, and it slowly passed from the tenements in which it at first appeared. Róisín had seen such fevers run through a herd on the farm and that at least prepared her for the exhausting days spent to get some control over it. Diseases were far too frequent in the tenements and far more disruptive than was the general flu.

Gradually, Róisín became comfortable in her role and did not look back whence she came, and it was not long before she became the preferred nurse for the pregnant Irish women (or mostly girls) who needed care after something went wrong, helping midwives and consoling those whose babies did not survive. And she became a regular presence on the streets that her cousin warned her against entering on that day she came to New York.

16.

Some months after Róisín started working at the clinic, and well into her routine, several men brought in a gentleman and a lady who, from all appearances, seemed to have been in an accident much like the one that first brought Róisín to Dr. Doyle's attention. This time, though, the blood on the lady was her own. The gentleman was bleeding and unconscious. They were directed to the examination room. There, while Doctor Doyle and Nurse Evans attended to the man, Róisín tended to the woman. She had lost much blood, but Róisín could find only one source, a gash along her forehead. She applied a cloth to it. The lady was coherent but woozy, and Róisín instructed her to press the cloth to stem the flow of blood.

She then examined the lady's body. She was very near Róisín's age but shorter by several inches. She had a pleasing bosom, and Róisín noticed the symmetry of her body. More immediately, though, was that her light brown hair was in spots darkened by her blood and there was the tracing of a drop that meandered down the side of her face to her shoulder, where it dried. As Róisín ran her hands along the sides, she found several places where the lady suffered obvious bruises. Róisín placed the screen between the two examination tables.

The lady nodded when Róisín asked if she could look at her skin. Her cream-colored artistic dress had a loose, swooping collar that allowed Róisín to pull the top down to the lady's waist and then untie and remove the simple corset. Stepping back, Róisín saw several bruises on the left arm and stomach. The lady was chilled by the Irish woman's hands as they applied pressure in places on her abdomen, eliciting several groans as she did. Róisín told the lady that she suffered some bruising and that her skin would become increasingly discolored for several days.

When Róisín pushed in various spots, she was glad that the lady did not react, which suggested no significant internal injuries, something she would confirm with Dr. Doyle.

"Do you feel any discomfort in your legs?"

"No. It was my upperparts and my head that got hit."

"How did it happen?" Róisín was still studying the patient's body.

"The gig slipped on the pavement, and my fiancé could not control the horse as it began to slide. Before I knew it, the gig was nearly on its side. He was silent, and I feared that he was dead. Several people rushed to help, and one called out that he was still breathing. And we were brought here. I do not remember much else."

"Well," Róisín said, "I think you at least were lucky. I do not think the blood is significant, but you must rest for several days so that you can regain your strength. Dr. Doyle will examine you, but I do not think you suffered anything else on your body but bruises."

"Thank you, nurse."

"Ah, I am not quite a nurse yet. I've not been here long, but Dr. Doyle is an excellent teacher."

With that, Róisín stepped around the screen. She saw that the lady's fiancé was still unconscious, and it was clear that he suffered terrible injuries. His body was broken as many of his bones had taken the brunt of the crash. It was a blessing that he was unconscious. Róisín wondered whether any man could tolerate the pain he would surely experience when he awoke. If he awoke.

Nurse Evans went from the room. She called to a boy who did errands for the clinic and told him to rush to the German Hospital for an ambulance to collect the gentleman. When she returned, the three—Dr. Doyle, Nurse Evans, and Róisín—stood over the body, each thinking of the horrors the gentleman would encounter.

Róisín bid Dr. Doyle look at the lady, and the two stepped around the screen.

"Doctor. How is my fiancé?" She lifted herself to pose the question.

"Oh. He is your fiancé. I must tell you, miss, that he is in a very bad way. He is not awake, which is a blessing. We have sent for an ambulance to take him to the German Hospital, where he can get the care he needs. But I fear that he has injuries that will affect him for the rest of his days."

"God. He is such a fool. Trying to show off with his skills in a gig. Planning to race against his cronies uptown. A fool." She lay back down.

It was not clear to whom this observation was addressed, and both Róisín and Dr. Doyle were embarrassed by the vehemence of its delivery.

"He is Edward Meade. His family is very prominent. Someone must be sent to inform them. I will provide the address. I assume that they should be told to go to the hospital?"

"Yes, miss. That is right," the doctor said.

He turned to Róisín.

"Take the information down and get it to a boy to give the message," and she wrote what the lady had to say and left the room briefly. Before she could return, Róisín heard the clang of an ambulance, and she stepped to the sidewalk to direct the crew in. She held the door as they carried a stretcher in and followed them to the examination room.

Dr. Doyle told them the patient, a Mr. Edward Meade, was unconscious and suffered significant injuries in a gig accident. The ambulance crew delicately and skillfully lifted Meade to the stretcher. The lady insisted on seeing what was happening to her fiancé, and after Róisín cleaned away the blood and helped restore the corset and dress to their appropriate places, she moved the screen completely to the side.

The lady sat transfixed by the lifeless form. He was rushed out, and she asked if she could accompany him notwithstanding her condition.

There was not room enough in the ambulance, but Róisín offered to take her to the hospital, and Dr. Doyle allowed her to go and gave her some money for a cab. He found a coat to cover the lady's blood and applied a bandage to her forehead. The pair arrived shortly after Meade and were directed to a dark corridor near where he was being treated.

As they sat waiting, the lady said calmly, "This may be a blessing."

Róisín looked at her, but she stared into the distance.

"I do not love him. He is brash and a bully and a braggart. But he has money, and that is what my parents see in him. I have one sister married and I am the second and last and so I must marry as well." Róisín was embarrassed, listening to this confession, but the lady continued.

"My parents, my father at least, encouraged the match with his family. They are business colleagues in some way I do not understand. So, I must marry an ugly, horrible man I do not love and bear his children."

She turned to Róisín and attempted a smile.

"You do not know, I think, how fortunate you are to work for yourself. I hope you are not attached to a man you do not love, and if you are, I feel sorry for you. Very sorry for you."

She turned again to stare into the distance.

Before Róisín could respond, though in truth she had no idea how she would respond, the pair heard hurried footsteps in the hall. The lady stood and Róisín followed, the former whispering, "These are his parents."

The mother, who Róisín would only know as Mrs. Meade, rushed to hug her future daughter-in-law, oblivious to the other's presence. So, too, did Mr. Meade ignore

Róisín as he shook the lady's hand, asking what news she had.

The lady said she had none beyond what the doctor had said at the clinic. She added that they were fortunate to get care at the clinic after the gig accident and that "this woman," and she nodded to Róisín, who the Meades begrudgingly acknowledged, "accompanied me here. I was examined and told that I have no significant injuries. Edward, though, is in a very bad way. Very bad. He was still unconscious when the ambulance took him here. I am sure the doctors will be able to tell you more than I can."

Mrs. Meade said, "As to you, you must be properly examined here." With that, she and her husband stepped away, sitting on a bench some distance down the hall.

"They do sometimes say pleasant things to me, and I have come to like them," the lady quietly said, "but I am not marrying *them*. Edward, who I am marrying, is one of two children. He has an older brother, who married well, but because of his business relationship with my father, they think it appropriate that he marry me, although I am not of the stature of his brother's wife's family. Again. Sometimes I wish for simpler things."

The lady's hand was on Róisín's, in Róisín's lap.

"Now I must leave you. Thank you for coming here with me. I shan't keep you longer. I must do my duty and sit with them. They made it clear that they wish you gone. Thank you."

With that, Róisín rose and headed down the hall away from the Meades.

"Wait," the lady, whose name Róisín did not get, called to her. She reached into her purse and pulled out a bill. "Please take a cab back to the clinic. I am forever in your debt."

After handing the money to Róisín, far more than was necessary and insisting that it be taken, she turned and with a sigh headed to her future in-laws, still covered by the coat she borrowed from the clinic to cover her blood.

17.

Four months after beginning at the clinic, Dr. Doyle arranged to have Róisín spend one day each week at the German Hospital. She would learn more skills there, which she would bring back to the clinic. She was assigned to a surgical hall. This meant that she interviewed patients before they were taken to theater for their operation and helped with their initial convalescence.

She developed some friendships, more acquaintances, with some of the nurses. Because she was employed at the clinic, they had no fear of her supplanting them and were generous in their advice and support. Soon she went twice a week, and Dr. Doyle retained another woman to help at the clinic.

On a summer afternoon in 1873, Róisín was at the hospital when a boy who ran errands for the clinic rushed up to her.

"Please, miss. You be needed."

She looked at him and after telling the nurse, she rushed the eight blocks, nearly half-a-mile, south. When she entered, Nurse Evans went to her.

"There is someone in your room."

Róisín could not imagine who it could be or why things were so urgent. When she went through the door, she saw a girl of about eighteen sitting on a chair, staring out the window. As the girl turned, Róisín recognized her sister Sophie. She was sometimes Sadhbh at home but in America, she would be Sophie. And she stood as Róisín rushed across to her, putting her hands on Sophie's upper arms.

"Oh my God. 'Tis you. But what are you here for?"

Sophie pulled away and stepped to the bed where there was a satchel and next to it a letter. She picked the letter up and brought it to her sister. It was sealed and addressed to Róisín.

"Mamma gave me your address. She wrote this for you." She sat back down, turning the chair to watch her sister.

My Dearest Róisín,

I could only get this news to you by having your sister bring it. Sophie is with child. It don't matter how it happened, and you can't blame her too much for it. She didn't want to leave, but your daddy and I saw no choice.

'Tis something I can only ask of you as my daughter and her sister. That you care for her as best you can. She be wild at times, but she is still in her heart a good child.

I know you will do what is right. You must decide whether to tell your cousin Jimmy. My sister, his mother, knows about this. So does your father. But no one else. Not even the child's father.

Please may God
be with you,
Mamma

When Róisín looked up from the letter, Sophie was staring at her.

"Do you know what mamma wrote?"

"Not exactly. But I know she told you of my...condition. I hope she told you not to blame me. Please, Róisín, don't be blaming me. It was wrong and stupid. But I promise to do better. I promise."

Sophie was eighteen, the age Róisín was when she came to New York. Róisín approached her sister, who stood. She ran her hand across Sophie's tummy.

"Do you know for how long you have been with child?"

"It was only the once. Three months ago."

After stepping back again, Róisín realized that on Sophie's thin and lanky body, it would not be long before her pregnancy would be evident. Perhaps a matter of weeks. Surely no more than a month.

"Well, the first thing we must do is get you settled. You will stay here, of course. I am sure that Dr. Doyle will permit it. He will examine you. We will need to get a second bed. And...and we will see what will happen. For now, please try to get some rest. Have you eaten?"

When Sophie admitted she had not, that she was too nervous to keep anything down, Róisín said she would get her some food.

The girl rushed to her sister.

"Oh, Róisín. I was so afraid you would put me out on the street, and I would be a beggarwoman and put in jail or die on the streets. Some girls on the boat. They said I could do something to be rid of my baby, but it is his baby too and I will never do that."

Róisín stopped the babbling with a series of taps on Sophie's back, whispering, "I know. I know. You are my baby sister. It is for me to care for you like I did at home."

The clinic was still busy when Róisín went downstairs so she went to the avenue to buy some food. That done, she returned to her room. She found Sophie asleep on the bed, breathing lightly and in a ball. Róisín barely recognized her. She was fifteen when she last saw her. She was a pretty girl, but too often lacked any sense, and had not improved since Róisín came to America.

Róisín ran the back of a hand across her smooth cheek, moving with her breath, wondering what had possessed her to do something so stupid, something that could lead to her and likely her family's ruination in the village. She was a stupid girl, and she was now Róisín's responsibility. There would be time enough to decide what to do. For now, she must tell Doctor Doyle and Nurse Evans. She sat on the chair watching over the girl till she, too, nodded off.

Róisín was awakened from her uncomfortable sleep by Sophie, who had devoured the sandwich her sister brought her. Sophie sat on the side of the bed.

"Oh, Sophie." Róisín shook her head slightly. "What're we to do with you?" The tone was soft, and Sophie was not offended, and the sisters reached to hold each other's hands.

"We'll have to figure it out," Róisín said. "For now, though, I must speak to the doctor about you."

"I heard them come up the stairs not long ago," Sophie said.

"Good. I will go see him. Stay here."

With that, Róisín left the room and walked up the flight of stairs to the doctor's rooms. Rapping lightly, she was told to wait a moment by the doctor. Shortly he answered the door, and Nurse Evans was with him.

"I need to speak to you about something," Róisín said when she was in the apartment.

Nurse Evans made to leave, but Róisín said that she should hear it too.

There was a sofa in the doctor's living room as well as several chairs. He had a small kitchen and then two bedrooms. Róisín sat on the sofa while the other two were in chairs.

"The girl who came here today is my sister Sophie. She is just over eighteen years old."

She paused.

"My mother sent her to me because she is with child."

"How far?" Nurse Evans asked.

"She says it is about three months. She has just begun to show signs, but it appears she is past the initial illness. My mamma put her into my care, and I do not know what I can do. I think she is a good girl, and so my mamma says, but I have not seen her in over three years and so much may have changed. She was not the sweetest of children, but I agree with my mamma that I think she is not a bad person.

"I would like her to stay in my room if possible. We can give her work in the clinic, but I fear the consequences should her condition become known. I do not know what else to do. I do not know her intentions for the baby. I do not know anything, but I know that the two of you must be told."

Róisín looked up only occasionally while she spoke. Now her eyes went from face to face.

"Well, you must allow her to stay in your room. That is clear," the doctor said. "What happens later, we shall see. I am sure we can find work to keep her occupied, at least for a while. I will examine her now, and we shall see what we shall see."

With that, he and the others rose. Nurse Evans reached over to Róisín, touching her wrist.

"God willing, it will be alright."

Dr. Doyle did examine Sophie and found her to be in good condition and assured her that she would be safe under his roof. And Sophie spent her first night in New York sharing her sister's too-small bed and hoping for the morning.

When that morning came, the sisters ate their breakfast quietly, with Róisín telling Sophie about her experiences in New York and Sophie telling her sister what happened in Hospital since she left three years before. Later that day, a second bed was found and moved into the room. Sophie was given loose-fitting frocks and her condition remained a secret. She provided help in the clinic and accompanied her sister on trips around town. Róisín decided her Cousin Jimmy should be told, and Sophie had no objection, so they visited him in his small flat late one Saturday afternoon not long after Sophie's arrival. He barely knew Sophie but was sympathetic to her and her plight. He promised he would do what he could if Sophie needed it, and the women were glad they told him as it eased some of the burden that Róisín felt.

The issue of what was to be done with the baby wore on Róisín. At times she thought it was a greater concern of hers than it was of Sophie's. She wondered whether she was as naïve as her sister when she first came to New York at eighteen and did not recall having such a luxury.

Róisín was aided by the one person in whom she most confided. She had her regular constitutional with Mr. Henry, although not as frequently because she was also walking with Sophie on Sundays after mass.

"It is going to be difficult," he said when she told him about her sister. "Putting aside the physical birth itself. If all goes well. They will be after her."

They both knew who "they" were. On the one hand, the Catholics would seek to take the child, deeming Sophie a harlot and a sinner. A fallen woman undeserving of compassion. On the other, the Protestant matrons who were ascendant would also want the child and also think of Sophie as undeserving and they would find a good Protestant home to raise the child, perhaps hundreds of miles away.

In either case, it was unlikely that Sophie would ever see the child after he or she was born. Neither Róisín nor Mr. Henry, though, knew whether that would be a bad thing for either the mother or the child.

Mr. Henry insisted on meeting the girl. On the ensuing Sunday, after mass, he walked to the clinic, and after Róisín saw him, she and Sophie went down. They found a four-person cab on the avenue and took it to the Park, with Mr. Henry sitting facing the sisters. It was less than a month after Sophie's appearance, and she leaned heavily against her older sister and gripped Róisín's hands. He spoke kindly to Sophie as they rode north, and Sophie did not understand the relationship he had with her sister, but so much was new to her in New York. She appreciated that there was genuine affection between the two. It was almost as if they were brother and sister and that he relaxed Róisín.

Shortly after reaching the Mall, Mr. Henry led them to a well-dressed man with a slight, well-groomed beard, who doffed his hat as they approached. He was a New Yorker, although born in Dublin. He was called Stephen Cassidy. The women were at first surprised by his presence, but Mr. Henry assured them that discretion would be maintained, and the four enjoyed their stroll up-and-down and on the shared cab ride back downtown.

18.

everal days after that walk, Róisín was sitting at their table when her sister came in, and she turned to look at Sophie, waving a piece of paper.

"Is this him? Is this the one who did this to you?"

After a long pause during which Sophie's eyes were daggers, she said, "Of course it's him. He loves me. I love him. I hate it here. I hate you. I want to go back. I want to be with him, as far from you as possible."

Róisín stood, now taunting the other with the sheet of stationery. "You are such a fool. I did not realize how much of a fool until now."

"I'm the fool? You're the old witch who has never known what love means. Who will never know it as you shrivel up here in this hell hole. I am—"

Róisín quickly closed the distance to her sister. When she reached her, she gave her a slap across the face, letting the letter drop.

Sophie, stunned for but a moment by the impact, threw herself to the floor to pick it up.

"You had no right," she screamed. "This is nothing to do with you. This is between us. Only us. Not you. Not Doctor Doyle or Nurse Evans. Or that Henry man you seem so fond of. Not mamma. Or papa. Only him."

Róisín was taken aback by the vehemence of the words and even more by Sophie's countenance. For a moment Róisín thought her sister would kill her if it meant she could be reunited with the boy she loved. Or thought she could.

The stand-off was brief. Sophie fell into tears and collapsed.

"I am so unhappy here. So alone. There are millions of people and none for me. Where is my man? I have the child from the man I love and I will never...see...him...again." She looked up. "Why? Why, Róisín, why?"

The older woman was next to her sister. She placed her arms around Sophie as she bawled. Yes, Sophie was a fool. But she was an innocent. A romantic who thought a moment's passion would lead to a lifetime of joy and was slowly realizing how horribly wrong it had all gone. Whether she and the boy loved each other no longer signified. What did was the reality of what would have happened to Sophie had she stayed in County Limerick and what was going to happen to her in New York. For hundreds of thousands of the Irish, the two worlds were like night and day, as it was with Sophie. And, truth be told, with Róisín. But Sophie was in America now. Her life and future were in America now. Róisín just had to find how to make her sister happy. Or at least less miserable.

Róisín hadn't intended to read it. She came upon her sister's letter to the child's father quite by accident when she was cleaning up. Sophie had been working on it for some time—it was full of romantic delusions—and hid it in the back of her drawer for safe-keeping. Róisín found it when she was rearranging the drawers. She was hesitant to read it, but several words caught her eye, and she quickly understood what the letter was. It was then that she confronted Sophie about it.

She left the letter with Sophie, but she knew Sophie never finished it and never sent it. Sophie made sure that her hiding place for it was discovered by Róisín so that Róisín would understand. She loved him, and he may still love her, but that childish part of her life was forever gone, and she thought of him coming to her less and less. There would soon be another person deserving of her love, and at times she vowed that her child would be the only person she would ever again love.

Sophie took to slipping out on days when Róisín worked at the hospital. Mostly she walked the streets, absorbing the city. She would ignore the boys who said inappropriate things when she passed and envy the girls who were accompanied by boys. More than Róisín had, she took in the sights and smells and sounds of the tenement district. So much humanity. More in one block than she would see in a lifetime at home. Yes, she was a romantic, though the reality of this world was encroaching. There were times when she was tempted to connect with one of the boys she saw on her travels, but she had the lingering hope that her true love would come to her and was determined to remain faithful to him and to their child.

Soon it was clear, though, that Sophie could not be free anymore. Her condition was becoming obvious, and Róisín was concerned that word of it would lead well-meaning types to latch onto her. She and Doctor Doyle and Nurse Evans were well experienced in assisting with births, and they would care for Sophie when her day came.

Dr. Doyle arranged for some piecework to keep Sophie occupied while she sat in the room, confined hour after hour. He often did that for pregnant patients who could not venture out. Róisín insisted that Sophie use the time to improve her reading and writing. Sophie was in some respects a common girl and arrived with just a passable ability to read and somewhat less of an ability to write. Róisín found that romance novels did much to improve the former and that a required weekly letter home helped with the latter.

19.

The baby was due in less than five months, and Róisín and Sophie had yet to resolve what was to happen when it arrived. Róisín shared the progress, including her arguments with Sophie, with Mr. Henry on their next walk, one taken on an overcast, almost cold day when the pair took a cab to the Park and strolled along the Mall.

Almost immediately after they began their walk, her friend said quietly, "I can think of several things she could do. There are women she could see that would assist her in ending the matter."

Róisín stopped him at once and lowered her voice. "She heard girls on the boat talk of such a thing, but she insists that she loves the baby and the father, and she will never do it. Never. And I have too often dealt with the aftermath when things go wrong."

Mr. Henry tapped her arm. "I understand, my dear. I was not suggesting it by any means. I think it needed to be considered and now that the decision has been taken, we will speak no more of it. That leaves, as I see it, two other options. She could say that she is taking care of the baby of a woman who died in childbirth. The problem with that, though, is that there will have to be records. You can't just produce a baby without tracing whose it is.

"The alternative is that she gets married."

This stopped Róisín.

"Married? Who, for God's sake, is she supposed to marry?"

"Do you remember the man who walked with us in the park when I met your sister?"

"Vaguely. He seemed nice enough, but I never understood what he was doing there."

"He was deciding whether he liked her enough to marry her."

She looked at him. "Are you suddenly insane, my dear Mr. Henry?"

There was an empty bench, and they sat.

"I am dead serious. He has no particular desire to be married. But for various reasons, it would be beneficial for him to have a wife. And, as we know, there are reasons for your sister to have a husband. There would be no reason for them to have relations or even to consummate the joining. He is a good man at a good firm, and a marriage of convenience would be of use to both of them.

"In a way, you can think of it as a marriage that is little more than the consolidation of two family fortunes. You are surely aware that such things happen in New York."

Róisín, of course, knew of many such marriages, in which everyone knew that neither the wife nor the husband had the slightest affection for the other and had no physical contact with each other beyond what was necessary to keep up appearances in public and to propagate.

"A marriage would prevent her from marrying a man she loves."

"Yes, there is that. There is no reason why she could not fall in love with another man. She simply could not marry him. Arrangements could be made for liaisons, of course. As they would be for her husband. But the reality, my dear, is that your sister is about to give birth and the father is across the seas."

Róisín long admired her friend's analytical mind, and now it was in full flower, with his hands gesturing in time with his words.

"She is not married, and she will be ostracized. There is every chance that the good sisters will try to take the baby from her. If she were married and with what appears to be a loving husband—and I assure you that he could be fond of your sister based upon his initial impression of her—I think she can keep the baby and the level of ostracism will be reduced.

"He is a good, responsible man. She will be kept in a style far superior to what she would otherwise have. She would be free to come and go as she pleases, within limits, of course. All I ask is that you think about it and if you think it might be possible that you broach the topic with her. I fear we have little time remaining, so you must be quick."

They got up. The idea was growing within Róisín.

"I assure you, Róisín, that he is anxious about the prospect. He did enjoy her company and would like to see her again. Perhaps the theatre and a nice restaurant."

"Well, I will have to get her a proper dress for that."

Mr. Henry reached into his vest pocket and removed a card.

"Of course." He handed the card to his friend. "I have presumed to make arrangements here. They will prepare two dresses for her. They are expecting you."

"For such a young man, Mr. Henry, you are such a sneak."

"Only when it serves, my dear Miss Campbell. Only when it serves."

And after he slightly bowed his head, they continued their stroll, arm-in-arm until it was time to hail a cab and return home.

20.

"**B**ut I could never love him."

"That is the point. You do not have to love him. He does not have to love you. Sophie. This could be your only chance to have your baby and keep your baby."

"But he will come. I know he will."

"And if he doesn't? What life could you have? They will take the baby from you. You will not work except in the most horrible place."

"I cannot love—"

Róisín went behind the chair in which Sophie sat and wrapped her arms around her sister. With her lips close to the other's right ear, she said, "We all suffer and struggle. I believe that this is what you must do."

"But I am too young."

Róisín got up and returned to her seat.

"You ended your youth when you lay with that boy at home. We cannot always decide when it is that we grow up. But you did then, and now there are consequences for that decision. You will be forever known as a fallen woman, a harlot. People of good character, or at least who pretend to be of good character, will have nothing to do with you. And, I fear, with me either."

"So, you are making me do this for you."

"I have long since given up on going out in any type of society. What others think of me is beyond my control. It is beyond my concern. But it is real."

"I suppose you are right. But I so much wanted to stay in love."

"You will have a child to love. Were you not to do this, you might lose it forever."

Sophie rose and walked about the room.

"I will do as you say. I will again meet this man."

"Stephen Cassidy."

"I will meet this Stephen Cassidy and I will hope to like him and I will hope that he will be a good father to my child. That is all I can do."

She stood, her hand dropping down so Róisín could hold it.

"It is all you can do. But I think that you must do it."

On the weekend, Sophie got the two dresses, accompanied by her sister. They were cut loosely around her midsection but remained fashionable and camouflaged the condition of her stomach. The seamstress said she had "a fair amount of experience" making such dresses. Sophie went to dinner and the theatre with Stephen Cassidy.

Cassidy was far different from the men and boys she knew from Hospital, the Irish town she was forced to abandon, and her occasional trips to Limerick City. He was closer to thirty than twenty. In his demeanor, he acted in the manner that Sophie read in her novels a gentleman should behave, a world apart from those at home, including her lover.

In virtually all respects, Stephen Cassidy was infinitely more sophisticated than was Sophie. He was born in Dublin, the second son of a prosperous attorney, and like Henry, he had come to America to make his fortune and had done well and was a junior partner at a Wall Street bank. He could afford his own brownstone and several servants. It was on Wall Street that he became known to Mr. Henry. The two were about the same age, and Cassidy was more taciturn than Henry. They enjoyed one another's company well enough, but Mr. Henry told Róisín that his relationship with Cassidy was no more than that. Cassidy, Mr. Henry promised her, was a true friend and honorable man and would do well as Sophie's husband.

Mr. Henry told her that Cassidy found her sister "rough" in parts, befitting an Irish farmgirl, but that he thought he could grow to like her very much. Made aware of her medical condition, Cassidy expressed an eagerness to participate in the raising of a child. It was with these assurances that Mr. Henry approached Róisín in the first place about the prospect of a marriage.

With marriage agreed upon, Róisín thought to speak with Mrs. Flanagan. On the next Sunday, she went to mass at Immaculate Conception, the parish church she attended when she first arrived and sure enough saw her erstwhile landlady. As she was alone, Róisín approached her, and before she could say anything, she found herself in Mrs. Flanagan's grasp. They separated with greetings. As they reached the sidewalk and turned west, she asked, "To what do I owe the pleasure of your visit?" which hurt Róisín slightly.

"It is a matter calling for discretion."

Mrs. Flanagan could not help looking at Róisín's stomach.

"No. It is not me, I can promise you. It is my sister."

"You have a sister here?"

"That's just it. My mother sent her when she was…was compromised at home."

"That is unfortunate. Things will not be much better here for her than at home."

"I know. But the boy is there, and she is not."

"Aye, there is that."

Róisín resumed, "Before you go on, I need to tell you what we have come up with."

"We?"

"Well, it began with someone I met on the boat. He is just a friend."

"He?"

"Yes. He is upper crust and works in investments. He suggests that my sister, whose name is Sophie, that Sophie marry as soon as possible."

"I guess that is one solution. But it requires that there be a groom, does it not?"

Their stroll was interrupted periodically by people greeting Mrs. Flanagan as they walked. The number of girls who boarded with her was extraordinary, and she recalled all of their names. But seeing as she was deep in conversation with Róisín, most merely gave her a hello and a nod and moved on.

"Mr. Henry, my friend, has found someone."

Mrs. Flanagan stopped and looked at Róisín.

"Let us wait till we are inside. This is sounding very complicated."

"It is complicated."

When they reached the boarding house, Mrs. Flanagan and Róisín once again went to the kitchen to get tea and when they did, they brought it to the sitting-room with which Róisín was so familiar and sat on the sofa. Mrs. Flanagan asked Róisín to explain her scheme.

"It concerns one of Mr. Henry's friends. He is in his twenties, late twenties, and has no intention of getting married."

"I understand," Mrs. Flanagan said.

"Good. But he would like the chance to raise a child. It is difficult to explain, but it would be a marriage of convenience and they would both be free to pursue their other interests. It is not ideal for my sister but far better than any alternative I can think of."

"You are probably right there. Can this gentleman afford a wife?"

"He can. He is well enough off. I have met him, and Sophie has spent time with him, and she believes she could come to like him. She still hopes that the father of her child will come here, but I told her that is not likely to happen and that the longer she waits the—"

"For how many months has she been with child?"

"It is just above four months. She promises me that she knows exactly when it happened."

"Well, I suppose your solution is better than any other, assuming she wishes to keep the child."

"She does."

"And if she is not married there will be all sorts of do-gooders seeking to take it away. And is she agreeable?"

"As I said, she still hopes her boy comes to her, but she is coming to accept the reality. She believes she could be happy with this gentleman and is coming to see that it is the best opportunity for her."

"So, what do you need of me?"

Róisín paused.

"Ah. I see. How does she get married?" She poured more tea into Róisín's cup.

"It is not as uncommon as you would think. Though usually the groom is the child's father. But no one need know that he is not. We must act quickly. Father Dawson will accommodate provided it is done quietly. When can they do it?"

"She is seeing him this afternoon with me and Mr. Henry. We go for strolls together in the park. I think we can agree that it be done as soon as possible."

"Mr. Henry?"

"The friend from the boat."

Mrs. Flanagan sat back. "Yes, I understand."

21.

Cassidy's marriage to Sophie began as soon as possible. The wedding was a small affair, attended only by the bride and groom and Róisín and Mr. Henry. It was performed by Father William Dawson at a side altar of the parish church. Under the circumstances, of which Father Dawson was fully aware, the church did without wedding banns in the interest of quickly creating a couple married in the eyes of God.

Sophie moved into Cassidy's brownstone. It was five stories high with a stoop to a double front door to the left that opened to a long hallway. To the right was a comfortable sitting-room with a fireplace surrounded by a molded mantel with a fine landscape above it, and straight-ahead from the foyer was a traditional dining room with a window that overlooked a small garden and connected to the kitchen to its right.

The second floor, reached by a central staircase, featured a large drawing-room that looked out over the street with its three large windows. An oriental rug dominated the floor, on which sat a comfortable sofa and several wing chairs to the right—where there was a large fireplace surrounded by an ornate mantel—and several smaller seating areas with small, occasional tables to the left.

Mr. Cassidy's wood-paneled study was to the rear of the second floor with a mahogany desk and a mixture of bookcases and charcoal portraits along its walls. The house was finished out with two large bedrooms on the third floor and four smaller rooms on the fourth, with three rooms for staff—his man (Fisher), Cook, and the maid (Sally)—on the top floor.

Although made of brick, brownstone was placed to the front, rendering it much like the similar houses on the block. Or in the neighborhood, for that matter. A bedroom was prepared for Sophie's arrival, down the hall from his. A second room on the fourth floor that looked out across to the rear of the brownstone a block to the north was prepared as her den, newly painted in pink and newly furnished with a loveseat, two chairs, and a desk.

It was in this house and in these rooms that a pregnant Sophie Cassidy settled into her new, married life in New York.

22.

With Sophie married, Róisín could resume the long walks she often took alone on Saturday afternoons. She had no specific route. Instead, she would almost randomly select which streets or avenues to walk up and down. Sometimes she walked and walked until exhaustion enveloped her, and she took a trolley home.

At times, she headed to the area near Mrs. Flanagan's. It, and she, were special to her, and she visited her former landlady every few months. Sometimes Róisín found herself near The Thistle. It was a popular tavern where she went that horrible morning when she was dismissed by Mrs. Geherty, and she liked to interrupt her journey with a late-afternoon ale before heading to her flat. On one such Saturday, as she sat alone at a small table along the sidewall, she was within earshot of the bar, and her attention was grabbed when she heard reference to the Geherty family. She recognized the speaker as a footman at the house.

She did not recall his name, but he was animated as he told his fellows of his master's losses in the Northern Pacific Railway scandal and that he had invested all he still had in a speculation about a Bolivian railroad.

"He has gentlemen come by and I hear them talk 'bout how many dollars they'll all be making on it. Sometimes one'll say he might just be risking too much but he laughs at them, says they're acting like frightened girls."

The others, also in service, spoke of their own masters' foolishness. Soon the topic turned elsewhere, and Róisín lost interest.

It happened that Róisín was on her normal Sunday walk with Mr. Henry the next afternoon. She mentioned what she heard, not identifying why she might have an interest.

"I, of course, know of the losses with the Northern Pacific Railway. I believe I have also heard of the Bolivian railroad investment. Some of the not-so-smart money is invested there. It sounds too good, so I have kept far from it. Would you like me to make inquiries?"

Róisín thought a moment. "I should appreciate that, Mr. Henry. I may know someone who might be involved."

With a doff of his hat, Mr. Henry assured his companion that he would do so and with that, they turned to other topics. As always, Sophie and Cassidy being chief among them.

Two weeks later, during their next walk, Mr. Henry raised the topic of the speculation. He said that it was widely considered a very risky scheme, perhaps even a fraud. A not insignificant group, though, insisted that it was as good as gold. But, he said, he was informed that several insiders were getting out. He said many of the new investors were desperate to make back the losses they felt when the Northern Pacific Railway collapsed setting off a full panic in New York, Chicago, and San Francisco.

"I assure you, my dear. If you know of anyone who has put money into the Bolivian scheme you must persuade them to remove it at once. I do not think that it shall end well."

"Thank you," Róisín replied, and again the conversation veered elsewhere.

23.

The door was answered promptly after Róisín rang. It was opened by Mason who, after a moment, recognized her. It was the Saturday afternoon after her recent walk with Mr. Henry.

"I am sorry, miss. But the servant's entrance is to the side. As you know."

"I am here to speak to Mrs. Geherty, Mr. Mason. On a matter of personal importance."

He paused a moment before nodding and turning to his side, allowing her entry. In the foyer, he showed her to the sitting-room and advised her that he would see if Mrs. Geherty were available and begged that she sit.

He closed the door when he left but it was presently opened. Mary McNabb entered. Róisín got up.

"Mason said you were here to see mother. I happened to be visiting, and I could not believe it. So, I came to see if it was true and I fear it is. Of what would my mother possibly want to speak to you?"

"It is a matter of some urgency."

"What could you possibly have to tell my mother that is 'urgent'? I hoped never to have to set eyes on you again."

"It is for your mother."

Mrs. McNabb walked around the room, examining several items on the mantel before returning her gaze to Róisín.

"You are with child. Confess it. And you require my mother's charity. I bet it is with some stock boy at Lord & Taylor. Confess it."

"I am not with child and I am not here to take anything from your family, charity or otherwise."

"You wish to have a position here? Even you would not be so forward."

"I merely wish to speak to your mother on a matter of some urgency."

"I assure you that there is nothing that you can say that would be of the slightest interest to her."

She turned back to the mantel.

Instead of feeling dismissed, Róisín stared at Mrs. McNabb's back.

"Why do you hate me so?"

"I do not hate you. I am completely indifferent to you. Now that I am married, I am no longer concerned about your attempts to seduce my brothers and my father and my husband."

"What are you talking about? I did nothing to any of them."

Mrs. McNabb, holding a small piece of cut glass she lifted from the mantel, turned. "You think I am stupid as well as blind? I am no fool, and I saw how Mr. McNabb looked at you, lusted after you."

"Peter? You must be joking. I barely noticed he existed."

"'Peter'? You dare to call him 'Peter'? You have forgotten your place. Farmgirl. You may have fooled mother and that cow at Lord & Taylor but—"

"I am no longer there."

"Oh, did they finally realize what an immoral creature you are?"

"No. I work as a doctor's assistant in a clinic."

"What? Caring for the Irish too poor and helpless to stay at their homes in I-re-land? Oh, I am sorry. That applies to you, don't it?"

"I don't need to tolerate this from you or anybody. If you have delusions about the faithfulness of your husband, Mrs. McNabb, that is no concern of mine. If you cannot provide what your husband, Mr. McNabb, requires of a wife, that is no concern of mine either."

Mrs. McNabb had never witnessed such insolence. And from a peasant girl.

"You harlot. How dare you speak to me in such a manner?"

Gripping the glass orb, she rushed to the door and flung it open.

"Mason! Mason!"

Róisín heard the butler's "Ma'am" a moment later.

"This creature is finished with her business in this house. Show her out. And do not allow her admittance in the future."

With that, Mason looked into the sitting-room, but Róisín was already on her way to the door.

"No need, Mr. Mason. I know my way out and have no reason to believe I shall ever grace this house again."

With that, she opened and went through the front door and to the sidewalk and quickly walked to the avenue so she could return to her home.

She was not far from the house when Mrs. Geherty came down the stairs and saw a befuddled Mason and a livid Mary.

"Is Miss Campbell not here? I was told she wished to speak to me."

Mason remained confused, and Mary remained livid, but able to calmly tell her mother that for some reason unbeknownst to her, Róisín simply got up and left while she, Mary, made polite conversation and she had no idea why she did so.

As she walked south, Róisín convinced herself that either what Mr. Henry said was unfounded or, more likely, that she would not have been listened to in the Geherty House even if she said what she planned to say. In any case, it was not her fault that Mary McNabb treated her so badly and it was in part the entire Geherty family's fault that they reared such a horrible person as Mary McNabb, née Geherty.

<h1 style="text-align:center">24.</h1>

On a Monday morning in December 1873, it began as a rumor that ricocheted back and forth among the buildings that lined Wall Street. By Monday afternoon, the sight of somber-faced gentlemen established it as fact. The Bolivian railway speculation was collapsing. Many wagered all (or more than all) in it, hoping to recoup losses suffered in the domestic panic that hit three months earlier.

Charles Geherty was among them. With his war profits, he'd sold his inventory and goodwill for a fine price and formed his own firm to manage the family's money. It gave him an excuse to leave the house each morning and hobnob with gentlemen of a similar ilk on Wall and its neighboring streets. When the initial rumors reached him at his office on Broad Street, he thought they could not be true. Must not. It was a supremely safe investment. Hardly a "speculation" at all. It would put him and his family to rights for a generation.

He was barely bothered as he lunched at his downtown club where things were more somber than usual, even for a Monday. But at three, shortly after his return, John Wilson, the man who put Geherty into the speculation, rushed into Geherty's office carrying a crumpled telegram.

"What is it, Wilson?"

Wilson threw the paper on Geherty's desk. Geherty smoothed it out.

"ALL IS LOST."

"What does this mean?" he asked.

"It means we are ruined, Geherty. All of it. All gone. 'All is lost.'"

Wilson dropped into one of Geherty's chairs. Geherty sat immobile in his, the paper dropping to the floor.

"You heard the rumors this morning. It was our chance to get out of the hole. It was a certain thing. The government guaranteed it. It was a certainty."

"Is there not anything left?"

Wilson stood. He walked to the side of the desk and bent down to pick up the telegram. He placed it on the desk and attempted to smooth it out.

"ALL IS LOST." He pointed.

"The money must be somewhere."

"Somewhere we will never find it. Face it, Geherty, we are goners. I just hope you siphoned off enough so you can at least keep your house if not your reputation."

"I will not starve, Wilson. As I am sure you will not. Perhaps some of the others you induced are not so fortunate as you and I."

"Some probably will put a gun to their heads and pull the trigger. But they were fools not to have enough. I have no pity for them."

"Or their widows?"

Wilson looked at Geherty. "Or them." He again dropped to the chair and looked over.

"Where will you go? You cannot have enough to keep that house of yours."

"I expect the sheriff will be on it soon enough," Geherty said. He turned his chair so he could look out the window. "We will escape to Stockbridge. It will be boring and tedious, but it will suffice."

"It will have to."

"Aye. It will have to."

With that, the two men stood. Geherty stepped around his desk. They shook hands, and Wilson went to hasten his retreat to whatever place was set aside for him should something like this occur.

Geherty sat back down. He stared at the telegram. Wilson was right. No ambiguity. He expected that his creditors were already racing to grab what could be grabbed. Geherty's solace was that there were likely many more exposed men in the two or three blocks surrounding his office. Creditors would be diverted, perhaps, by chasing after them first.

It did not matter. They would get to him and they would find him. They would take everything.

He rose again and removed his overcoat from the coat rack by the door. He put it on and removed his gloves from its right pocket and placed them in his left hand. He opened the door and looked back into his office. He then walked out and closed the door. He did not bother to lock it.

By the weekend, the staff was all dismissed, except for Mason and Collins. The pair were offered positions at the Stockbridge house at dramatically reduced wages and they had no choice but to accept. They were old, and they would not be retained in a decent house in the city. Miss Elizabeth, who'd long since returned from her European sojourn, promised Biddy O'Casey, who took care of her as she had before Mary left the house, that she would do what she could to help her get another position, which she did with an acquaintance whose own maid found herself pregnant and rushing to the altar.

All of the furniture was spoken for as, of course, was the house in town. Mrs. Geherty salvaged the silver and some fine linens, as well as numerous dresses that would never again be worn—Mary McNabb's were stored somewhere in her new house—but little else of consequence except an assortment of jewelry.

They left it for their lawyers to battle it out with the creditors.

Miss Elizabeth and her parents took a final ride in their carriage to the Grand Central Depot and from there embarked by train to Stockbridge, Massachusetts. Mason and Collins would follow with the belongings they salvaged. The carriage and the horses would soon be sold.

Mrs. McNabb did not appear. She had an appointment she could not break.

25.

As the train rocked its way north, Elizabeth Geherty sat across from her stoic parents. Neither of the pair spoke as she watched what quickly became countryside pass. She took this trip often, but this was far different. She envied the bare trees tilting in a slight wind in their simplicity and their freedom.

Her father had sent a telegram ahead to Johnson to open the house. Jacob Johnson was a local farmer who often did chores for the Gehertys, and he prepared fires in several rooms to take the cold off the long empty space before he went to get the three at the station. The house was off a main road and down a winding driveway. Its most noticeable feature was the sloping lawn that led to a small wood. A terrace off the sitting-room was where the family spent most summer evenings when the bugs were tolerable, but all of the outdoor furniture was put in storage months before. It would be too cold to use it anyway.

Elizabeth's favorite spot in the house was also closed off. This was a room in the north-west corner of the ground floor with windows looking out in both directions and a variety of plants in plain or ornate pots sitting on tiered shelves. Her particular spot was an armless chair sited to allow her to look north or west, and she often spent summer afternoons, especially rainy ones, with a book. This became her favorite pastime in Stockbridge, and the other members of the family knew to leave her undisturbed in her reading, though when she was bored Mary frequently ignored the injunction and sought to draw her sister into a walk or some other activity that was more to Mary's liking. Her importuning became less frequent when they were ignored and so they were largely ignored.

The wood, visible from Elizabeth's spot, was also naked, the leaves long gone except for a row of small pines that drooped down to the east.

It was a good house. Charles had it built some five years earlier in the flush of his war profits. A large porch spread across its front. Its Mansard roof was its defining characteristic, styled after the buildings built along the avenues of Paris. The windows were elaborately encased, and a tower rose in the center with an iron rod reaching to the sky. It made quite an impression as one approached it, exactly as was intended.

It was in a part of Stockbridge where the neighborhood and the neighbors closely matched those in the monied parts of the East Side of Manhattan. Most of the families were like the Gehertys: second- or third-generation Irish who made out well in trade during the war. While two or three had a son or a brother lost, the rest did very well by the hostilities. As had the Gehertys.

The Geherty sons, though, showed little interest in becoming actively involved in their father's firm. Charlie, who avoided serving in the war by paying a commutation fee, especially found the notion of work repulsive, preferring the company of like-minded fellows and the occasional broad-figured woman. It was periodically rumored that he would become engaged, but he bristled at the notion. Through his father, he had employment at a Wall Street firm, but the employment consisted chiefly of massaging the concerns of nervous investors. Charlie was rarely home. Unmarried still, he preferred spending his nights at his club with friends or the wives of friends (rarely) or whores (often), not arriving back until after dawn, and then sleeping into the afternoon.

His brother Michael was far more serious. His mind tended to the intellectual, and he was a member of several New York clubs that held symposia and sponsored expeditions, though he lacked the capacity for playing a meaningful part in either of those. He, though, did marry. Kathleen Bancroft was from a family like the Gehertys, and their marriage had the benefit of being shrouded in mutual affection and was blessed with a baby daughter some ten months after the wedding. Michael found work, again thanks to his father, in a shipping company, and he earned enough to maintain independence from his family.

The post-war prosperity continued (for some) with the peace, and more and more of them invested in the building of railroads out west. Several sons decamped to California to care for the operations out there, but a flurry of bankruptcies recently flooded Wall Street and investors in Chicago and more and more of the Berkshire houses were expected to become refuges, as the Gehertys' had.

Now while Johnson drove them in a hired carriage to the house, Elizabeth again sat across from her parents. All three had blankets covering their laps. If her parents said more than a dozen words to one another the entire trip, Elizabeth did not hear them. Each looked out as the dusk filled the air on the two-mile trip.

There was a decided chill after the sun went down, and after thanking Johnson, Elizabeth rushed past her parents to get into the house so she could stand before the fire in the sitting-room. It warmed her thoroughly.

Johnson had packed some food for the family. The kitchen would not be open until Mrs. Collins arrived. She would hire a local girl to handle the cooking, but that was for later. Now, Johnson carried in a large picnic basket containing various sandwich meats and bread and several bottles of beer.

Elizabeth did not know for how long she was lost in the fire but was returned to the house when Johnson coughed and said, "Miss Elizabeth, if you please. The food is set out in the dining parlor, and I must return to me farm. I be coming back in the morning with the missus to reset the fires and clean up. The master has asked us to."

Elizabeth, who turned as Johnson began, thanked him. "Johnson?"

"Yes, miss?"

She paused. "I do not think we could survive without your help and that of Mrs. Johnson."

Johnson bowed as he started to back out of the room.

"It is indeed our pleasure, miss. But thankee for saying that. It means the world, it does."

He was a good man. His wife was a good woman. They abandoned whatever they were doing to cater to the Gehertys. Elizabeth meant what she said. Were he not there, she doubted the discomfort of the return to the house would have been tolerable.

Elizabeth went up to her room. Johnson had made a fire and lit the candles. It was in the northeast corner of the second floor. Mary's, at the southeast, had the superior view and though it was not occupied and had not been since Mary became Mrs. McNabb, Elizabeth was forbidden to enter it. By her sister.

Mary rarely came to Stockbridge since her marriage. She preferred summering with the McNabbs. They had a far finer place outside of Lenox. While Lenox, where the McNabb's father and son had houses, was the town just to the north, it might as well have been on the other side of the world. The Gehertys could and would visit Lenox, but it was the rare occasion when the McNabbs returned the favor. This was not unique to this family. It was the order of things and almost exactly translated to the order of things in Manhattan.

As in New York, there would be shared pleasantries when those from one community happened upon those from the other, but all parties were aware of the superiority of the one and the inferiority of the other.

True, it was not quite as it had been before the war. There was a growing number of men making money in speculations out west and in New York real estate much as there were those who did so during the war. Some of the older families were beginning to understand that whatever the source, some money was better than none and a lot of money was better than not-quite-as-much-as-it-once-was money.

There was thus a sense of change to come. Alas, for the Gehertys, the changes they faced were likely to push them further down. It was surely the case that their standing in Manhattan had burst. How it would fare in Berkshire County remained to be seen.

On her first morning, Elizabeth awoke soon after the sun cleared the wood. She opened the drapes and saw that a slight snow passed through overnight and there was a white coating to the grass and trees. Her room was cold, and she shivered when she came from under the covers. She relieved herself, put on a pair of slippers, and went to the hallway, which she found even colder than her room.

The house was quiet. Quieter than she had ever known it. All the times she was there before there had been servants and noises of the house and of the woods, though she never was up so close to the dawn. Johnson and his wife would be coming soon to light the fires, and Mason and Collins were expected at midday. They would take care of the organization of the house for the family's exile.

Elizabeth wrapped herself in a shawl. While the sun was beginning to enter, it was still dark and she used a match to light a candle, which guided her way to the kitchen. She found some cold bread from last night's meal in a cupboard. It was hard, but she was hungry and gnawed on it while she sat at the table the servants used for eating when the house was open (and there were servants). She doubted it would be used again in that way. At most, it would be Mason, Collins, a cook, and a scullery girl. For a while at least. For the while when they could remain at the house and for the while they could afford to keep such servants.

Elizabeth gazed out a window to a snowy vale and rustling trees. She had little notion of money. Her mother did, with her responsibilities for running the house in town and the one here. Elizabeth, though, had no such responsibilities. Indeed, Elizabeth had no responsibilities of any kind.

Except one.

She was to be a good wife who would be fruitful and would be a good if absent mother to the resulting issue. Now that responsibility was gone. The decision about going through with marrying Edward Meade was no longer hers. The Gehertys' failure would make such a match impossible. She was glad of it. But the failure also made marrying even more important to Elizabeth for financial reasons. She rued the irony.

Her thoughts were interrupted when the rear door opened. She hadn't noticed the wagon that came to the back bearing the Johnsons.

"Oh, Miss Elizabeth," Mrs. Johnson chirped when she saw the girl. "How are you up so early? And nothing to eat? Let me fix you something."

Johnson rushed in, promising to make the fire in the sitting-room so Elizabeth could be comfortable as Mrs. Johnson turned to begin the makings of a fire in the kitchen.

"Please, both of you. I am quite fine. Indeed, I think I shall go for a walk."

She turned and left the kitchen, and the Johnsons looked at one another.

Mrs. Johnson said, "A walk? In this cold?"

"Shall I go with her?"

"No, Jacob. She knows what she's about. Takes after her mother, this one does."

Elizabeth heard none of this. She went to the third floor, where the family's clothes were kept. There were a few things of hers, mostly for summer, but she found a dark green winter visiting dress. Its two pieces were wool, and she hoped it would be warm enough for her walk, with the addition of a coat. With her wardrobe not yet arrived from town, she was fortunate to find a little-used wool coat in the back and a bonnet on the shelf.

It was nearing eight when she made her way down the stairs. The fire was lit in the sitting-room, and she was tempted to remain there until her parents were up but was resolute in going out. Johnson was carrying wood for the upstairs fireplaces as she prepared to leave, and she told him she was quite determined to walk to the village. She had never walked to Stockbridge on her own.

"It's near two mile, Miss Elizabeth. I will take you in the wagon."

"No, thank you, Johnson. I shall be invigorated by the walk. Please tell Mrs. Johnson and my parents when they come down. I do not know how long I shall be."

With that Elizabeth went through the thick front door and down the steps from the porch. The only gloves she found were white, for evening, but she had them on with a bonnet pinned to her hair as well as a scarf around her neck.

The path itself was clear, the day having warmed enough for any traces of the pre-dawn snow to be gone. Although she was slightly chilled because it was only a light coat, she felt warm enough by the time she reached the road. It was a quiet walk. The road was lined with low stone walls and trees that made a canopy in the summer but whose branches now provided nothing but a shadow of their past and future selves.

Two wagons passed her heading to Stockbridge. She pulled to the side as she heard their approach. She did not recognize the farmers who drove them, but they recognized her, and each offered to take "Miss Elizabeth" into the village. She declined, assuring both that it was a "wonderful morning for a walk and I should regret not taking advantage." They waved as they left, and she watched as they disappeared around a curve and out of sight.

After half-an-hour, she began to feel her feet. Her shoes were accustomed to the smooth sidewalks of New York, not to the sometimes rough stretches of Berkshire County. Perhaps she should have accepted the farmers' offers after all? But her discomfort faded and her spirits rose as she recognized how close she was to the village.

Elizabeth's eyes fixed on a large inn with a porch. She had been there many times for social events, but she never saw it so quiet and so early. She climbed the five steps and through the door, and a woman rushed to her.

"May I help you, miss?"

"I am sorry, but my walk was more of a strain than I anticipated. Might I sit briefly?"

"Of course. And shall I bring you some tea?"

Elizabeth realized she had not brought her purse.

"I am sorry, but I do not have any money."

"We shan't worry about that, miss." With that, the woman led Elizabeth to a small table by the fire.

There were only a few others in the room, all in pairs, all dressed better than she was.

"Might I sit by the window?" she asked, and she was taken to a square table set beneath a window overlooking the porch, and the woman left. Elizabeth removed her gloves, bonnet, scarf, and coat and draped the coat and scarf over the chair on the other side of the table and placed the other things on the table, and sat. She watched wagons and carriages and a few intrepid pedestrians pass until the woman returned with a tray. She placed a cup and saucer and a small plate of biscuits on the table. Then she poured tea from a teapot, which she placed on the table with milk and sugar.

"Will that be it, miss?"

"Oh, yes. You are very kind."

The woman put the tray below her arm and went to lift Elizabeth's coat, scarf, bonnet, and gloves.

"Oh, please do not bother."

The woman smiled, "'Tis is no bother, miss," and she took them away.

The first sip of tea was an elixir, and Elizabeth felt herself relax and warm immediately. She glanced out at those passing by.

"You are Elizabeth Geherty, are you not?"

The woman who stood next to Elizabeth and broke her trance was two or three years older and dressed more formally than was Elizabeth.

"I am."

"May I sit?"

Elizabeth nodded.

"I do not mean to startle you in this God-forsaken place, but I was in the grocer when a farmer mentioned seeing you on the road to town and I just had to find out for myself. I thought this would be where you would go. I am Emily Connor, and we, too, are hiding out from our creditors."

Elizabeth could not place the woman.

"Oh, you wouldn't know me. I was a great friend of your sister until she discovered Peter McNabb and his little circle and then, *poof*, I ceased to be a great friend of your sister. You were in Europe at the time, I believe."

"Well, Miss Connor, you surely have the advantage over me."

"Oh, it is 'Emily,' for goodness sake."

The woman at the inn came to the table. "May I get you some tea, Miss Connor?"

"That would be delightful, Mrs. Neal. Have you met my good, dear friend, Elizabeth Geherty?"

"Ah, Miss Geherty. I have heard the name. I am sorry. I did not recognize you."

"Mrs. Neal, do not be troubled. I sometimes do not recognize myself."

Emily chortled at this, and Mrs. Neal turned with a smile to get fresh tea for the women and a cup and saucer for Emily.

"I think our fathers must have been in cahoots with this Bolivian or Brazilian or whatever it was railroad thing. Leave it to men to ruin everything."

"Are you ruined?"

"Financially, yes. I do not know for how long we can hold out before I may have to find work. Socially? I have been ruined for years." She lowered her voice. "You see, I am not married."

"Nor am I, *Miss* Connor."

"Ah, the cripple. I have heard all about him. You need not worry anymore about him. There is that."

"Yes. Financial ruin is so liberating."

Mrs. Neal returned as these words were spoken, and she re-filled Elizabeth's cup and poured Emily's tea.

"I do think we shall be good, dear friends," Emily said as she gently ran her hand along Elizabeth's left cheek.

Walter Connor was, in fact, one of those chosen to invest in the railroad speculation. His family had come to Stockbridge the day before the three Gehertys arrived. Their house was to the east of the village. If Elizabeth's path ever crossed Emily's, neither recalled it. When their tea was gone and Emily paid, the two headed out into the cold. They crossed the street to get the sun, and Emily placed her arm through Elizabeth's as they strolled as if they were heading to Arnold Constable or Lord & Taylor on Broadway. There was little to see in town, but the air did them good.

After chatting amicably for some time, they turned back until they neared a carriage. It was an everyday brougham, not nearly as fancy as would be seen in town, with two horses and one coachman. Upon seeing Miss Connor, the latter jumped down to open the door and fold down the steps. Emily said, "I shall convey you home. We at least still have this though I truly did not know of any reason to leave the house until I came upon you sitting there all alone in the inn. Perhaps there will be more of us orphans here soon and we can compare notes on the men we haven't married."

"Or who have not married us," Elizabeth replied, earning a fit of laughter from her companion.

As they entered the carriage, Elizabeth sat facing the front and Emily Connor sat facing Elizabeth. Emily leaned closer, putting her hands on Elizabeth's knees as the carriage began to move.

"How is your delightful sister?"

Elizabeth was flustered for a moment. Emily continued, "Is it true that she had one of your servants dismissed because McNabb took an undue...interest in her? The girl was completely innocent in the affair, but Mary did not care. What is more, she ran into her working at some ball or other at her new place and got her dismissed from that position as well. I heard she never worked in service again. Your sister refers to it as her 'greatest triumph.'"

"I believe I was away in Europe when that must have happened, so I cannot say anything about it."

"Perhaps it is just gossip. Mary ended up marrying him anyway so all's well that ends well, yes?"

"Indeed."

Elizabeth looked out the window at the path she walked earlier, the sun now shining through the bare limbs. She had not heard that particular story but knew it must be true. She had been sent to Europe for as long as she was so as not to interfere with Mary's marriage prospects, however unlikely it was that someone interested in Mary would have the slightest interest in Elizabeth and vice versa.

Elizabeth was glad for Emily's interruption until it circled back to her sister.

"What happened to us happened very suddenly. Surely you could have stayed with the McNabbs."

"Oh, no. That could not happen. They are having a party tonight, and, well, they were too occupied to be diverted by the needs of our parents."

"And your needs?"

"I assure you. They were not considered."

There was a pause, which Emily again broke. "Surely you could have remained for the party?"

"Even were we asked, which we weren't, my father could not tolerate the feigned words of sympathy and the whispering in the corner about how they always knew that he was a fool."

The talk again reached a quiet spot as the carriage continued, and both women looked out the windows, both looking to their rights, until they finally were in front of the door to the Gehertys' country house.

When Emily sought to follow Elizabeth from the carriage, the latter asked her to remain.

"I should not like my parents to feel embarrassed by having a lady visit them so soon. I will walk into the village on Monday morning again. I will be in church tomorrow."

"Walk? Surely not. I have this carriage. I shall come to pick you up."

"No, please do not. But I will wait for you at the entrance to the Carlyle Farm. We passed it about half-a-mile ago."

"I will find it and I will be there at ten o'clock on Monday. If you are not there when we arrive we shall continue until we are again at your door and we will bang loudly on it to awaken you for our journey so you had best be at the Carlyle Farm at ten o'clock or I shall surely embarrass you as being lazy and slothful."

In a moment Elizabeth regretted not knowing Emily Connor when she lived in town. She promised she would be at the Carlyle Farm at ten o'clock on Monday, and she hoped she would see Emily Connor at mass the following morning.

26.

"At times I am glad I did not marry."

The pair was walking arm-in-arm along Stockbridge's main road on Monday.

"Who? The cripple?"

"Stop calling him that. No. I mean just in general. I'm afraid I do not see myself becoming a wife and raising children and doing—"

"You do not raise them. You have a nurse for that."

"I know. At least when we had money. And I do like children. In fact, perhaps I would prefer to raise children without the complication of having to be married first."

Emily looked at her friend.

"Having a child without a husband is not anything that even I would recommend."

"I do not mean that. I mean that I like the idea of having a child but would not do something that way. I am thinking of becoming a nun."

Emily stopped.

"You are what?"

"I am thinking of becoming a nun."

"What? With the habit and everything?"

Elizabeth continued, and Emily rushed to catch up.

"There is no opportunity for me to marry respectably," Elizabeth said. "I am a burden on my parents. I am sure my sister would take me in. But," and she turned to face Emily, "but I hate doing nothing and doing nothing here in the middle of nowhere where everyone from town pretends to be in town with all of the nonsense of being in town.

"No. I wrote to several orders inquiring about them. Mason, our butler, brings me their responses without telling my parents. He is very good at discretion."

"He is a butler. That is what butlers do."

"Well, yes. But he is good at it."

They were entering the inn for a bite, and Mrs. Neal gave them the table by the window. Their voices lowered.

"You must not tell your parents or anyone."

"I promise."

Emily was focused and helpful once she recovered from the shock of what she was told. Frankly, she could see nothing wrong with what she was being told. For her, children were not much of an attraction, but Elizabeth was not her.

27.

Sometime after Elizabeth met Emily, in the new year Róisín Campbell saw Charlie Geherty die, one more of the many deaths she witnessed since that washerwoman was hit in the head by a horse's hoof. Many from the effects of an opium overdose, which is what killed the Geherty heir. He, as was often the case, was found collapsed in an alleyway not far from the clinic. Someone dragged or carried him to the clinic's door in the night and began banging repeatedly on it. Róisín looked out the window into the dark and saw a lifeless form in a gaslight's glow and the other person rushing down the block. She hurried to the street in a robe and found Charles Geherty, Jr., barely breathing.

Soon Nurse Evans, who was also awakened by the banging, joined her. She had a key and opened to door to bring him into the clinic. Róisín then ran up to the third floor to get Dr. Doyle. When the two went into the examination room, Nurse Evans was rubbing Charlie's head and his breath was short and he was struggling. Finally, he heaved, but it was too late, and he soon was dead.

"I know him," she said. "I worked for his family. I thought they were gone from the city long ago."

Dr. Doyle, studying the dead man's expensive but soiled clothing, said that he looked to be living hard, perhaps on the streets, likely abandoned by whatever friend or gambling companions he had when he was flush with money.

"Well, there is nothing to be done for the poor soul now," the doctor said. "We will put him in the room and contact the morgue in the morning. I am sure the police will be able to locate the family so that proper arrangements can be made."

Róisín studied the face. It seemed well older than the thirty-one or so years Róisín knew it had of life. It seemed a peaceful face. It lacked the smirk it often displayed to her and the other servants in the Geherty House. It was, in the end, a sad and miserable face. The morgue collected the corpse in the morning, and Róisín learned that he was buried in Queens after a small funeral mass at St. Stephen's.

By this point, Mr. Henry was no longer pushing Róisín to marry. From the first, he was concerned she would end up alone and destitute. As to him, it was long clear that he would not be a match, suitable or otherwise, for Róisín. The gap between the two, he being from Cork City and in finance on Wall Street and she being a farmgirl working as a nurse in a small clinic on the east side, was far too broad to be bridged. And Mr. Henry gave no indication that he wished to wed. He was happy in his bachelor's existence with his bachelor friends, and he understood that Róisín, too, was content with her situation.

Still, at times he wished she would at least once give a chance to one of the men she laughingly told him attempted to meet her, generally up-and-comers among the new Irish who were training to be lawyers or bankers or who were clerks that saw her in church. But she insisted that she lacked the requisite desire for such a companion. "Do not speak to me of such things," she retorted more than once, "when it is abundantly clear that a man such as you must be in want of a wife," although they both understood that that was something for which *he* lacked the requisite desire.

Now he realized her growth at the clinic where Dr. Doyle certified her as a nurse provided a career for which a husband was neither necessary nor particularly desirable. She had some friends. A few were lightly maintained from Lord & Taylor, though many of the women she knew there were gone and married and bearing children. She had friends from the parish, but, again, they were married and raising children.

Róisín was content with her work and with her reading. She often sat at the small park near her flat and read a novel she obtained from Nurse Evans's small collection or from a little bookshop around the corner, sometimes in the company of Deidre O'Sullivan, the governess she met in the pocket park near the flat she had while at Lord & Taylor.

She still visited Mrs. Houlihan or Mrs. Flanagan on some fine Sundays, and the older women had become something of mothers to her. They were in some ways more like her than was Róisín's mother, to whom she still wrote at least once a month, as her mother did to her. But she found her mother's letters with their local gossip and tales about siblings being married and having children of little interest.

And at least once a month her Cousin Jimmy, still looking for a bride, insisted that she come to his small apartment for Sunday dinner after mass.

28.

And, of course, there was Sophie. Róisín often walked to Cassidy's house after mass, sitting with Sophie and going for a walk if the weather was pleasant. As her sister grew, though, Sophie bristled at what she considered interference but Róisín considered care.

"You ain't mamma," Sophie began to say more frequently and as often as not Róisín was told by Fisher, Cassidy's man, at the door that Sophie was not up to seeing visitors and Róisín would leave, though not without a glance at Sophie's window, sometimes seeing the girl, sometimes not.

At least every two weeks, Róisín wrote to their mamma to say how Sophie was progressing. Sophie stopped writing when she became Mrs. Cassidy, so Róisín's letters were their family's only source of information. Sophie refused to open the letters her mamma sent to her, and Róisín was left to read portions of her own letters aloud to her sister that contained information their mother wanted Sophie to have. Largely information that would be of use to a pregnant girl had she the slightest inclination to listen to it.

Róisín spoke to Mr. Henry of all of these things.

"She is a woman," he said to her, though he, of course, was not. "You must let her be one. I know she is just a child, too, especially to you. But she will not permit you to mother her and she will not forgive you for having her marry Cassidy. At least for a time."

He said this to her with some frequency, especially as the pregnancy was progressing and the refused entrances more frequent.

Róisín's connection with her sister was so tenuous that she did not learn of the birth of the boy until several days after the event.

Sally, the maid who answered the door on the following Sunday, a cold day with several inches of snow that fell overnight, said, "Please, miss. The baby, a boy, is born and everything is quiet—" at which Róisín pushed past her, taking the steps two at a time to the third floor.

The door to the left, Sophie's room, was open, and her sister slept peacefully, with a tiny bundle in a bassinet beside her. Róisín removed her bonnet and coat, holding the former and draping the latter over an arm. As she looked around the room, in the corner, rocking slightly, was an older woman, who put a finger to her lips when she saw Róisín. Fearful of making noise, Róisín turned and went down the stairs.

On the ground floor, the servant girl was waiting.

"Thursday was when he was born. It was a surprise to everyone."

Róisín suddenly recalled that Mr. Henry was on the sidewalk. She draped her coat across her shoulders and placed her bonnet on her head and told the girl she would just be a moment before opening the door and hurrying out. Mr. Henry was moving side to side in a small amount of snow when he saw Róisín rushing headlong towards him, and he feared she would slip until he could steady her by the waist.

"You must come, Henry. I am an aunt. A boy. You must come and see him, though he is asleep."

She turned and reached back so he would take her hand. Walking more slowly now through the slush she pulled her friend with her and up the stoop. As they were about to reach it, the door was opened by Sally, and they entered the warmth of the house. Sally closed the door and took first Róisín's bonnet and coat and then Mr. Henry's hat and coat.

"Can you please remain here," pointing into the sitting-room where a fire attracted the visitors, "while I get the master?"

Róisín and Mr. Henry pulled two comfortable chairs closer to the fire and put their shoes on the fender to take the freeze from their toes. Mr. Henry never saw Róisín so animated. At times he thought a frown had been sculpted on her face. That was gone as her eyes looked into the small flames that warmed them.

"Isn't it wonderful, Michael? I am an aunt. I never thought I would care, but now it is all that seems to matter in my little world."

Without turning from the fire, she asked, "What do you think they shall name him?"

"Stephen, Jr., I would suppose."

"Yes. I suppose. But she will never call him that."

Mr. Henry did not understand. Before he could ask, Cassidy himself entered. He had a coat over his left forearm and gloves in his right hand.

"Henry. Miss Campbell. You must excuse me for keeping you waiting on this horrible day. I should have remembered you, Miss Campbell, would be making your usual Sunday visit and I regret not having told you the news. It was a failure for which I am entirely to blame."

Both the guests stood before him, their backs now warmed by the fire.

"Mother and son are, I must tell you, doing fine. She claims that he takes after his father, but I, of course, am in no position to agree or disagree with her on that."

"I presume he is Stephen, Jr.," Mr. Henry said.

"Indeed he is, sir. Indeed, he is. I am told he is sleeping so I fear we may not disturb him. I, alas, have a significant prior engagement to which I must attend, so I must take my leave of you. You, of course, are free to remain as long as you wish, at least until the child awakens.

"Sally," he said to the servant, who was standing anxiously by the door. "Please see to it that my guests have whatever they desire."

"Yes, sir."

"Very good." With that, Cassidy put the coat and gloves on. "Again. I regret that I must be off," and beyond slight bows and Róisín's slight curtsey, his guests did nothing until they heard the front door close.

"Well he, at least, will not allow the addition to his family to alter his life," Róisín said.

"Róisín. You knew that it might be so."

"Yes, of course, Henry." The two turned back to the fire after Mr. Henry asked Sally to bring them some coffee while they waited. After sitting, Róisín continued. "But it is less than a week. I had hopes."

"I agree. 'Tis not a good sign."

Shortly after the coffee and some cakes were brought, Sally returned and told them that the missus and master Stephen were awake, and they could go up to see them. "But," the girl said, "'tis best not to call him 'Stephen' as the missus don't take kindly to it."

Róisín's climb was more deliberate now, with Mr. Henry behind. On the landing for the second floor, they stepped into the drawing-room at the front of the house. It was the formal salon and it faced the front, though that did not signify as the windows were covered with a layer of dampness from the morning's snow. Sophie sat in a chair by the fire, which was set since Róisín's abrupt arrival.

She ignored the guests as she mumbled to the infant until they were very close to her.

"What do you think of Diarmaid?" Sophie asked.

The other two looked at one another.

Róisín stepped closer to her sister. She told her that he was a very handsome baby, and she reached a finger towards his face, but Sophie swatted it away.

"He is precious. We cannot risk his health. But you may sit," and she nodded to a chair set up near her, also facing the fire, "there."

As Róisín sat, Mr. Henry complimented Sophie and the baby, asking how they both fared.

"We are tolerably well, sir. It came really sudden and it hurt but we came through it, didn't we?" This last was to the baby, to whom Sophie made a face.

As Henry carried a chair so he could be closer to the ladies, Sophie said, "I am sorry, Róisín. But I cannot share Diarmaid with anyone. He is all I have, and I shan't risk losing him. I am sorry."

This was the last thing Sophie said for the next ten or fifteen awkward minutes during which she ignored all of the attempts by the others to engage with her.

Finally, Róisín stood.

"Are you leaving so soon?" Sophie asked.

"Yes, sister. You are tired and must get your sleep. I will call on you tomorrow evening if I may."

"You can if you want," Sophie said. "It don't matter to us." And that was the last thing Sophie said to her guests that Sunday.

29.

When Róisín returned on Monday, Fisher told her his mistress was indisposed with the baby and could not see visitors. This was repeated on the following three nights. On Friday, Róisín was granted entrance, but instead of being shown upstairs, Fisher took Róisín's bonnet, coat, scarf, and gloves and asked that she enter the sitting-room.

It was smaller than the drawing-room on the second floor, but it was more comfortable. It was where their recent encounter with Cassidy took place. The weather was colder than it had been on that Sunday, though the snow had largely melted away, and an attractive fire drew Róisín in. Only then did she notice Cassidy standing by the tall window, looking out onto the street.

"She will not see me," he said, without turning. "Her nurse and Sally. No one else. She will not leave her room since you visited her with Henry on Sunday."

He turned, a brandy snifter in his right hand.

"She knows I could love the boy as my own, but she will not permit it. She does not even allow me to see the child." He turned back to the window, extending the snifter away from his body and holding it there. "I simply do not understand her. He is gone. I am her husband."

Róisín could see his shoulders slump. "I am her husband."

Cassidy put the snifter to his lips and drank. He again turned to Róisín, who was anchored where she first saw him.

"Miss Campbell. I am being remiss. I shall have Fisher get you something to warm you."

Fisher, who was standing in the doorway through this, stepped forward. Cassidy looked at Róisín.

"What would you like, Miss Campbell."

"If it pleases you, sir, I am perfectly content."

"Nonsense." He looked at his man. "Fisher. Go ask Cook to prepare that warming concoction she does so well, for Miss Campbell."

After the man was gone, with a bow, Cassidy directed Róisín to the chair she used on Sunday when she appeared with Mr. Henry. It was placed so that her feet could rest on the fender. As she sat, he walked to a long and narrow table that held a series of crystal decanters and refilled his glass. He placed it on a table between the chairs as he took the one Mr. Henry recently used.

Each looked into the fire until Fisher returned with a mug, which he placed on the table next to Cassidy's snifter and closer to Róisín.

"Thank you, Fisher, you may leave us," and Fisher, with a bow and a "Very good, sir," left and closed the door behind himself.

"I do not know what it is, but when I come in from the cold, Cook makes this for me, and my innards warm from the inside out. She will not tell me what it is and what is in it. She thinks of it as a form of job security. Please."

Róisín looked at the mug as Cassidy lifted his own glass. It had a handle, and she moved it to her lips, feeling the heat of the drink in its first drops. She blew on it and then placed the mug on her lower lip before taking a testing sip. She paused and took a second, longer draw, and then a third before pulling the mug away.

"Did I not tell you?" Cassidy said. "'Tis a miracle drink."

After a fourth sip, Róisín returned the mug to the table. Cassidy kept the snifter lightly between his thumb and the fingers of his right hand, moving it just enough to swirl the liquid around.

"I truly do not know what I can do. I knew I could never properly love her, but I hoped to love the child, whosever it is. And I have become very fond of your sister. But I do not believe she feels anything for me, even fondness, beyond anger for being me and not him."

"I am very sorry to hear that, sir."

"As I am sorry for saying it." He gulped more whiskey and turned to her.

"Miss Campbell. We are related. I do wish you would call me by my Christian name."

Without taking her eyes from the fire, she said, "I shall call you 'Stephen,' Mr. Cassidy, if you will call me 'Róisín.'"

"Then we can agree on that. Miss Campbell."

After several moments, she said, "I did not know my sister very well. She was but a girl when I left Limerick. When I speak to her, I fear she remains too much the romantic."

"And that she dreams of being rescued by her lover."

"Exactly, Mr....Stephen. Exactly. I fear, too, for the position in which I have placed you."

"You were honest with me. It has not gone as either of us envisioned."

"For now, at least."

He again turned, and she did as well when she felt his eyes on her.

"Do you think there might be hope? That things would be as...calm as I expected. That she and I could have our lives together, and with Stephen, Jr., as well as our lives apart. That is what I hoped for when I agreed to marry her." He turned back to the fire. "I am such a fool."

Róisín stood and walked around her chair so she could be behind his. She placed her arms so they crossed his chest. "You were not a fool, Stephen. I shall always love you for what you did."

He tilted his head, so it lay upon her right arm. "You are my sister now, more I think than before the baby. And I will always love you for that."

Both looked into the fire until Róisín was forced to stand as she began to stiffen.

"Perhaps I should go."

He rose and rang for Fisher, who brought her things, and Cassidy showed her to the door.

"Good night, Róisín."

"Good night, Stephen."

And with that, she left and walked back to her apartment.

Sophie relented on Sunday afternoon when Róisín appeared, alone, after mass.

"Mistress will see you, miss." Sally surprised Róisín in saying this, and Róisín followed the girl to the drawing-room on the second floor. It was cold, though not as cold as it had been, and Sophie sat where she had the Sunday before. This time Sophie looked at her as she went in.

"I see you are alone today."

"I am alone today. I was alone each night I came to see you during the week, but I was told you were indisposed."

"Yes. I am told it is part of having a baby."

When Róisín got close to her sister and her nephew, Sophie did not shoo her away.

"You can hold him if you want."

Róisín did want to and bent to lift the tiny creature. She often held infants at the clinic or hospital or in flats in the tenements, but she cradled Stephen, Jr. more tightly than she had with any of them and carried him to the other chair.

Róisín returned each of the following three nights to sit with her sister and the baby. Cassidy suggested that she move into the brownstone instead of having to leave in the cold to go to her apartment. Róisín took a small room with a bed on the fourth floor and did what she could to make it comfortable. But the only time she spent there was when she slept. She left for the clinic or the hospital only after looking in at Sophie and the boy and went directly to either the drawing-room on the second floor or Sophie's room on the third when she returned each night.

Sophie allowed her sister more and more time to hold the boy, and each evening the two sat in the drawing-room at the front of the house in the chairs that faced the fireplace, and Cook allowed Sally, when her work was done, to sit in a corner sewing and watching. Róisín kept quiet unless Sophie spoke to her, and when she did, Sophie spoke of her ambitions for the child. Róisín did not dare mention Cassidy, hoping Sophie would but she never did, and each morning Róisín reported this to Cassidy before he left for his office. If he were home, and he usually spent his evenings at his club, he kept himself to the sitting-room on the ground floor where he kept his liquor.

This was the routine the house had settled into until several days after the boy's one-month anniversary. That night, Sophie burst into Róisín's room, clutching her child.

"He's not breathing!" she screamed, "he's not breathing!"

In a moment, Róisín was up, grasping the boy from her sister's arms.

"He started to choke and cough, and I rubbed his back and rubbed his back and then he just stopped! Do something! Please, God, do something!"

She placed her mouth on his, as she had seen while at the hospital, and blew, hoping to replace his air but he still did not move. With a kiss on the forehead of the infant, Róisín placed his body on her bed and lowered herself to her sister, who was collapsed on the floor. She put an arm around her and promised, "He's with God now," and then stayed motionless until her sister somehow fell into a sleep.

30.

Sophie could not attend the mass or watch the small boat cross the river bearing the tiny bundle to its final resting place in Queens. Only a small group attended. In addition to Róisín were Cassidy, Sally, Mr. Henry, Nurse Evans, and Róisín's (and Sophie's) Cousin Jimmy. Sophie stayed in her room for a week after, refusing to see anyone but Sally, and then only for meals. If she saw someone when she went to the toilet, she retreated until that person was gone.

Though Róisín went into work, she was allowed to leave each midday, in case her sister would agree to see her.

It was two Sundays after Stephen Cassidy, Jr., was put to rest that Sophie came down the stairs. Cassidy and Róisín were at mass together, and she was waiting for them upon their return. She refused to speak to them—was perhaps incapable of speaking to them—but she stayed with them as they read in the sitting-room for over an hour before simply rising and walking up to her room.

"I do not know what I am to do with her," Cassidy said when his wife was out of earshot. "She will not see me. She will not let me comfort her. As with you."

Róisín remained silent, at a loss for what to say. She well knew the distance that Sophie was creating between herself and the world. It was worse for Róisín than for Cassidy. Sophie, Róisín thought at least, loved her.

After several weeks, Sophie came downstairs. She woke early and sometimes went for a walk in the neighborhood though it was still cold, neither looking at nor waving at people she saw on the streets. She returned while Cassidy and Róisín were at breakfast and said "good morning" to them before returning to her room for most of the day.

In the evening, she came down again after Cassidy and Róisín had supper. She still only ate in her room. Each night, Cassidy and Róisín sat in the sitting-room after supper. The two either read or wrote letters and chatted about the little things that one living in the city spoke about. Róisín had taken to writing letters to the members of her family in Ireland and England, more than she had because of her being in the unusual circumstance as a resident of Cassidy's house.

A chair was positioned for Sophie, and at first, when they heard her on the stairs, they stopped what they were doing, mid-sentence of a letter if necessary, and stood awaiting her appearance. They soon realized that this form of greeting was uncomfortable for them all, so they reverted to simply continuing what they were doing. The chair was still there for her, always left empty, and she took to sitting in it.

After initial efforts at speaking to Sophie failed, the other two treated her as if she were not in the room, though acutely conscious that she was. The charade only ended when Sophie spoke. It was about a month after her child died. She was in the chair, looking into the fire. It snowed significantly in the afternoon, likely the last time for the season, with flurries still coming down. Both Cassidy and Róisín had struggled to get to the house, and the normal sounds of passing carriages were muffled by the accumulation. Each had one of Cook's rejuvenating concoctions.

Sophie was in the chair, looking into the fire.

"Someday I shall be with him."

At first, it was the sound of Sophie speaking that shocked the others to attention, and then it was what she said. Róisín, who was sitting at the secretary continuing a letter to their mother she began the day before, jumped up and sat in the chair beside Sophie, which normally was left empty in the evening. She reached across to gather Sophie's hands, but her sister would not offer them. Róisín decided to remain silent. After several minutes, marked by the hallway clock, Sophie turned to her sister, whose gaze remained on Sophie throughout. "I love you."

With that, Sophie got up, and the other two watched her leave the room and heard her heavy steps on the stairs. When they knew she reached her room on the third floor and shut herself in, Cassidy sat in the chair Sophie vacated.

"What shall we make of it?" Cassidy asked.

Róisín, whose eyes had not ventured from the spot where she saw Sophie begin to go up the stairs, said, "We shall need to watch her. I fear she is despondent, and we must help her recover."

"Sometimes she be out for hours, miss, and I think she won't be back."

Sally stood, shaking slightly, in the sitting-room. It was a particularly nice late winter Sunday, and the window was open, and the noise of the street was reintroducing itself. Róisín had asked Fisher if she could speak to the girl about her sister. She promised Sally that she would not let Sophie know about their conversation, but Sophie was not in when she and Cassidy returned from mass.

"She made me promise not to tell anyone, miss. Especially you."

Róisín dismissed the servant and stood looking out at the people passing by on the sidewalk. She did not know what could be done about this information. She could not broach it with Sophie. Sophie was coming out of her shell little by little. It was her absence that day that led Róisín to question Sally.

Róisín weighed telling Cassidy. He was becoming more distant about both Campbells with each day. No longer was he trying to engage with Sophie, and it was weeks since he spoke to Róisín about his concerns. Often in the evening, he sat with a book in his favorite chair, the one near the window with a slight view of the street, reading the same page over and over, usually with a whiskey tumbler on the small table beside his chair.

Sophie did not come home that Sunday afternoon nor that evening. Róisín sat alone in the sitting-room. Cassidy was told of his wife's absence when he came in shortly before the sun went down and after a quiet supper with Róisín, he went out for what he said was a prior engagement.

With the sun going down, it was cold, and the window in the sitting-room was firmly shut. In Cassidy's absence, Róisín sat in his chair, the one with a view to the outside, where she could see Sophie when she came home. But she did not come home.

At nine, with the street quiet and only Fisher, Cook, and Sally in the house, Róisín was nearly out of her senses. She raced to the closet in the hall and grabbed a coat and bonnet. She put her head into the kitchen, where Sally and Cook sat over some tea and biscuits and told them she must go out.

Cook told her to wait.

"Sally, here, will go with you."

Before Cook finished, Sally was up and went to a rack along the hallway to get her own coat and bonnet.

"Yes, miss. You canna go out alone."

Róisín did not protest.

Their first stop was the local precinct, but the sergeant at the desk told them that they'd not seen a woman alone and in distress. He suggested they go to the taverns by the water, and the two had no better luck at any of them.

"Perhaps she be home, miss," Sally said.

Róisín agreed, but when they returned some hour-and-a-half after having left, Cook said Sophie was not back. The natural next stop was the morgue at Bellevue. Fisher insisted he accompany her, and it was nearing midnight as the two went through the gate and banged on the door. A young, lanky man in a leather apron answered.

"What be you wanting?"

"Please. My sister. She is gone and none can say where she is. The police. The taverns. She is very low. We're afraid about her."

"Well if she done herself off, miss, she probably wouldn't be here yet. That's the truth. But we's got two women that was brought in tonight. You free to look. How old be your sister?"

Róisín could not hear what she was being told.

"Miss. How old be your sister?"

Fisher did not know how old Sophie was, but that, "She just had a baby."

The man's attention turned to him.

"Ah. And the baby died? Yea. We get some new mothers. 'Tis really sad."

Róisín heard, and Fischer realized she was swaying slightly. He looked crossly at the boy as he reached to prevent Róisín from collapsing.

"That'll be enough from you," he said. "Are there any women about that age?"

"Nah," the boy said in his matter-of-fact way. "They both be older. Ugly women they both are. I guess they may have been pretty some time. But they ain't no more."

Fisher barely let him finish before he led Róisín to the cooling air of the street, with a slight breeze coming from the river.

Róisín looked east, towards the river.

"What if she's there, Mr. Fisher? Floating away? What if she's—?"

Fisher, continuing his streak of uncharacteristic sympathy, gripped her tightly and Róisín would have fallen had he not. He led her down the street to the avenue. After a wait, they found a cab and rode to Cassidy's in the quiet streets. Cassidy was back when they returned. They found him sitting in the sitting-room in his chair looking out his window.

"Did you find her?" he asked without turning his head.

"Why do you care?"

This outburst from Róisín caused him to turn to look at her. Neither liked what they now were to each other. He had been more than kind and generous and now his wife for all he knew or cared might be drifting slowly down the East River. She saw him in a way she had not before and did not find it attractive.

By then, Fisher had backed out of the room and closed the door. Alone, Róisín spoke first. "We did not find her. I shall resume my search in the morning," and she walked up the stairs to her room.

The next morning, Róisín told Dr. Doyle she could not work and the reason, and she spent Monday and Tuesday repeating her journey to the local precinct and then walking to as many others as she could find. Each afternoon at about four-thirty, she headed to Bellevue and the morgue. She received more consideration from the pathologist than she had from the boy who was there overnight. But she received no news about Sophie. Other bodies appeared. None fit Sophie's in any way.

On Wednesday, as she ate some toast to prepare her for the day's work, Sally told her there was someone at the door to see her. Róisín rushed, half dreading, half hoping. It was a girl she did not recognize but who appeared to be in service.

"Be you Miss Campbell?" When Róisín said she was her, the girl handed her a note, curtsied, and left before Róisín could give her a coin.

My Dear Miss Campbell,

You will not recall me, I think, but I believe you assisted in my care when I was in a gig accident with my former fiancée, Miss Elizabeth Geherty. I have the honor of advising you that I have undertaken to provide protection for your sister from the brute to whom I am aware she is nominally married.

She has advised me of all of the circumstances of her marriage and those of the tragic loss of her child.

I assure you, Miss Campbell, as I assured your sister, that I will place her care to the foremost of my thoughts and efforts and that she shall be safe.

Your humble servant, &c.
Edward Meade

P.S., Please know that your sister insisted that I not contact you or anyone else. I could not, in good conscience, abide by that request, knowing how concerned you surely are about her well-being. I have not told your sister of this communication to you and do not intend to tell her. It is therefore with some regret that I must insist that you refrain from attempting to contact her. She is, as you can surely imagine, in a very bad way.

I will endeavor to keep you apprised of her condition and, I hope, of any improvement in it. Please defer to my judgment in coming to visit her. Again, I assure you that she is safe and that her well-being is foremost in my mind.

EM

Sally, who was watching her mistress (as she believed Róisín to be) read the note, rushed to her when she watched it slip to the floor, just in time to again prevent her falling. She collected the note without reading it—Sally was not a proficient reader in any case—and led Róisín to the sitting-room.

Cassidy was long gone, leaving well before he normally would, as he also did on Monday and Tuesday. Sally went to ask Cook for tea and biscuits for Róisín and returned as soon as she could. She found Róisín standing at the window, looking out at the people passing by and slowly rocking side to side. The weather continued warm from Sunday, though clouds suggested that rain was on the way.

"Please, miss, if you please. Is Mrs. Cassidy...alive?"

Róisín turned at the disturbance.

"I am sorry, Sally?"

"Mrs. Cassidy, miss. Be she alive?"

"Yes, Sally. She is alive. But I do not know when I will see her again. I fear she will never grace this house again."

Sally had placed Meade's note on the mantel, and Róisín saw it when she finished what she said to the sweet maid, who was already heading to the kitchen to gather the tea and biscuits. She picked it up again. She understood what it said and was yet to process what it meant. She looked at it and found her eyes drawn by two words.

Elizabeth Geherty

She had never gotten the name of the woman she accompanied to the hospital after that second gig accident, the one who spoke of disliking the man she was destined to marry. Meade called her his "former fiancée." Róisín mentioned that accident to Sophie, among other things that occurred at the clinic. About a man horribly injured showing off in a gig to his fiancée. Sophie must have connected Edward Meade to the accident and thus to Róisín herself and said something to him about it.

Róisín was reminded of Charles Geherty, Jr.'s death in the clinic after she discovered him against its door. She was told that his mother and sister visited while on a day when she was at the hospital. She assumed it was Mary. Could it have been Elizabeth? She had not thought to ask, having long since surrendered any interest in that family when she left its house following Mary's onslaught. Róisín knew about the speculation's collapse and thought it would have adversely affected the family, as it surely did. It was a subject in which she had little interest beyond some regret for having failed to protect Mrs. Geherty in the matter, regret lessened by Mrs. Geherty having dismissed her without her, Róisín, having done anything wrong or inappropriate. No matter what Mary said.

Whatever thoughts she had of the Gehertys, though, she put aside. With her mission of searching for Sophie completed, albeit in a manner that was unsatisfactory but not as unsatisfactory as she feared it could have been, Róisín sat in Cassidy's chair, looking out. She did not know how the two, Sophie and Meade, came to be together, but what mattered was that they were together. Shortly, Sally interrupted her trance with her tray of tea and biscuits, which she placed on a table beside Róisín.

"I am sorry, Sally. I was taken by surprise by the note. I am advised by a gentleman that he has taken Sophie under his protection. I do not know what that means, exactly, but she appears to be safe. I am told not to attempt to see her, at least for now. That is all I know."

"Thank you, miss," Sally said before curtseying and turning to leave. Róisín asked that she tell Fisher and Cook, and Sally left after promising she would do so.

Róisín did not know what she would say to Cassidy. She did know that she would not show him the note. Of that, there was no doubt.

With that decided and there being nothing more to be done for the time being concerning her sister, Róisín's thoughts drifted back to those two words. "Elizabeth Geherty."

32.

"**G**ood riddance."

Róisín should not have been surprised that this is what Cassidy said when she told him that Sophie was now with Edward Meade, but she was.

"You think that harsh of me, Miss Campbell?"

"Well, Ste...Mr. Cassidy, I am afraid that I do."

"Do not be afraid."

It was the Wednesday night, and Cassidy had just come home. With his coat and hat taken by Fisher, he went into the sitting-room and directly to his bar. He removed the top of a crystal decanter, the one with a dark whiskey, and poured it into a tumbler. He took an immediate, long draw and moved to look out the window. When she heard his arrival, Róisín came down from the drawing-room on the second floor.

When he heard her enter, Cassidy turned. He pointed his glass in the direction of the bar, but she shook her head. He asked, "Have you had any word?"

"She is, I believe, safe."

He took a gulp of whiskey.

"That is good to know. She is alive then?"

"Yes. She is alive. She has found a way to Edward Meade."

"Edward Meade? I do not believe I have had the pleasure."

He went to the chairs by the fireplace and indicated that she should join him. The rain came in earlier and with it a cold air, so the fire was comforting.

"I happened to have met Mr. Meade when he was in a horrible accident some years ago."

"My God. Edward Meade. He is the cripple?"

"Well, he was seriously hurt in that crash."

"Of course, of course. The cripple who went to Europe and whose fiancée refused to marry him, or at least they never married. It may have been that her family lost all of its money, and then some, in some railroad swindle or other."

Cassidy took another long drink.

He looked again at her and lifted his glass. "Are you sure?" and again she shook her head.

"Edward Meade. Well, he is welcome to her. Good riddance is what I say. Good riddance."

He looked at the intricate etchings in his glass as it reflected the flames.

"We shall have to get her things to our friend Mr. Meade. You will help Sally with that, won't you, Miss Campbell?"

She looked at him, somewhat surprised at his brusqueness, and could only say, "Of course, sir."

"And you shall be leaving us, too, I daresay. Not that I will not regret *that*. But it is of course necessary." He smiled. "I cannot be seen living with an attractive woman who is not my wife, now, can I?"

With all the day's swirling, Róisín had not given this the least thought but knew it was inevitable. She would bring it up with Dr. Doyle on the morrow.

Cassidy was as good as his word. By Friday, all of his wife's things were packed and a note sent to the home of Edward Meade, which was his parents' home about a mile to the north, that "Mrs. Stephen Cassidy's belongings are packed and available to be retrieved." The boxes themselves were kept in a small room on the ground floor of Cassidy's house.

For Róisín, her room at the clinic had long since been taken by a second doctor who was hired. Nurse Evans, however, offered to cede her rooms to Róisín, having decided to move into Dr. Doyle's. He had two separate bedrooms and (in theory though not fact) she could have one of them. As to a scandal, it was common knowledge among the community that the two had a *de facto* marriage, a real one being prevented by the accident of Nurse Evans having married some twenty-five years earlier a man who promptly headed west for the California gold rush and had not been heard from since.

33.

Róisín went to mass the following Sunday at Mrs. Flanagan's parish and walked with her to the boarding house. She wanted to thank her for her kindness to Sophie and to tell her of the developments with her sister. The older woman already knew of the loss of the baby and expressed her condolences. She insisted that they sit again for tea.

"I trust that you remember Mary Bette Flynn?"

"Of course." She was the woman with whom Róisín shared a bed when she was first at Mrs. Flanagan's. A poor girl from County Mayo.

"I suppose you haven't heard. But things have been very hard for her."

"Hard?"

Mrs. Flanagan took a long sip of her tea.

"She's been arrested several times for public vagrancy."

Róisín understood this to mean prostitution, which was not itself illegal. It was a lucrative but dangerous business, the greatest risk being contracting a disease that could not be cured and resulting in a lingering and painful death.

Róisín very much liked Mary Bette and still savored the memory of the small intimacies they shared when they were in the bed on her first hot August nights in New York. She had not kept abreast of what she was doing after she was mentioned a few times when Róisín visited Mrs. Flanagan while she was at the Geherty House. She had not seen her since the day she first left the boarding house.

She knew it was not uncommon for a girl who could barely survive doing piecework as a seamstress to turn to prostitution. It was an offense that resulted in the immediate ostracizing of the woman, though never the man. If Mary Bette were arrested, surely she was cast from the Catholic community. Hundreds of gentlemen's brothels dotted the city, but Mary Bette may not have met the standards for the women in those establishments and was too old for some of the lesser ones.

"Is there nothing that can be done for her?" Róisín asked.

"Now, of course, she will not come here. She knows what it would do to me and the house were she to be seen. I do not know where she goes when she is out of jail. I am sure it is one of the tenements close to the docks. Where she does what it is that she does. I have those who tell me about her. Currently, she is in jail and, frankly, that might be the best place for her. She will not get out for several months. All I ask is that you keep her in your thoughts and prayers and that if you come up with a solution for her you share it with me."

For someone who thought she was finished with solving the problems of others, Róisín suddenly found herself thrust back in. She made sure to have her walk with Mr. Henry the following Sunday. He was without a response when Róisín told him of her friend Mary Bette Flynn, and the two were largely silent for the balance of their walk beyond his "That is a bad business."

34.

In Massachusetts, Elizabeth Geherty was settled into a life of boredom and anxiousness. She saw Emily often and they shared some afternoons at each other's houses. The Connors—Emily's parents—were not nearly as despondent about what happened to their money as Elizabeth's parents were about what happened to theirs. As Emily predicted, several more bankrupt families found their way to their Elba, and Emily orchestrated regular get-togethers in the village and at the inn, extending to several awkward parties in the latter's ballroom.

At first, Mr. and Mrs. Geherty spent little time together, chiefly at meals, as they each kept mostly to their respective studies. When the weather was pleasant, they sometimes strolled up to the road, arm-in-arm. They rarely ventured into Stockbridge itself. The couple did not marry in anticipation of wealth or society, yet both attached themselves barnacle-like to the Gehertys.

While Mrs. McNabb invited them to the city for Christmas and New Year's, it took but a moment for them, with Elizabeth, to agree to remain in Stockbridge. Charlie came up once shortly before Christmas, but he was a foul mood and begged to return to town just one day after his arrival. It was clear that he was having a terrible time of things, but he would not hear about it. A letter from Michael gave some assurances, more in hope than expectation, that he would monitor his brother or at least try to, and after Charlie's death, Michael more than the others would be tortured with thoughts of what could have been done differently for that poor soul.

Even the faux levity of Emily's events could not survive an early January blizzard. Johnson had filled the house's storage with dry goods that would keep the Gehertys fed and when the storm hit, he and Mrs. Johnson were safely on their farm. When the roads cleared, the time in isolation affected the family dramatically.

Mr. and Mrs. Geherty found it difficult to remain distant from one another and discovered, or re-discovered, that they enjoyed one another's company. To preserve wood, they remained in the sitting-room most of the day and when a ready supply of firewood appeared after the snow was gone, they continued to remain in the sitting-room together.

Elizabeth spent those days sitting on a window seat, reading in the wan winter light, and gazing out over the whiteness of a New England snow that highlighted the contours of their property. She missed the diversions Emily offered, but as her parents found that they liked each other, Elizabeth found that she liked herself. It was, frankly, no revelation. It was a comfort to be reminded of it.

As the trees began to bud, Charles Geherty sat with his wife and Elizabeth in his study. It was clear, he said, that they could not last much longer in Stockbridge. He showed them a telegram he received from Peter McNabb. In it, McNabb assured the Gehertys that there would always be a place for them in his house in Manhattan.

"I shall have to accept it, of course. It riles me, this reliance on him or anyone else. But it must be so. We must prepare ourselves and what few belongings we shall have after all of this is done."

With that, he folded the telegram and restored it to its envelope.

The news was hardly a revelation. Abigail Geherty rose to step behind her husband. She wrapped her arms around him and told him, in a voice just loud enough for Elizabeth to hear, that having each other was all she wanted or needed. For the first and only time, Elizabeth saw the glimmer of a tear in her father's eye as he held his wife's hands close to him.

Elizabeth rose to leave the pair to themselves.

"Father. You will never be blamed. I will always love you."

With that, Elizabeth went for a walk in the garden where the slightest hints of blossoms had begun to appear.

35.

It was not long after her husband's telegram to his father-in-law that Mary McNabb summoned her sister back to New York. Elizabeth's normal disdain for being forced into company with her sister had sufficiently withered away in Stockbridge that she was glad to be done with it. She doubted she would return to that village, seeing as how the debts were accumulating even in western Massachusetts and the butcher, the baker, and the candlestick-maker were increasingly unwilling to extend credit to the Geherty family.

Emily Connor, whose family was in similarly desperate straits, had already decamped to Greenwich Village, moving in with an unmarried friend who had artistic aspirations.

On her second Sunday at the McNabb's, Elizabeth was in her lightly-furnished small room on the fourth floor. She was still in bed when her sister burst in triumphantly and without knocking.

"Surely she is ruined now. And we must thank that cripple of yours for it."

Elizabeth sat up. She did not know her sister to be up this early on a Sunday, or on any day for that matter.

"Mary. What on earth can you possibly be going on about?"

"Ah, yes. You never had the misfortune of meeting that harlot who once worked for mother when father had the house. It seems that she had a sister who got pregnant in Ireland and was sent here to separate her from the Romeo who did it to her in some form or another, probably in some dank barn or field with cows looking on."

Elizabeth put her legs to the side of her bed watching Mary pacing left and right, left and right.

"Well, she got here, and someone arranged for some kind of marriage, in a church no less. There was no love between them. They just met and his thoughts went, well, in another direction. So, four months after the wedding out popped Romeo's bastard child." Mary shot her index finger into the air after using it in her mouth to make a popping sound.

"A little boy. Little boy, though, was sickly and didn't survive much beyond a month. And the harlot's sister—"

"The harlot being?"

"The harlot being the one I got mother to dismiss. And I got her dismissed from another house, that dimwitted Marilyn Reynolds's house, as well. So, the bastard dies, and what do you think happened?"

"Mary, please, you're talking about a dead child."

"My talking about it isn't going to make him any deader now, is it? It won't bring him back, will it?

"So, the mother runs away. And guess who she runs to. Guess."

Elizabeth stared at her sister, wishing desperately that she was back in the Berkshires with her parents.

"With your Edward, of course. She is now in his protection after she told him horrible things about her husband. They will probably get an annulment, seeing as there was one would think no consummation. *Quel scandale!*"

Mary sat on her sister's bed.

"What's it to do with the sister, the one you got mother to dismiss?"

"Don't you see? She is the one who engineered the whole marriage thing. It seems her sister just showed up off a boat and had a note from their mother which told the whole, sad story. And the sister, the one I got dismissed, had some friend who knew this Cassidy fellow, the husband, and together they set it up, but her sister went crazy when the baby died."

"That's all very sad. But what's it to do with me?"

"You? It has nothing to do with you. I just wanted you to know how right I was in judging the harlot."

"What would you have done if I were her, with a note from the mother?"

"But you would never be her. The idea of you getting pregnant?"

"Mary."

Mary was laughing, slapping her sister. "I can never see *that* happening, but if it did, I shall know nothing further of you. I shall throw you to the wolves, so be forewarned. You shall walk the streets alone, and not even mother would know you. I surely would not. You? Pregnant?"

She laughed more and rose to leave.

Elizabeth, knowing Edward Meade better than most, and especially better than her sister, felt for the girl, whoever she was. Seeking him for protection was like a Christian seeking the same from a lion in the Coliseum. Yes, this girl was wrong. But she was a mother who lost her child and did not deserve the likes of Edward Meade.

But Mary was having her fun, and being as it was Mary's house, Elizabeth would just have to let her. Mary would talk again and again of the accuracy of her opinion of the former servant—and Elizabeth was aware that Mary confirmed the story Emily told—and label herself an astute observer of other women.

After mass, Mary insisted on sharing her triumph with her *coterie* of friends. It was a warm late winter day, and they elected to walk together to a nearby park where they could spread across a path with their children being taken home by their nurses and their husbands adjourning to another park for their cigars and peacocking.

"Elizabeth," one of Mary's friends said when they passed the park's gate. "You must know her. She is the one who found poor Charlie."

"That's right," Mary said. "She works at that clinic where Charlie died. I forgot. You must have seen her when you went to thank them for doing what they could with him. Something Campbell was her name."

Elizabeth recalled visiting and meeting with a doctor and a nurse, but the woman who found Charlie was elsewhere that day. But, she was told, her thanks would be passed on to her. Shortly before Elizabeth left, Dr. Doyle asked if she was involved in a gig accident, and when Elizabeth said she had been, he said the nurse who cared for her—Róisín—was the one who found Charlie.

Elizabeth remembered her, and their talk at the hospital, and that she promised to return to the clinic to speak with her, but had not had the time to do so before she and her parents returned to Stockbridge following Charlie's funeral. He was a casualty of the Gehertys' financial collapse since his money dried up with his father's and those with whom he entertained himself and on whose hospitality he availed himself for a place to sleep (when not in his brother's sitting-room) soon tired of him and left him to his own devices to use whatever money he found for whoring or visiting opium dens. It was a trip to one of the latter that killed him.

So that was the woman Mary had dismissed. Twice. Her sister was jealous and vindictive, but till she put a face on the dismissed servant, Elizabeth never felt a connection to Mary's victims.

The conversation among Mary and her friends soon ventured elsewhere, and Elizabeth moved to the edge of the group and half-listened to what was being said. Having no interest in the intricacies of pregnancy and stories of the pain and suffering these women endured for their children, at least before they came into the world—though Mary had yet to experience that notwithstanding many attempts—Elizabeth's thoughts drifted to the woman who was kind to her, recognizing that she never told the woman her name. Elizabeth wondered whether the woman's attitude would have been different had she known Elizabeth was Elizabeth Geherty.

She decided to visit this woman in the morning.

By that Monday morning, the news about poor Sophie had percolated through much of the Irish community. She was already labeled "Meade's Whore" in more than a few places. Róisín could tell from the lowered voices when she came into the waiting room that she was likely the topic of conversation. It could not be helped; she had a job to do. Shortly after eleven, an elegantly dressed woman entered. Róisín was heading into the back as the door opened, but Elizabeth recognized her from the rear. She called out,

"Miss Campbell."

Róisín turned, fearing who with such a voice was beckoning her.

It is likely she would not have recognized Elizabeth but for the reference in Meade's letter to her and the memory it dislodged.

"Miss Geherty."

It was Elizabeth's turn to be surprised. How was she known by name? Róisín opened the door to the rear and called in that she needed to step out briefly for a matter of some urgency. She then went to Elizabeth and asked her to go outside with her.

The weather had turned, and it was almost frigid although it was spring. Elizabeth was in a coat, but Róisín's was at the clinic. She decided not to retrieve it. She could not be gone for long, but long enough to sit with Elizabeth at a bakery on the avenue, which had seats and passable tea as well as more than passable German pastries. They hurried there in the cold and found seats at a small table by a hearth.

"You have come because of my sister and Mr. Meade, have you not?"

"Yes. But only in part."

"I did not know that the word of my unfortunate sister would travel so fast. And so high. It is all the news in the clinic."

A waitress brought a pot of tea and two strudels, and when she was gone Elizabeth said, "I did not know who you were when you were kind to me."

Róisín, after swallowing the first bit of strudel, said, "I do not know what you mean."

"That you worked in our house while I was away." She took a sip of her tea and felt her companion's stare. "And that my sister said horrible things about you to get you dismissed."

"It was so long ago," Róisín said, waving it off, "that it would not have mattered had I known."

"I am nothing like my sister. I think that is what I want to tell you."

Róisín laughed. "I would not believe you were Mary's, I mean, 'Mrs. McNabb''s sister in a thousand years had you not told me."

They were quiet as they ate their strudels.

"I should like to see you again," Elizabeth said when their pastries were gone and their teas were growing cold. "I know few people in New York, but I should like to know you."

Róisín could not understand. Why would someone from a family such as the Gehertys, or at least before everything was lost, wish to know her, especially with her unfortunate sister?

"Yet," Elizabeth added, "I do not even know your Christian name."

"It is Róisín," she was told. "But I must tell you something."

Elizabeth noticed the change in Róisín's voice.

"I could have saved your family. But I did not."

Elizabeth was mystified.

"Saved? How?"

Róisín had to be back at the clinic but this could not wait. It would be false not to speak it. She told of learning of the speculation by Charles Geherty and of being warned about it by Mr. Henry—described as a "dear friend"—and attempting to speak to Elizabeth's mother about it but being chased off by Mary.

"I should have been stronger. I should have at least written to your mother about it. But I was too proud. I am sorry."

Before Elizabeth processed the words and could react, Róisín was out the door, and Elizabeth saw her rush down the street to the clinic. It was stunning, the news she received and the way Róisín fled. She finished her tea and left money on the table. She put her scarf around her neck and her coat and her bonnet on and walked out into the cold.

Róisín still regretted not having done more about the speculation before. Now, having met Elizabeth, or at least realizing that Elizabeth was Elizabeth, she was in tears when she reentered the clinic. Nurse Evans noticed but thought it best to stay silent about it as Róisín resumed her duties.

36.

As Róisín was continuing with her day, Elizabeth walked to the McNabb house. She did not understand Róisín. Why she let what happened to her family happen. She understood Mary's toxicity. She knew Mary was as much if not more to blame than was Róisín, who Mary drove away before she could speak to their mother.

When she got to the house, she went to her room. It had a window with a view to the mansion across, and Elizabeth put a chair by it so she could look out. Though it was still cold, she opened it wide. It was past one and she barely moved when a parlor maid knocked on her door.

Elizabeth opened it. "Miss Elizabeth. Cook wonders if you will be eating lunch today."

The maid was in a formal outfit befitting a member of the McNabb staff.

"Tell Cook I shall be down presently, but I only require some bread and sliced meats and coffee. I will come to the kitchen for it."

"Yes, miss," and the girl was gone with a curtsey.

When Elizabeth entered the kitchen, Cook said that bread and a collection of meats and some coffee were set out in the dining room for her. Elizabeth assured her that she should not have bothered. Elizabeth was well used to making her own lunch at the Stockbridge house. She succeeded in making her sandwich and sat at a chair on the side of the dining table. As she ate, she heard someone racing down the stairs.

"The prodigal sister returns," Mary said when she noticed Elizabeth. "I was told you went out and came back and went straight to your room without coming down for lunch. It is reassuring to see that you have returned to us."

Elizabeth thought a moment.

"Was the 'harlot' you mentioned Róisín Campbell?"

Mary paused, suddenly glaring. "Yes, it was. Why is it of consequence to you?"

"Did you cause mother to dismiss her and cause her to be dismissed from the Reynolds House?"

"She was a horrible cow and deserved what she got."

"And the speculation. Did she come here about that?"

"The speculation? The one father threw his money away on? Well, frankly, I have no idea and less interest."

Elizabeth looked at Mary, who was adjusting her coat and examining her gloves, growing impatient about being delayed by her sister about this Róisín Campbell.

"Did she come to see mother about something, and did you insult her and send her away?"

"Insult her? I did not. I simply told her the truth about what she was. Did you speak to her? Did she say I 'insulted' her?"

"Did she tell you why she wanted to speak to mother?"

"I do not think she told me what she wanted to say but it didn't matter. I told her whatever she had to say could not possibly be of interest to anyone in the house."

"Did you know that she had learned that the speculation was a fraud and that father would lose all of his investment if he didn't get out? Did you know that?"

"What is that to do with me? She came to the house, I was offended that she had the nerve to do so, and come through the front door—Mason will vouch for me on this— and pretend she had something that could be of the slightest interest to mother."

With that, Mary began to pull on her gloves. "If that is all, I have an engagement I am already late for and I shall blame you for being so."

She turned and, in a moment, the front door slammed, and Elizabeth saw her walking east to do whatever it was that Mary did on Monday afternoons.

37.

While Elizabeth sat in her room that evening thinking of Róisín, Róisín was doing much the same about Elizabeth. She would have liked to have been Elizabeth's friend. In New York, she was neither rich nor poor, or at least not the poor of those in the tenements. Her nature was to be an introvert, and she rarely ventured to the pubs and taverns that sang on weekend nights of the old country, of people too often resigned to their fate in their new one.

But she was also far beneath those, of which Mr. Henry was an example, who were sufficiently educated and had sufficient resources and connections to enjoy a relatively comfortable life, with their own house and one or two domestics to cater to them.

Perhaps her only friend was the governess, Deidre O'Sullivan, and they saw each other rarely. She felt there was something different about Elizabeth. But having confessed to what she had not done for the Gehertys, she knew she would never find out what that was, and while she regretted the missed connection, she little knew Elizabeth Geherty and it would be an easy thing to continue with her life as she had lived it for some time without knowing of the existence of someone called Elizabeth Geherty.

38.

The more she thought of Róisín on Monday, the more Elizabeth knew she had to find answers from her parents, so the next morning she was on the train to Stockbridge. She did not expect to be returning so soon, if ever, but she was unsettled by her conversations with Mary and with Róisín. When she got off the train, she hired a carriage to take her to the house. Elizabeth, at least, had enough goodwill to be able to get a ride.

Her parents were sitting in separate rooms in the house. Mason and Collins remained, albeit without pay, and the former told Elizabeth that her mother was in the sitting-room. When Elizabeth entered, Abigail Geherty looked above her glasses and from her needlepoint and smiled.

"Lizzie. Why are you not with Mary?"

"Mother. I need to speak to you."

Her mother removed her glasses, and watched Elizabeth sit in a chair beside her. To her daughter's query, she said, yes, she dismissed Róisín. Yes, Mary had said some things about her, but she questioned Mary's motive. She was almost certain that Róisín had not done anything inappropriate with anyone at the house.

"But I felt your father might be susceptible to the attractions of a young, beautiful girl fresh from Ireland. He had infatuations before, and he was always morose when they ended, usually with the poor girl none the wiser about his affections for her. So, I shooed her off to another family, though not one of my friends. I made that clear to Róisín. That she not seek a position with an Irish family, and she did not."

"Do you know that she worked for the Bradford Reynoldses—?"

"Yes, I heard that. I was glad of it."

"Do you know that Mary got her dismissed from that position? That Mary accused her of doing improper things with Charlie and Michael and even father?"

"She said something to that effect at Lord & Taylor."

"Lord & Taylor?"

"Yes. I don't recall when it was but obviously after whatever happened at the Reynolds's, but Mary and I were there, and Mary saw her working and asked to see her superior. She, Mary, said all manner of awful things about Róisín, but the superior, a nice, Irish woman she was, did not believe any of it. So Róisín was still there when I was at the store again, though I do not believe she saw me, but Mary refused to return and I understand convinced some of her friends to go to Arnold Constable instead."

Elizabeth was surprised at the degree of her sister's ill-will. Róisín did not strike Elizabeth as a fountain of innocence. She was too clever for that and displayed too much empathy for that when they met days before. But why Mary's vindictiveness?

There was one more thing.

"Did you know that Miss Campbell tried to warn you about the speculation."

Mrs. Geherty's manner hardened.

"I know nothing of the sort."

Elizabeth repeated Róisín's claim about coming to the house and being sent away by Mary. That Mary had confirmed the fact of the visit but claimed not to have done anything that would lead Róisín to have left and that why she did so remained a mystery to her.

"Róisín said Mason was there."

Mrs. Geherty rang for the butler. When he arrived, she asked about the alleged incident.

"Yes, ma'am, I do recall Miss Campbell coming to the front door and insisting on seeing you on a matter she would not disclose. I sent her to the sitting-room to await you, but Miss Geherty, I mean, Mrs. McNabb, insisted on speaking to her. A short time later, Mrs. McNabb called for me and instructed me to see Miss Campbell to the door and out of the house, but Miss Campbell was already leaving before I could do anything. Shortly after that, you will recall, ma'am, you came down, but Miss Campbell was already out of the house. That is all I know, ma'am. I cannot say why Miss Campbell came to see you or what she and Mrs. McNabb may have said to each other."

"Thank you, Mason," and with that, the butler was quickly gone.

"I do not understand why she did nothing further about it. Did she hate us that much?"

"Mother, she regrets it. She said she was 'too proud.' It weighs on her, and when she told me she fled, and I think I may never see her again because of it."

"And that matters to you?"

Elizabeth shrugged. "I don't...I don't know."

Mrs. Geherty reached for her child's hands.

"Well, there is nothing to be done about it anyway. I very much doubt your father would have listened to what a servant had to say to him about one of his investments. It would not have signified. But, my dear, why do you mention it? We have moved on with our lives, and she has with hers."

"I learned that she was the woman I mentioned to you, who tended to me when I was in that horrible accident with Edward. She was a great comfort to me, but I did not know who she was, and she did not know who I was. She was also the one who found Charlie by that clinic's door and tried to save him."

"The same woman?"

"Yes. She was not there when we visited that doctor and nurse about it. Remember they mentioned someone else? That was her."

Mrs. Geherty had long since put her needlepoint on the table beside her.

"Why this sudden interest?"

"It was Mary. Again. On Sunday she was crowing about this Róisín Campbell's sister. You will not have heard, but she had a younger sister."

Elizabeth explained the chain that led her to seek Róisín out.

"Are you certain she never did anything inappropriate as to father?"

"I asked him before I dismissed her. In some ways, I wished she had. It would have made things easier for me. He recalled only a single conversation with her, in his library, and that she did nothing but listen to him rant about one thing or another when she came in to check the fire, not knowing he was there."

Elizabeth rose and leaned down to kiss her mother on the forehead.

"I must speak to father. Please do not tell him about what she did. I fear he would never forgive her and..."

"I will not," Mrs. Geherty assured her, and she watched her daughter go to find her husband.

39.

When Elizabeth reached her father's study, she lightly knocked on its door, and he told her to come in. There, he sat at his desk, which faced out into the room. It was cold, but there was no fire. Papers were strewn about, and if there was an order to them, he alone knew it. Even the picture of Charlie that was always there had been pushed over by the papers. It was early afternoon, but he had a glass of whiskey. He had not placed the top of the decanter back.

Before she said anything beyond a greeting, he asked her to sit on the sofa. He rose to sit by her.

"I spoke to your mother about it," he said when she sat across from him, "and I told her I would speak to you."

He explained that the end was near and unavoidable. He would surely have to file bankruptcy and the creditors would get everything.

"Perhaps we may keep the clothes on our backs. I don't know."

The house in Stockbridge was already spoken for, sold effective May 1 with the proceeds, all the proceeds, going to creditors. He said he hoped he at least could pay the debts he incurred in Stockbridge but was not even certain of that.

"That railroad speculation was my last hope, after the losses in the market from the panic. And you know what became of that."

He took a sip and then a gulp from his glass.

"Father. If someone told you that the speculation was a fraud, would you have gotten out?"

"I don't know. Everyone echoed everyone else. We were all in it together. And we all—what is it?—hanged separately. But if someone I knew and trusted said something, I might have thought about getting out. We'll never know, will we?"

He emptied his glass and pushed back his chair to get another. As he poured, he looked at Elizabeth.

"Do you know of such a person?"

Elizabeth waited a beat, and then said, "No, father, I do not."

He sipped his new drink as he stepped back to his chair. "We'll never know."

He thought.

"Perhaps we do. I was such a fool. Thank God McNabb took Mary on. By then, it was too late. I couldn't afford how we were living. Mary's clothing alone began to eat into my capital. You were the sensible one."

"But what of my year abroad?"

"That was costly, true. But I did not have to pay for all the gowns even you would need in New York. No. You were the sensible one. Mary was not. And I wasn't. Or the boys. Only your mother. Bless her. I would not have gotten as far as I have, pitiful as that may be, without her support. I do not deserve her."

He took another gulp. "She is 'magnificent,' as someone once called the house. I do not tell her often enough."

Elizabeth had barely moved since he began. She did not normally drink alcohol, but she asked if she might have some of his whiskey. He was surprised by the request, but he rose to pour her some. He warned her to be gentle with it as he handed her the glass.

"No, Elizabeth. I wouldn't have listened to anyone. I was too stubborn, and it was our only hope. Had the pope warned me, I wouldn't have listened. No. It was our only hope. My only hope."

His second daughter put the glass to her lips and let some of the firewater course down her throat. It sent a wave through her, and she took some more. She found it a comfort. She waited, sitting stiffly with the glass on her lap between her hands.

"About now. Michael's circumstances have been significantly compromised financially. He and Kathleen and their girl have found a brownstone. It is not in a fashionable area, but life would be miserable for them if it were, seeing what people would do when they walked down the street. I begged him to live on his salary and not to speculate." He took another draw from his glass. "I shall always regret mentioning the speculation to him or accepting the money he insisted on having me invest for him.

"So, it is Mary. Our lucky Mary"—he took another sip, and his words were beginning to slur—"who is to be our savior. Peter has been considerate enough to allocate us some space in his house. It is humiliating, of course, but we have no choice, the alternative being living on the street or in the park. The people I knew no longer know me. So being out of fashion does not matter.

"My biggest regret is you. More than Michael. We knew you had few feelings for Meade, but it would have been an advantageous match, and had you made it you would not be talking to me about moving into your sister's husband's house with your poor, stupid father."

Her parents could never know that sleeping in the park was preferable to Elizabeth to sleeping with Meade. No, if there was any *bright* side to this, it was being rid of Edward Meade. Elizabeth knew they would end up with Mary and McNabb. There was no alternative. And her father was already at bottom socially so there would be less of a sting when he was reminded of it.

Her mother would, Elizabeth thought, be relieved to be free from the grind of the fashionable life, however many pegs it was below Mrs. Astor's Four Hundred.

She lost Charlie when he committed the sin of indulgence that led to his addiction. Mary remained an enigma to her, a product not so much of indulgence but of insecurity. Only Michael and especially her Lizzie turned out to resemble what she hoped they would when she brought them into the world.

Her father's mention of Meade led Elizabeth's thoughts to drift to that afternoon she sat with Miss Campbell in the hospital in dried blood and was comforted by her mere presence and found it easy to speak of things she never spoke to another about, before or since. A woman who, through no fault of her own, was an outcast. Before she thought too much along those lines, she realized her father was asking her something.

"I asked whether you have given any thought to finding a position for yourself."

In some respects, it was a preposterous idea. Elizabeth was the daughter of a family that not long before was among the fashionable. Her sister married into a family that was still fashionable. The Gehertys suffered financial difficulties. No more. The notion that she would be farmed out as a nurse or governess for some newly well-to-do family in New York was laughable.

But it was also something that had to be considered. Elizabeth had few, if any, marriage prospects. Perhaps had she the beauty of her sister she might have found someone on the ladder who would be interested in her. But she was neither pretty nor sociable enough and always was destined to marry for social position more than anything.

Even her age spoke against her.

That thought also led to one about Róisín. Her parents confirmed all she said. Yet there was the stigma of Sophie. For the moment, those thoughts had to be put aside in light of more immediate concerns. The three—Mr. and Mrs. Geherty and Elizabeth—were soon to be without a home and would be relying on the generosity of Mary and, especially, Peter McNabb. Elizabeth knew it would be important to Mary that her position as mistress of the house be understood and accepted by all without question. She would not permit the others' presence to alter her life. The McNabbs' house in town had more than enough room, but Mary more than her husband bristled at having to again live under the same roof. Still, her friends would credit her for her charity.

Mary would fear that Elizabeth, without her own prospects, would attach herself to her more successful sister and to Mary's friends and, worse, their brothers. *That* she would not tolerate. Elizabeth would have to find her own way as Mary (in her own mind, at least) found hers. Were she to become a dependent spinster, as seemed likely, it would be no fault of Mary's.

40.

Mrs. McNabb was not at the house when a cab brought her father, her mother, and her sister from the Grand Central Depot. It was a Saturday afternoon, over a week after Elizabeth returned to Stockbridge to speak to her parents about Róisín. But Mary always took tea with a group of five other women on Saturday afternoons. As the six sat having their tea and sandwiches in the lobby of the St. Nicholas Hotel, Mary mentioned that members of her family were moving into her house that very day. It was said only in passing—and the others showered her with the appropriate praise for her sacrifice—and the subject quickly disappeared as they continued with more important business.

When Mary returned to her house, she stood in the foyer after Bradley, the tall, balding butler, bowed and took her coat, bonnet, scarf, and gloves. Her eyes briefly fixed on the landing at the top of the broad staircase that flowed up the right wall and that was lined with ornate landscapes—the money being too recent to have portraits of ancestors. Seeing it empty, she turned to Bradley. "Do they not know that I have arrived?"

Bradley, who was waiting for Mrs. McNabb to leave the foyer so he could carry on with his duties, said, "I will send someone to inform them, ma'am. And where shall she say you will be for them?"

Mary looked from the stairs into the large room to the right.

"Tell them I shall be in the sitting-room, Bradley, and do bring me some sherry," and with that, she went there and the butler went to find a maid to alert the others of her majesty's arrival.

Mary sat with her sherry admiring her sitting-room. She had done nothing in its design and less in the application of the design to the space and took great pride in having the insight to employ those who did. No one failed to compliment her on it when they came in. The room had a chair with a high back that was positioned in such a way that its occupant could as easily look out onto the street as look across the room, and it was exclusively used by Mrs. McNabb. It is where she sat awaiting the family members she assumed had by then been summoned to attend to her.

Brutally aware of their position, Mr. and Mrs. Geherty cursed themselves for not hearing their daughter arrive. But their room was in the back of the house, and they were resting from the long train journey from Stockbridge. They hurriedly dressed in the style of the city, which they were glad to ignore in their months of sequestration. Mary heard them starting down the majestic staircase from the second floor, beginning quickly and slowing to a dignified pace as they neared the bottom. She turned to the window so as not to look at them as they entered the room and she turned only when her father coughed.

"Oh, mother. Father. I see you have arrived." She stood and directed them to sit on the sofa. The sofa was, in fact, the least comfortable piece of furniture in the room, and Mary learned from her husband the benefit of imposing it on those one wished would quickly terminate their visit. Mary's parents, regrettably, were not visiting, but the sooner they left the sitting-room the better.

Mary sat in a second wing chair that was across a coffee table from the sofa, holding her glass with its sherry in her right hand and offering them nothing.

"How was your trip back to town? I am sure you have missed it terribly."

There ensued a conversation barely above that of strangers meeting on a train platform waiting for a delayed express train to take them their separate ways. Through it all, though, Mary seethed. *Where was Elizabeth?*

Finally, she could restrain herself no more.

"And Elizabeth? How is my dear sister?"

"She was very quiet as we came down," Mrs. Geherty said. "She may be napping."

"Oh, that is fine then. I shall see her later."

With that Mary rose, indicating that the uncomfortable interview was at an end. She rang for Bradley.

"Bradley, my parents are weary from their trip. They shall need to prepare for dinner. Will you see that they are made comfortable?"

Bradley bowed and confirmed it.

"And Bradley, does my sister still sleep?"

"I am sorry, ma'am. Miss Elizabeth is not in. She went out shortly after arriving and changing into walking clothes."

"Yes? Why did you not tell me?"

"I am sorry, ma'am. I did not realize you wished her to have an audience with you. I understood it was your parents you most wished to see."

"Yes, yes. True enough. My parents are my parents."

She looked at them. "Thank you, mother. Thank you, father. I shall see you at dinner."

With that, she walked past them and began to head up the steps.

She stopped and turned.

"Tell me, Bradley. Do you have any idea where my dear sister went?"

"I am afraid she did not say, ma'am. All she said was that she should be expected to return by dinner time, ma'am."

"It is of no moment, Bradley. I shall go up now."

Which she began to do before again stopping. Over her shoulder, she said, "And mother, father. Do not forget that we dress for dinner." She resumed her climb and did not again stop, the other three watching her take each slow, deliberate step up.

As dusk came, Mary sat at a window seat in her bedroom that offered a view to the house's gate. The temerity of her ungrateful, forever ungrateful spinster of a sister. She should have been there to thank Mary for all she had done, was doing, and would be doing for her. As her parents had, albeit tardily, which she excused because of their age and her generosity. Elizabeth was not independent of Mary and would need to understand and accept that reality were she to remain in Mary's house. Eating Mary's food. Breathing Mary's air.

These thoughts cascaded through Mary's mind countless times when she saw a figure approaching the gate from the east and then turn in. She got up and rang the bell. A chambermaid appeared promptly, and she curtsied after Mary told her to enter.

"Yes, ma'am?"

"Alice. My sister has just deigned to join us. Could you please go to her when she gets to her room and ask her if she could spare a moment to see her sister before we go down for dinner?"

When Alice was gone for her task, Mary paced briefly before sitting on a chair at her vanity. She was not there long when she heard a hard knock at the door. She directed her visitor to enter. It was, of course, Elizabeth.

That looked at each other in the mirror.

"Ah, Lizzie, dear. So kind of you to come to thank me and Mr. McNabb. You may do it properly when we are down for dinner. But thank you for coming down. I will see you presently."

Their eyes locked for a moment, or perhaps less. Elizabeth turned and left, without, they both noticed, a nod. And without, they both noticed, uttering a word.

41.

"**E**lizabeth. In the future please remember that we dress for dinner in this house. Perhaps we can spare someone to help you to get dressed."

Mary was beyond enjoying being Mrs. McNabb as they stood in her sitting-room waiting for dinner to be announced. The only people eating were she and her husband, her parents, her brother Michael and his wife, and Elizabeth. All but Elizabeth were in formal dress; if Elizabeth had something appropriate, it was stored away and likely being sniffed over by a creditor at that very moment.

"I am sorry, Mary. I do not own a suitable gown so what I wear must suffice. I fear that you must give me leave in this regard."

Mary was not alone in noting the condescension in what she was being told, but she responded with a smile, "I presume we have no choice then. 'Tis a pity you are so…short and broad or you might be able to wear one of my old ones."

With that, the subject passed as Mary turned to her brother and sister-in-law and Elizabeth turned to look out the window. Things were no warmer while they ate. At one point after the soups were cleared and the salads placed, Mary looked from her perch at one end of the table to her sister, who was to the left of Mr. McNabb on the other.

"Elizabeth, I am sorry that you were unable to greet me when I came in this afternoon. Bradley told me that you were out on some errand or another."

"Yes, Mary, but we were able to speak after I returned, as you will recall."

"I do. Yes, I do. May I ask the nature of your errand?"

"You may. It was to see a friend."

Elizabeth's tone made it clear that she would not be going further, so Mary let it drop as if she did not care.

Later in the meal, though, her father said to Mary, "Lizzie was asking about that girl we dismissed a while back. One of the new Irish ones. Asking me if she'd done anything improper. I said not that I recall." He looked across at his wife. "Isn't that right, Abby? She was pretty, and I don't recall why you dismissed her."

Mrs. Geherty glared at her husband and lied and said she did not recall. It must have been something, but whatever it was, was lost to her.

Elizabeth's face stiffened, and Mary caught it from the other end of the table. She paused briefly but it was not long before she addressed her sister.

"Is that who you went to see, sister? That Irish farmgirl?"

Elizabeth contemplated the food remaining on her plate. She then pushed it away and stood. The room was silent except for the sound made by a footman as he rushed to pull her chair from the table.

"Róisín Campbell is her name. And, yes, I saw her." She was glaring at her sister, who was sitting with an expression that Elizabeth could not read. "I apologized for some things I and this family did to her."

Elizabeth threw her napkin to the table and left the room before anyone could respond. All eyes turned to Mary. Even the staff's.

"I daresay Elizabeth has things to apologize for. I do not." With that, and after directing that all traces of Elizabeth's recent presence be removed from the table, she cut her meat and kept her fork in her left hand so she could eat in the French style.

Elizabeth sat in her room, declining a maid's offer to get her something to eat or to do anything else for her. About an hour later, her door opened without a knock. Mary.

"I don't know what you think, but while you're under my roof you'll do what I instruct you to do and not do what I instruct you not to do. And I instruct you never to see that whore again."

With that she turned and left, leaving the door open so Elizabeth could hear her go down the hall and down the stairs to the large drawing-room on the second floor where the others were presumably gathered for the evening and waiting for the return of their benefactress.

42.

Róisín was half-reading a novel in her room. She was trying to grasp the meaning of Elizabeth's visit earlier in the day. It was mid-afternoon, and she was reading in her flat when Elizabeth knocked at her door. She'd gone to Dr. Doyle's apartment, and he directed her to Róisín's. The nurse was shocked by the visit, given what happened when they were last together weeks earlier, when she confessed to failing to warn Mrs. Geherty about the Bolivian fraud. They returned to the café, where they ordered tea and cakes and Elizabeth said she was sorry for how they left things.

"I cannot say you were right in what you did. But I spoke to my parents and in the end, my father admitted, as he put it, that the pope himself would not have convinced him to end the speculation. We were in such a deep hole that the speculation was our only hope, he said. Even if he took the money out, we still would be broke."

Róisín felt a weight lifted. What she was told did not alter that she had erred in her actions, but it did salve some of the guilt.

"Does this mean I am not forever cast from Eden?"

"Eden?" Elizabeth said. "Being my friend is far from that. Perhaps 'tis even a *'Cerci dell' Inferno,'*" which to Róisín's confusion she explained, "'Circle of Hell,' from Dante." Róisín knew the reference.

Now, some hours later and with things very much in the air, hearing the knock, Róisín put her *Agnes Grey* down and stepped to the door. When she opened it, she was disarmed by a distraught, sobbing Elizabeth Geherty.

"I have nowhere else to go," Elizabeth said as well as she could. All she held was a satchel not unlike the one Róisín carried from Ireland, though of a higher quality. At a loss, Róisín stepped aside to let Elizabeth in.

Róisín's room, which was Nurse Evans's before Róisín returned from her tenure at Cassidy's, had a parlor in the front and to the right. To the left was a kitchen, with a stove, a small table with chairs, and an icebox. To its right was a door to a bedroom that reached to the front of the house. There was a four-drawer dresser along the wall next to a wardrobe and near the window a small desk and a single chair. The bed itself was larger than the one Róisín had when she was in her first room above the clinic.

For now, though, Elizabeth dropped onto a threadbare sofa that was against the main room's right wall. The room had two large windows, and there was an oval mirror between them. A small coffee table sat between the sofa and two also well-worn armchairs. The fabric on the three pieces matched, a green with swirls of ivory, and blended in with the somewhat worn maroon Persian rug that covered most of the wooden floor, though less with the blue patterned wallpaper that had long graced the room's walls.

Róisín got a hand towel from a drawer in the kitchen and handed it to Elizabeth, who used it to dab and dry her eyes.

"Tell me what happened."

Elizabeth relayed the horrible dinner. She thought she escaped her sister's inquiries about where she was that afternoon, but her father mentioned Róisín and it lit her sister up like a firecracker. It was clear from the first syllable that passed Mary's lips that she would not permit Elizabeth to ever see Róisín.

"I went to my room and she came in when everyone else finished dinner. She did not even knock. She told me that I was in *her* house and had to obey *her* rules, and one of those rules concerned you. I was silent as she left. I knew I would be a slave to her were I to stay. When she was gone, I filled my satchel with some things I knew I would need and went down the servants' stairs to the kitchen. When no one was there, I went out the servants' entrance and walked here.

"I did not know where else I could go or who else I could go to."

Elizabeth was twisting the towel one way and then the other as she spoke. Róisín was dumbfounded.

"You can stay as long as you require. But we cannot decide anything now. You have had a very long day. We'll sleep and speak in the morning."

The two women shared Róisín's bed, with Elizabeth falling asleep quickly and Róisín listening to the other's breathing as she struggled to fall off. But she did and awoke to find Elizabeth was gone. Her heart recovered when she heard her in the kitchen.

In the morning, the two went to the ten o'clock mass. Róisín was well known but there were whispers aplenty about her companion. She was completely unknown to all save Doctor Doyle and Nurse Evans, who had seen her several times at the clinic. When the mass was over, all four strolled back to the clinic together. Shortly before they arrived, Nurse Evans suggested they share a light dinner, so the four went to a restaurant on the avenue.

With it being unseasonably warm, Róisín and Elizabeth left the others after eating and went for a walk, heading east to a nearby park. It was crowded with all manner of the east side, but Róisín saw a being-vacated bench and the two ran to claim it. Till then, they had spoken of general things, but their moods changed when they sat alone in the company of dozens of strangers.

"What shall we do with you, my dear Miss Elizabeth?"

Both sat stiffly. Elizabeth looked at her hands, folded neatly in her lap.

"What shall become *of me* is the better question, my dear Miss Róisín."

Since neither could know the answer, they were quiet until Róisín suggested they head "home," and the pair strolled arm-in-arm back to the flat, doing nothing more than engage in idle chit-chat as they walked.

43.

Michael was the emissary of the family. He arrived by cab that Sunday night. It was unknown whether this was the first or tenth place he went searching for Elizabeth. It was the last. A tavern was open on the avenue, and after Elizabeth insisted to Róisín that she was happy to hear what Michael had to say, she and her brother walked there.

"I know she's wrong." Each had a pint of ale, and Michael took a long sip of his, and the foam tinged his mustache in a way worlds apart from the seriousness of the conversation.

"Why is she so hateful?" his sister asked.

"I fear I may have had a hand in that."

Elizabeth did not understand.

"It was when Mary's engagement to McNabb was announced, at a party at the house. You were in Europe. The girl—"

"Róisín."

"Yes, Róisín. Róisín came into the drawing-room doing something or other of her duties and both McNabb and I noticed her. I said something, and I am not proud of this, something like, 'Could you imagine?' and Peter said, 'Believe me, Michael, I have, I have.' I mean, she *is* awfully attractive. I believe Mary overheard at least some of what we said as I saw her rushing across the room after we said it.

"She immediately went up to Mason and said something, and a moment later Mason said something to Róisín, and Róisín quickly left the room. Never to be seen again, so far as I know. Or at least I never saw her again except a few times in passing until just now when she opened the door. I must say that she still is quite attractive."

"Do you know Mary got her dismissed and also from the Reynolds House?"

"I did hear something like that."

Seeing his sister's reaction, Michael said, "I told you Mary is wrong in this."

"Did mother ask you about Róisín before she was dismissed?"

"Well, now you say it, she did. But I said she never did anything untoward, to me at least. I did tell her. I was an ass with her at times—you know me—but she never behaved improperly. She was clear that she had no interest. In me or Charlie or any of our set. Or, for that matter, in Peter."

Elizabeth did not doubt it.

"You know Mary will not change," Elizabeth said.

"Frankly, she is only getting worse. Kathleen and I would much rather be alone than see her, but there are times when it can't be avoided."

"I shan't go back. I cannot say whether I will stay with Róisín. Or even if she will let me. I just don't know. But I do know I will not sleep again beneath Mrs. McNabb's roof, and I am sorry for mamma and papa, who have no choice."

"Lizzie. What choice do you have? Really?"

In this instance, her brother—who told her he could not accommodate her for physical and political reasons related to Mary—was practical. Elizabeth had given no thought, thinking that leaving that horrible house was her only choice. But where was she to stay? Why would Róisín want to have anything to do with her? They'd met only a few times, the first when neither knew who the other was. How was she to eat?

"No, Mícheál," Elizabeth answered, using the Gaelic version of her brother's name, "I must trust that she will let me remain until I can find another place and a situation that I can use to support myself." She put her glass on the table. "I must go back now."

Michael did not react. He watched his sister walk from the tavern, wondering when he might see her again.

When she returned to the flat, Róisín assured Elizabeth that she would not be put out on the street. It was not a spontaneous utterance. She gave it much thought as she looked out the window while Elizabeth was with her brother. Seeing her come down the block, Róisín ran to the stairs and down to greet her on the way up.

"As long as you wish," she said as she hugged Elizabeth. The two spoke late into the night about what was happening, and Elizabeth promised Róisín she did not regret giving up whatever she was giving up by siding with her against her sister.

Mostly, though, the two spoke about Sophie. Elizabeth had only third- and fourth-hand gossip to inform her. She agreed with Róisín's assessment, that being with her ex-fiancé was not reassuring. She knew more about Edward Meade than she wanted to thanks to her sister's and, to a lesser extent, her mother's informing her of every tidbit of information they received.

When news of the downfall of the Gehertys reached him in Europe, he wrote a letter to Elizabeth. In it, he expressed his concern for her well-being and health and told her that he could not compel her to retain her obligation to him in light of his severe injuries. He made no mention of the downfall of the Gehertys but placed the termination of their betrothal entirely on his concern for her.

It was a fine letter, fitting for someone brought up as Edward Meade had been brought up, and it had little in the way of truth. It was not unexpected. Elizabeth knew its contents before she opened it—knowing Edward Meade—and its receipt and what it said were a relief to her.

Meade ensured that his chivalry was known far and wide, and he was admired for it upon his return to New York. He was badly altered, yes, but accommodations were extended to him wherever he went, and his dual misfortunes made him a far more popular and sympathetic figure than he was before. That began to change, though. The passage of time had chipped away at some of his newly-found credit, and word of his "protection" of Sophie Campbell quickly turned to approbation. She was a ruined woman (if she ever had anything to ruin) and his taking advantage was recognized by all.

But he did not care. He found her company amusing and physically stimulating. They were in separate rooms on the third floor of his family's brownstone. More accurately, they began each night in separate rooms but on most, he quietly entered hers and shared her bed.

Quiet as he attempted to be, the liaisons were not unnoticed by the staff and in under a week, the nature of Edward Meade's protection of Sophie Campbell was known by virtually everyone. "Everyone" did not include his parents but did include Mary and the latter's knowledge of it set in play the chain of events that saw Elizabeth speaking late into a Sunday night with Róisín as they sought in vain for a solution of what was to be done about Sophie.

44.

The Immaculate Conception Church on East Fourteenth Street was a typical Manhattan church. Much like St. Stephen's, where Mary married McNabb, it was in the middle of a block and between two buildings. Several steps led to it and an antechamber and a second set of doors brought one into the nave. It was a simple church with simple stained-glass windows towards the ceiling, high enough for the sun to reach inside. The altar was marble, and the crucifix above it grand.

Róisín returned to it after her time with the Cassidys. She was known and liked there for the work she did at the clinic and at times in the tenements. Often, she went to mass with Doctor Doyle and Nurse Evans, but she elected to go only with Elizabeth on their second Sunday together.

Just as the circumstances of Sophie's being with Meade were quickly known, so too was the presence of Elizabeth Geherty with Róisín Campbell, so by the time the pair entered the church that morning, most of the congregation knew of it and the entirety of the congregation knew of it by the time they were seated along the aisle on the right side of the church, near the Eleventh Station of the Cross.

45.

When the pair got back in the late afternoon, they went to the third floor and knocked on Dr. Doyle's door. They were invited in and sat with the doctor and Nurse Evans. The clinic, the doctor said, needed skilled help in addition to the second doctor who worked there now. He said that he and Nurse Evans discussed it at length after Róisín suggested it a day or two before and agreed that Elizabeth would be taken on a trial basis if she wished.

Róisín and Elizabeth independently reached the same conclusion. It was natural. As with Róisín, Elizabeth understood she had few options to earn a living and thought caring for the sick something she would find worthwhile. She had, after all, flirted with entering a religious order when she was first in Stockbridge, an idea quashed when she came to doubt the religious part of such a devotion. At the clinic, she could live with Róisín (since there was far more room than in Róisín's original flat, enough for a second bed) and retain her independence from Mary.

Although her lack of experience, even the limited experience that Róisín had when she began, was a difficulty, Elizabeth soon became comfortable dealing with patients. She was adept at organizing, and her primary task was taking down information about patients and ensuring that they saw the doctors as efficiently as possible. She proved a willing ear to the talkative ones anxious about whatever they came to the clinic for, including more and more who came so they could speak with her.

So, she, too, entered into her routine with Róisín. The pair spent their time off together, Elizabeth joining in the lengthy strolls to which Róisín had become accustomed since she returned from Cassidy's, and the two were often accompanied by Mr. Henry on trips to Central Park. Once his role concerning Sophie and Cassidy and his lack of any interest in anything romantic with Róisín were explained, Elizabeth came to cherish how important he was to her friend and hoped he would someday also become important to her.

46.

It was a Saturday some weeks after Elizabeth started working at the clinic, and she and Róisín had the rare day off. Sleeping well later than usual, the pair finally roused themselves and got dressed and it was half-past nine by the time they reached the sidewalk.

"Shall we walk?"

They were both quiet, with Elizabeth putting her arm through Róisín's, as they went east, Róisín telling the other that it was like Irish weather, either changing or on the verge of changing with unseasonable gusts coming from the north.

"We'll go to the café for some tea and toast," Róisín promised.

It was their favorite small establishment on the corner of the avenue, where they had their earlier conversations. There were three tables and six chairs set up on the sidewalk, but they were, of course, empty as the wind sometimes blew hard in gusts down the avenue. It was not clear why they were put out in the first place, always in danger of being blown away.

Inside, the air was somewhat close. Several stood at the bar with their tea or espresso, but when a hostess asked the two women, they asked for a table. They waited several minutes before a man and a woman rose and left, and the hostess cleaned the table and waved for them to come.

When they were seated, Elizabeth told Róisín of her life after leaving New York when her family went bankrupt.

"We could only remain in Stockbridge for the winter. Things were so bad as to money that we resorted to the support of Mary's husband, Mr. McNabb. Nearly all of our property was taken, and we scurried back to town with our tails between our legs, and we were offered rooms in the McNabb House. As you know. A prison, but my parents had no choice. My mother tells me my father spends his time in a chair that he found among those relegated to a storage room. Very unhappy."

She punctuated what she said with sips from her cup.

"My mother goes for hours and hours of walks, alone as no one knows her. Were my sister to go out with her just once that would change, but she will not do so. So, my mother walks and walks while my father sits and ponders what went wrong as he fattens himself on Mr. McNabb's generosity. No one knows him either, of course. I think they have grown much closer, though, with only each other."

Róisín knew much of this from her time with Elizabeth, but this was the first time her friend sat down and told the story in such a, well, sad and resigned way. And she knew Elizabeth often went on walks with her mother on Sunday afternoons alone, and without Róisín since there remained tension between her friend and her mother that she hoped time would heal.

Róisín poured more tea into the cups. Elizabeth's attention shifted to hers, and she drank a bit more from it.

"I was never of my sister's world. Or my brothers'. When we were away, I became a great friend to a girl quite like me in some ways and quite unlike me in others. I should not have survived our exile without her. Emily Connor. You must meet her someday. She was briefly of my sister's world but was glad to be cast out when Peter McNabb approached. Her father squandered their money as mine did, though I think it was more her mother who did the squandering as Mary did with ours before she became Mrs. Peter McNabb."

"I never saw such things," Róisín said, "till I saw her gowns and dresses and such."

Elizabeth seemed not to have heard Róisín's interruption. "But we had money, or so I thought, and it was not money that was 'too new' so Mary had an easier time than some and that is how she was able to get McNabb. He was ensnared in some of those gowns and dresses and such."

She looked at her friend and her dour mood seemed to have vanished.

"Peter is nice enough. Sweet even. I think he has left the running of the house to Mary and she has done with her power what she has done with it. It is my parents I feel for. Whether Mary will take them to Lenox I cannot say. In some respects, I hope not. They will be as ignored there as they are in town and here at least my mother can vary the places she walks and not think of the lost house in Stockbridge."

With the tea gone and a couple subtly but unmistakably coveting the table at which the two women sat, they rose and tightened their coats and left. Though Róisín offered to pay, Elizabeth insisted that it was her pleasure to do so.

"I still have enough money to pay for tea for my friends."

When they were on the sidewalk and the two had buttoned their coats, Róisín asked, "Am I your friend?"

Elizabeth looked at Róisín. "I hope so," and with that, she crossed the avenue with Róisín behind as they headed to the river, with each woman tightening the string under her chin lest her bonnet fly forever away.

As they neared the water, they paused, their eyes following a couple bracing themselves against a wind gust until the woman's bonnet blew off and the man rushed to chase it down, running back with it and presenting it to her with a slight bow before the couple resumed their walk, with the woman retying the bonnet beneath her chin as the man anchored her with his arm around her waist.

"I do not know whether I would have liked to marry," Elizabeth said as they watched the lovers. "It was my fate until I ran away."

"Did you run away?" Róisín asked.

They resumed their walk and Elizabeth did not respond until the pair were leaning on a rail overlooking the water. The wind was enough to create small whitecaps. She put her arm around her friend and squeezed. "Perhaps I was running *to* something."

After a moment's reflection in each other's eyes, Róisín pushed away. "If that something was me, I fear you shall be greatly disappointed." That it was said with a disarming smile made all the difference, and Elizabeth's mood again lightened as they returned to looking over the river.

"Ah, my dearest. We have had enough disappointments. Let us hope for no more."

They stood silently for several minutes, perhaps unconscious that they were leaning gently against each other.

Róisín turned so that her back was to the railing.

"I do not see the need to marry," she proclaimed.

"Have you not thought of it?"

Róisín turned back to the water, again leaning lightly against her friend.

"I do not know that I have had the chance to think about it, and the thought has never arrived independently of my thinking about it. I am, well, me. I do not see the need to be with a man, to surrender me to a man. Nor have I encountered a man to whom I might wish to surrender."

"But children. Surely you have thought about that."

"Let us walk."

The sun appeared in streaks through the clouds, and it dampened the wind as the two headed west.

47.

Not many weeks after that walk, Dr. Doyle called Róisín and Lizzie into his office when the clinic was through for the day. Nurse Evans was with him.

"Do you women know about the nurses' training school at Bellevue?"

They knew of it generally. The first nursing school in America began the prior year at the hospital under the principles of Florence Nightingale. The two, of course, knew of her and the changes she had caused to be made at the hospitals in London and elsewhere in Europe. The first class had six women. Ten would be accepted into the second, and Doctor Doyle and Nurse Evans thought both Róisín and Elizabeth should apply. It would require that they leave the clinic, but it was an opportunity to become a new type of professional nurse.

When the girls agreed, Dr. Doyle wrote a letter for each, which he sent to Sister Helen Bowdin, a London nurse imported to run the program. A week later, each received an invitation for an interview.

On the following Wednesday, Róisín and Elizabeth took the trolley to the hospital, where Róisín had been on her horrible visits to the morgue. They were directed to a large building with its rear against the East River. A colossal brick building, they found the main entrance. Inside, a surly man called to them, "You must be the nurses," and when Róisín said that they hoped to be, he directed them down a long hallway. "Third door on the right," he said and resumed his newspaper reading.

Their heels echoed down the hallway. Elizabeth slowly opened the third door on the right. It took them to a large, open room lined with wooden benches. On them sat maybe twelve women about their age. Conversation stopped when they entered, but it quickly resumed, and they saw some whispering and some pointing towards them as they found an empty bench for themselves. Though both wore their finest dresses, it was clear that the other women in the room were from a higher circle than was Róisín. Each was likely the second or third daughter in a respectable family, many much like Elizabeth.

The pair sat, but it was not long before a woman entered through a door on the left. All talking ceased.

She spoke with a clear London accent. "I am Sister Bowdin of the All Saints Sisterhood in London. I am the Superintendent of the nursing school here. We are seeing many girls who wish to be part of our program, but only ten will be chosen. We have met with many girls already and will meet with many more. When you are finished with your interview, we ask that you leave and that you not tell the things we spoke about. We do not wish anyone to have an unfair advantage over anyone else.

"When I call your name, please respond by identifying yourself."

She called the names, and after Róisín responded, there was a slight murmur in parts of the room.

"Silence," Sister Bowdin barked. She got it. The murmurs appeared again when Elizabeth's name was called, ended in the same manner. In the event, there were fourteen women and three names on the list found themselves vouched for by no one.

When she was done, Sister Bowdin asked that Marigold Adams follow her. A tall, gangly woman rose. She looked back at the two sitting by her, took a deep breath, and silently followed Sister Bowdin into the room from which the sister had come.

When the door closed, the large room burst into noise. Róisín and Elizabeth spoke quietly, sitting on their bench. They picked up pieces of conversation, including one woman saying that her friend was interviewed and told her everything she was asked, "So I prepared myself," and the women she sat with begged to be told what they would be asked, and she refused to do it. "She is my friend, not yours," and the others wished she had not mentioned that she was told anything by anyone. They moved slightly away from her.

Marigold Adams came back into the room not long after she left it. She was stoic as she asked the next woman to enter. Then Marigold Adams was gone.

When that second girl returned, also looking stoic, she asked Róisín—*Roy-sin*—to go in. She then went to sit with the women she sat with before being summoned.

When Róisín entered the room, savoring the squeeze her hand received from her friend, Sister Bowdin was behind a desk. Another woman, younger than the sister, sat in a chair to her left, holding on her lap what Róisín later learned was a board clip on which there were papers and lifting a pen with her right hand.

"Please have a seat. You are Róisín Campbell?" The Englishwoman pronounced it—*roe-Sheen*—like an Irish native.

"Yes, ma'am."

"My, you have a very strong Irish accent. We have not had such a strong accent yet, have we Sister Taylor?"

"No, sister."

Sister Taylor, too, had a London accent.

"I like it in a way," said Sister Bowdin. "Makes me feel a little bit like home. I am afraid, however, that it might make you unsuitable for becoming a nurse here. As you probably saw from the girls waiting outside, you are quite different from them. But please tell me how you came to be here."

"In New York?"

"Well, in this room talking to Sister Taylor and myself."

Róisín told her story. She made sure to mention being in service and the reasons she was dismissed. The chance happening upon that first gig crash and working with Doctor Doyle and Nurse Evans.

When she was done, the two other women looked at one another, and Sister Taylor shook her head.

"Dr. Doyle has very complimentary things to say about you. It is why we asked you to come today. But I am afraid that you lack the...background we are seeking. I am sorry. Could you send in the next woman?"

Sister Taylor looked down at her list. "Rebecca Coolidge."

Róisín stood and thanked the two sisters. She returned to the room where the others were waiting. It quickly quieted when she did.

"Rebecca Coolidge. They wish to see you."

She saw a woman leap up from a far bench, her two friends releasing her hands as she started to the room Róisín just vacated. To a woman, the others studied Róisín's face. Róisín though only looked at Elizabeth, to whom she gave the slightest shake of the head before turning to the door and leaving.

Róisín stood waiting on the sidewalk as several other candidates left, pacing back and forth, for over an hour before Elizabeth emerged. And she was happy for her friend. She did have the proper background and was asked to return on Saturday for a final interview. Elizabeth put her arm around Róisín's waist as they began their walk to the clinic, more upset about the unfairness of it than was her friend.

48.

Just over two weeks after meeting Sister Bowdin, on a Sunday, Elizabeth sat with nine other students to begin her course of studies. She was in a residence on Twenty-Sixth Street, sharing a room with Estella Tompkins. Estella Tompkins was slightly taller and far thinner than Elizabeth. Her hair was long and black. She was the same age as Elizabeth, but they had never come across one another over the years. But Estella's knowledge of the Gehertys' misfortunes led her to resent the pairing.

Earlier, Elizabeth went to mass with Róisín but they had little time to stroll afterward. Elizabeth was due at the residence at two. They promised, though, that they would continue their weekly post-mass constitutionals when they could and walked together to Bellevue so that Elizabeth was not late. Róisín watched her friend enter the building until she saw a wave and a smile, and then Elizabeth was gone.

"I shall have this bed," Estella informed Elizabeth when she arrived, pointing to the one closest to the window.

"I am sorry, but that is my bed," Elizabeth advised her. "I was, after all, here before you."

"You do not know your place," Miss Tompkins informed Miss Geherty.

Elizabeth, sitting on *her* bed, the one closest to the window, looked at her. "My place is right here," she said, patting the bed.

In a huff, Estella Tompkins placed her things on *her* bed, the one away from the window. She did not deign to speak to her roommate further. Elizabeth sat on her bed silently, watching the other woman unpack her things.

"At least you do not have enough to take up much space in the wardrobe," she said as she hung her dresses up, pushing the four hangars that had all of Elizabeth's dresses to the side. Estella Tompkins's dresses were a rainbow of colors and styles. Elizabeth wondered just where she intended to wear them.

At eight o'clock on Monday morning, Sister Bowdin entered the room where the ten students ate their breakfast of cold cereal and hot tea. The prior year's trainees, all veterans now, sat at their own table, giggling at the newcomers they so recently were themselves.

Sister Bowdin stood by Elizabeth's table, and those at the other turned to listen.

"It has come to my attention that some of you are dissatisfied with the composition of your group. This disappoints me. Each one of you was selected because in our view you stood out among those who applied as being of the sort who would show technical skill and compassion to our patients. If you do not believe yourself capable of doing so, I ask you to withdraw from the school. I will be disappointed should you leave. But leave you must if you do not look upon one another as sisters."

With that, she left the room. Elizabeth kept her head down, looking into the bowl of cereal. The others with her remained silent, and the other table resumed its suddenly more interesting conversations.

When the group returned to its rooms before they were to begin the day's classes, Estella said, "It was not me. Some of the others contacted their fathers about you. They came to speak to Sister—"

"Estella. We shall either be great friends or we shall not. I am not so stupid to not understand why you treat me as you do. I assure you, none of your haughtiness can match what I have endured already and if you wish me to be of no moment to you, I'm happy for you to be of no moment to me."

With that Elizabeth grabbed some things and went to the bath at the end of the hall, hoping and finding it was vacant. She and Estella maintained a quiet truce when she returned.

The roommates put on the outfits they were given on Sunday afternoon. Each had four identical frocks and aprons as well as shoes. It was a process much like what Róisín went through at the House of Mercy, though the "sisters" at Bellevue were nurses and the "sisters" at the House were religious, the term "nun" being reserved for religious women who were cloistered.

When ready, the ten went to the room where they sat before being taken in to be interviewed by Sisters Bowdin and Taylor. They were in two rows of five chairs, with Elizabeth at the end of the second row. Four chairs sat opposite.

It was nine a.m. She and the others jumped up when they heard a pounding on the door. Sisters Bowdin and Taylor and two gentlemen entered. All but Sister Bowdin sat.

"Ladies. Welcome to the Bellevue Hospital Nursing Training School. You have all met Sister Taylor," who nodded to the girls. "With us are Mr. William Osborn and Dr. W. Gill Wylie. They are responsible for the formation of this school. Dr. Wylie is on staff at the hospital. Mr. Osborne is one of the great supporters of the school. They are here to personally welcome you."

With that, each of the aforementioned gentlemen gave a short speech. The girls were selected to take on a new task, the care of the sick. They were to learn the skills for doing so following Miss Nightingale's precepts and were expected to have the compassion to do so properly.

"This is a great experiment," Dr. Wylie said. "I have seen schools like this in Europe aid in the creation of nurses who are a necessary part of a modern hospital. Sister Bowdin has been selected to guide you. With God's blessing, we hope that you, too, will provide the care and support to which each and every patient at Bellevue Hospital is entitled."

When he finished, and Sister Bowdin led applause from the group, the two men left, and the girls remained with the superintendent and her assistant.

"Ladies, much is expected of you. You will prove the importance of women in providing proper and compassionate care to those in need. This program will be rigorous, and I will not tolerate those who are unwilling to devote the effort to become nurses. Nor will Sister Taylor. From this point on, you are our responsibilities.

"From this moment on, you will be together. You will eat, drink, and breathe together. You will rely and depend on each other. You are all equal here."

Elizabeth felt several eyes on her as Sister Bowdin finished, but she had no time to contemplate it as she and the others were led from the room, following Sisters Bowdin and Taylor.

Thus, the course began. Much of the job was mending and cleaning. Elizabeth fell into the routine and the iciness of her mates dissipated over time. There were one or two who remained distant, but the rest were pleasant enough.

As for Estella, she was turning into a friend. She was the third and youngest daughter of a family whose business was on Wall Street and she shared some of Elizabeth's resistance to the life expected of her. Her parents were indifferent to her coming to the school, and Estella was glad for that. The two often spoke after their candle was out and they lay in their beds.

"Have you ever been in love?"

Estella's question startled Elizabeth. As always, they could hear the din of traffic from the street, but each day ended with both girls exhausted and the noise never stopped them from quickly falling asleep.

Elizabeth thought about the question.

"Elizabeth? Did you hear me?"

"I did hear you. I don't believe I have."

"But you were engaged, were you not?"

"Yes, but I wasn't in love with him."

There was a pause, ended when Estella said, "I do not think I have been in love. I wonder what it would be like."

"Well if you stay here you shan't find out. You shall be removed were you to marry."

"But what of the doctors?"

"You would be removed even more quickly if you got involved with one. Nothing would come to them, of course."

"Of course. But can I not imagine?"

Elizabeth had heard Estella "imagining" a few nights before and assumed it was of one of the young doctors with whom the students went on rounds several times. Probably the tall, thin one with black hair and a well-trimmed mustache.

But, no, Elizabeth felt no interest in him or the other doctors.

"Yes, Estella. I think we can all imagine."

Love. Elizabeth had read about it in her books. She sometimes did imagine what love would be like. In all her years, though, she never felt the slightest tingling—which is what she understood from her books she would feel when love was involved—for any of the men she met. Especially not of the sort of her brothers' friends and their ilk. Especially not Edward Meade. The doctors were much the same. Not so entitled, perhaps. But decidedly superior.

Elizabeth's group had a variety of backgrounds, but all were raised in the proper fashion. Though their names were English or Dutch or Irish, they were all largely the same as one another. Some believed in entering a position in which they could be a benefit to others, while the other women saw nursing as the best option of the limited choices available to them. Several were repulsed by the thought of intimacy with a man, no matter how fleeting and infrequent it might be, perhaps no more than the minimum necessary to have issue.

The truth was that at least at first, the work for Elizabeth was drudgery in contrast to what happened at the clinic. It was, she understood, necessary to develop nursing into a profession for women in which there were few others on offer. The tasks were mundane. They each learned quickly the importance of cleanliness in a hospital under Nightingale principles, and they spent much of their day cleaning the puke and the piss and the excrement, and oftentimes the blood, of the sick and dying in the wards. They were fortunate in being the second group of students as by then a significant portion of the doctors had come to appreciate their intelligence and dedication and mostly the value they provided to both patients and doctors.

49.

With Elizabeth at Bellevue, she and Róisín missed their time together and only saw each other following mass on most Sundays and sometimes on Saturday nights where they attended an entertainment. Both were too engaged to dwell on it.

As Elizabeth was delving into life as a nursing student, Róisín had her own thing to address: Sophie.

Róisín was anxious about her sister but was abiding by Meade's dictum to steer clear for the moment. There was the initial flurry of gossip, but things quieted as the Irish-American public moved to some other scandal. Finally, three months after Sophie fled, a letter arrived from Meade.

My Dearest Miss Campbell,

I hope this finds you well. I am pleased to advise you that your sister is greatly improved from when she arrived at my doorstep and is moving forward in leaps and bounds. I expect she will be able to entertain visitors within a matter of weeks. Before that, I will endeavor to remind her of the kindnesses that you extended to her upon her arrival in New York.

She remains, naturally, apprehensive about Cassidy. I have communicated with him, advising him of the protection I offer his wife from him. For his part, he has behaved admirably, confirming to me that he will undertake no venture seeking his wife's return and assuring me that he will not serendipitously seek to contact her. He has provided her possessions to me.

I have conveyed this to your sister, and she is overjoyed by the news. I expect in short order I may venture to speak your name in her presence without it sending her into a bad state. She has not, I fear, referred to you by name since her arrival. I will not say what she has referred to you as because I am convinced it is done in a condition of extreme stress. But it has caused me to weigh when an appropriate time to mention you will arise. I do hope that it will not be long in coming.

When that occurs, I will have the great joy of conveying to you her desire to have you visit.

Your obedient servant, &c.,
Edward Meade

Róisín looked at the letter when she finished it and then re-read certain passages. She did not know whether it was good news or bad. When she showed it to Elizabeth the next Sunday, Elizabeth insisted that it was the finest of news under the circumstances. It was not truly her view, but there was nothing to be done about it.

It came as something of a shock, then, when two weeks later Sophie herself appeared at the clinic demanding to see Róisín. It was a day on which Róisín was at the German Hospital, but a boy was again sent to fetch her on "urgent business." Róisín did not know what that could be, but immediately understood when she entered and was told by Nurse Evans that there was someone in her rooms.

She hurried up and opened the door. There she found her sister sitting on a chair she had moved so she could look out the window at the building across the way and down at the street.

"I saw you hurrying here." Sophie nodded to the street. "I was glad you were so eager to see your wayward sister again."

Then she broke into tears as Róisín went to her, squatting to place her arms around the younger woman's upper chest.

"I promise you I will never stop being eager to see you."

Róisín was surprised at how endearing her baby sister's shuddering chest was to her. She leaned her head against Sophie's briefly, then gave her a slight kiss on the side of her head as she pulled away. She dragged another chair towards the window and placed it an at angle to Sophie's. She sat and placed her hands on Sophie's.

"He cast me out when I got sick in my stomach. He said it could not happen. When it did, he said he would take care of 'it,' and I slapped him. He said in that case I could remain in his house, at least for a while, but I was to stay in my own room when he was in the house and that I would eat, live, and sleep alone. When he was gone, I escaped. I thought he loved me. That he did not care that I was married to Cassidy. That I had and lost a baby. I thought he—"

The last was swallowed by renewed sobbing. Róisín pulled Sophie up and led her into the bedroom. She undressed her sister and placed her in the bed.

"You need to sleep now. I will watch over you."

"Like an angel."

"Yes. Like your angel."

When Sophie settled, Róisín kissed her forehead and then closed the drapes. She sat in a small chair and watched her sleep. She knew not to interfere with Elizabeth until Sunday, when she had the day off and could leave Bellevue. Dr. Doyle was generous in allowing Róisín time during the day to see to her sister. It was helped by having a competent Irish girl in the clinic who was retained when Elizabeth went to Bellevue.

Sophie rose each morning before Róisín did, and she sat on the chair that allowed her to gaze out the window and hear the sounds from the street.

"I know I have been foolish," she said on the first morning when she felt Róisín's hands on her shoulders. "I know I am ruined." Sophie pulled Róisín's right hand to her mouth and kissed its back. "I know I am ruined and that I have ruined you."

"We are only ruined in the eyes of those who will not see us," Róisín assured Sophie.

On the next Sunday, Róisín and Elizabeth walked to the river after mass.

"What shall I do with her?"

Elizabeth had no idea. Sophie remained in Róisín's rooms while her sister went to mass. Róisín did not mention her sister to her friend until mass was over and they were walking east. The two were, as usual, walking close to one another, with Elizabeth's arm through Róisín's. It was a warm day, at least for the season, and they were lightly dressed.

Upon reaching the promenade along the river, the pair found an empty stretch of railing. The river itself was quiet, it being Sunday, and the walkway was crowded.

"I must allow her to stay."

"Of course, you must," Elizabeth agreed. "She cannot go back to Cassidy."

Cassidy made it clear that he had no interest in resuming any relationship with Sophie, however much it was a façade. They would all have to address what was to be done about the sham of a marriage. For now, though, Róisín and Elizabeth agreed about Sophie staying where she was.

50.

It was not long after Sophie's condition became evident that Abigail Geherty appeared at the clinic to see Róisín. Róisín had not seen her since the unpleasantness at Lord & Taylor but recognized her at once. She asked to see Róisín alone, and after a flurry of patients cleared, Róisín walked with her to the café on the avenue where she often used to sit with Elizabeth.

"I said your beauty would be your curse," Mrs. Geherty recalled when they were seated. "I fear it may instead be your sister's beauty that will be a curse for you both."

Róisín looked across the table. "We must all bear the burden or reap the benefit of members of our family. And in the end, we must still love them."

The waitress appeared just as this was said, and their orders were taken.

"Sadly, while we love them, we must sometimes choose between them."

"Or be forced to."

Róisín liked Mrs. Geherty enough to know that she faced a Hobson's Choice as to Mary and elected not to push the point.

"I must ask you something that may be difficult to you," her erstwhile employer said.

Róisín placed her cup down deliberately. "You wish me to have no further contact with Elizabeth."

Mrs. Geherty looked across. She regretted dismissing her but knew she was far better off as a nurse than in service. She kept Elizabeth's confidence about the Bolivian disaster and came to forgive her, regretting but also understanding why she failed to pursue it and also knowing that Charles would never have listened, and he admitted to her as he had to Elizabeth the true depths of the family's financial troubles.

She had spoken to her husband after she was confronted by Elizabeth in the Stockbridge house about Róisín, and he repeated the story of their single one-on-one meeting, when he bemoaned being bled dry by his daughter and she lent a sympathetic ear. And no more.

"Yes. She is not in society and I am proud of what she is doing. But a continued connection with you, and hence with your sister, will end any chance for her to reenter it. While it will, of course, tarnish me and my dear husband, I promise you that I am past the point of caring. Look where it got us. But she is still young and may come to care about it. I do this for Elizabeth and no one else."

The visit was inevitable and so was Róisín's decision. She and Mrs. Geherty separated, leaving their coffees half drunk when Róisín made her promise, and Mrs. Geherty watched her leave much as Elizabeth did many months before, when Róisín earlier walked from her daughter.

Elizabeth perhaps understood it too. Róisín was not at Immaculate Conception for mass that Sunday—she went to a church to the south, the one attended by Mrs. Flanagan—and when Elizabeth went to her room, there was no response. Róisín had insisted that Sophie accompany her to mass and for a stroll afterward. Nurse Evans came down and told Elizabeth that Róisín was out for the day and would not be back till dark. The scene was repeated the following Sunday, though this time Róisín and Sophie were in the apartment.

Róisín was frozen in the rooms. She ignored Elizabeth's knocks and her plea to be allowed in and commanded Sophie's silence. Róisín knew her sister would have leaped to the door to cure the fissure that was her fault, but Róisín's glare kept her in place.

Then a second knocking and a third. Then a note was slid under the door.

> *I understand. I pray for you and your*
> *sister and the child.*
>
> *EG*

Elizabeth left, vowing not to disturb her friend again.

Róisín was determined, too. For her, it was to be faithful to the vow she made to Mrs. Geherty. They all knew it was for the best. Róisín tallied that as a further cost to her of her sister's conduct.

As to Sophie, Cassidy decided to evade the further scandal of seeking a divorce and an annulment. He had no interest in marrying again, so he and Sophie maintained the *status quo*. Sophie was resigned to never being able to marry, even were she to want to. And so, it suited this husband and wife to remain married but to never see or speak to one another again. How the baby's birth certificate would reflect this was not yet considered by either of them. There would be time enough for that.

It was well that Róisín and Elizabeth were soon too absorbed in their daily affairs to give much conscious thought about the other (at least during the day), and Mrs. Geherty's request and Róisín's compliance quickly faded.

Sophie was allowed to work at the clinic, more to keep her occupied than anything. She was at times sulky and at times ebullient, but she was kept busy and she contributed to the workings of the clinic.

The clinic, which was now financed in part by contributions from the Irish community and partly by city funds engineered by Irish politicians, was reaching the point where its space was too small. People were becoming more accepting of hospitals and the German Hospital and Bellevue were among the first hospitals in New York, were joined by others. It was important, though, that facilities such as the clinic provide more support for the growing poor population, particularly in the Irish and German slums that were growing on the east side and in Hell's Kitchen on the west.

Relief came from an unlikely source. An elderly Irish widow who had come during the Famine and married a man who made his fortune in the war but was childless left her house to a charity with the instruction that it be used as a health facility dedicated to the care of recent immigrants, not limited to the Irish.

The building was a large house on a block near the East River and in the high teens. It was near Bellevue but north of the clinic and thus not as convenient for the masses living as best they could in tenements on the lower east side. It had five floors.

In the basement was a large kitchen and a series of smaller rooms for storage and offices. The ground floor was grand. A tall sitting-room, with detailed molding on the ceiling, ran the length of the house. The drawing-room that dominated the second floor was broken up into one large and several smaller examination rooms, and the third-floor study retained that use with a collection of medical texts and the other two rooms on the floor were used as offices and for the storage of supplies.

The fourth floor was given over to three residences. Doctor Doyle and Nurse Evans were in one. Róisín and Sophie in the second, and the second doctor the third. There were three smaller apartments on the top floor, and these were occupied by the new nurse and two newly hired helpers.

The sitting-room on the ground floor had large windows on two sides and was broad enough to be used for dancing in its prior life. On the other side was the dining room, which was at the front, and a large den or library, which was to the back. The former had a large fireplace and mantel and molding as well on its walls and ceiling. Tall windows looked out onto the street and to the large house that stood to its east.

It was, in sum, a quite impressive place for an expanded clinic.

51.

When Róisín, with Sophie, returned to Mrs. Flanagan's church for mass several months after Sophie's reappearance, Mrs. Flanagan signaled her muted endorsement for the pair by being polite to them, and the hostility from the others became less overt than it had been.

Then, on a Sunday some weeks after this new arrangement started, Mrs. Flanagan waited outside the church before mass. When she saw Róisín and Sophie walking towards her, she rushed to them and told Róisín she was needed at her lodgings. The three hurried there and found Mary Bette Flynn on sheets in the sitting-room darkened with the drawn curtains. Róisín immediately saw the blood. It was a common enough sight at the clinic and in tenement flats, a girl seeking to end a pregnancy awash in her blood when she hemorrhaged in a botched procedure, one who could not afford the (albeit illegal) services of a skilled abortionist, usually a woman, to whom respectable, married women flocked and with whom their secrets were safe. Perhaps she was destined to Hell for it, but in those moments Róisín was a servant of the sufferer, as she now was with Mary Bette.

"She came in thirty minutes ago. I did not know what else to do but seek you out."

Another woman, about Sophie's age, was on the floor with Mary Bette, attempting to have her drink water and comforting her in her moans. Róisín knelt on one side and Sophie on the other. She gripped the bleeding woman's hand.

"Mary Bette. Remember me? 'Tis Róisín Campbell. We were together in Mrs. Flanagan, oh, years ago. You must recall?"

It took a moment, but Mary Bette recalled her friend. They had not seen one another in years. Róisín saw that Mary Bette had lost much blood. She told the girl who sat with Mary Bette when they arrived to rush as fast as she could to get Dr. Doyle. He would be at Immaculate Conception for mass.

"I am sure the ushers will know him when you arrive."

The girl rushed out as Róisín did what she could to stem the bleeding. It seemed an eternity, but Mary Bette was alive when Dr. Doyle came in with Nurse Evans. He had his bag. They, too, saw this often.

"Oh, had she been brought to the clinic," he said, not realizing how loudly he did so. But though there was much lost blood, he thought he could save the girl. Mary Bette was carried to a table used for dining after a clean sheet was spread across it.

When he was done stitching up the wound, he turned to the others.

"She will be weak for some time," he said. "But I believe she may survive."

Mrs. Flanagan offered a room for her. Mary Bette had not stayed there for several years, eventually living on the streets and in one tenement or another, but her onetime landlady could not permit her to return to a vagabond existence.

Róisín took Sophie aside. She explained the situation and asked that she remain with Mary Bette at least until she was stabilized. Sophie, now plainly showing and desperate for something to do, agreed. She was tired of being under her sister's control and beck and call and relished the limited freedom moving to Mrs. Flanagan's would afford her. She would share Mary Bette's room and care for her.

The others left Sophie with Mary Bette and adjourned to the sitting-room. Róisín expressed confidence in her sister's ability to care for Mary Bette, and Mrs. Flanagan agreed.

Dr. Doyle was right. Mary Bette recovered much of her strength over the next weeks, and it was not long before she and Sophie could venture on walks on mornings and afternoons. Sometimes they covered the mile or so to the new clinic, where Dr. Doyle assessed both of their conditions. Each time, he told Mary Bette that she was improving and Sophie that the pregnancy was going well. Róisín agreed to her sister's request that she be allowed to stay with Mary Bette.

Sophie and Mary Bette, though, soon tired of the monotony. Mrs. Flanagan was providing them with their needs, supplemented by things sent by Róisín, but they were bored and took to slipping out several nights a week even as Sophie grew larger and larger.

52.

For her part, Elizabeth was deep into her first year as a nursing student. It was February and it was cold, but it was Saturday morning, and as she got dressed for the day she discussed with her roommate, Estella, where they might go in the afternoon. Saturdays were a short day—Sunday was the only one with no work or training—and the two regularly went out with several of the others to museums and other events in the afternoon. The initial iciness she felt from the others for her family's financial losses was gone by Christmas—which Elizabeth spent at the hospital in case a nurse was needed while the others spent their day with their families—in the bustle of the shared training.

On this Saturday, the two intended to walk with three other girls and venture to the just-opened Metropolitan Museum of Art on Fourteenth Street. It was cold, but the sky was clear when they rose, and they expected the Museum would be warm.

Saturdays, though, were often very busy, particularly tending to the injured who arrived overnight. They were usually wounds of one sort or another obtained during a fist or knife fight between two drunks. Mostly it involved patching and isolating the patient until he (it was usually but not always a "he") sobered up and could be sent home or, in some cases, until he could be collected by members of the New York Police Department.

When Elizabeth, Estella, and the rest entered the second ward they would be going through that morning, several doctors were around a table on which a noticeably pregnant woman lay. She was unconscious—thank God— and beaten viciously around her face. Her clothes were largely torn into rags that barely covered her. One doctor was assessing her wounds while Sister Taylor was cleaning off the blood from around her face. She called for a trainee to get a robe to make her decent, and Estella ran down the hall to fetch one.

Elizabeth had seen much, but nothing like this. The woman must be eight months pregnant judging by her stomach. One of the doctors said, "I think she's Meade's Whore," and Elizabeth was stunned. She brushed past two of the other trainees to get close. Though she knew much about Sophie, she never met her. Could she see anything of Róisín in the visage?

She looked at the doctor who made the claim.

"How do you know?" she asked.

He was embarrassed, but not so much as not to laugh as he said, "I saw them several times at some restaurant or another, thick as thieves, and very noticeable. One does not forget the sight of a cripple like Meade dining with a woman with flowing red hair."

Another doctor said, "Yes, I believe he is correct, and that it is her."

"Ain't she married to someone?" This was a third doctor, the tall, thin one, but Elizabeth did not hear the balance of what was being said. She pushed again through the crowd around the table. Estella, having delivered the robe to Sister Taylor, noticed and went to her.

"I must tell Róisín."

"Róisín?"

She looked at her friend. "Róisín Campbell is her sister. I was once a friend of hers but...things separated us. I must tell her."

Estella got permission from Sister Taylor for the two to go to the patient's sister. They got their coats from their room, and the two left the hospital and turned south.

Both knew the clinic had moved to the house that was only a few blocks away. They hurried there and were directed to the second floor where they found Róisín assisting Dr. Doyle with a patient. They stood at the door waiting to be noticed, and when they were, Róisín was surprised. She did not know who was with Elizabeth.

"I must speak to you immediately," Elizabeth said.

Dr. Doyle looked from the two to Róisín and back.

"It's alright. I can do this," he said and nodded.

Róisín removed her apron and draped it across a chair and rushed to hug her one-time companion. In the hall at the top of the staircase, Elizabeth said, "It is your Sophie."

Róisín feared the worst, but Elizabeth immediately said, "She is alive" to try to provide some minimal comfort to Róisín, who needed Estella's help to remain upright.

"She was beaten terribly and is at Bellevue. I know no more than that. I came here immediately as I heard. This is Estella Tompkins, who is my roommate."

Róisín gave a slight nod to the woman but could do no more.

Elizabeth asked Estella to hold Róisín while she went to Dr. Doyle to tell him what happened to Sophie. He found Sophie a talented but undisciplined girl, much like her sister as to the former and much unlike her in the latter. Assured that she was getting the best of care, he insisted that Róisín be taken there immediately. Róisín went to her room for her coat, and the three, Róisín between the other two, were quickly on the sidewalk and heading to Bellevue.

As soon as they were through the door to the ward, Elizabeth ran with Róisín in tow. There was no longer a crowd in the hallway as Sophie was in a room, and when the three reached it, only a senior doctor and Sister Taylor were with her. Elizabeth introduced Róisín, who pushed through her emotions to confirm to them that it was her sister.

"How is she? And how is the baby?"

The doctor nodded, and Sister Taylor took Róisín into the hall. She gave no sign of recognizing her from the interview at Bellevue. With Elizabeth, they found a bench on which to sit, and Róisín grabbed Elizabeth's hand as they went there.

"I am a nurse, sister. Please tell me. She is my baby sister."

"She was badly beaten. The woman she was with was not as lucky as she was?"

"Another woman?"

"Yes. The police believe she and your sister—"

"Sophie. Sophie Campbell, sister," Róisín said.

"That Sophie and her friend went to a tavern near First Avenue and settled in with two Irishmen. They left at about ten. And that's the last they were seen. A boy found them in an alley not far from the river at about six and they were brought here straightaway. The other woman was dead before they arrived."

"I may know the other woman."

"The police have identified her as a Mary Bette Flynn." Róisín froze at the words. "She was a known prostitute but apparently suffered in an abortion and had been having difficulty plying her trade since. The police think the men they left the tavern with may have had certain...expectations and lashed out when they found she could not fulfill them."

"My sister was no prostitute."

"No, the police do not think she was. They had some ales with the men and were foolish enough to think they only wanted to take them for a nice walk along the river. But they are looking into it."

Mary Bette Flynn. One of her first friends in New York and the only person with whom Róisín shared a physical intimacy. Beaten to death. With her barely-alive sister.

Sister Taylor rose, and let Róisín and Elizabeth sit together. She asked Estella, who was standing discreetly to the side, to obtain something to sustain the other two.

Róisín did not leave her sister's bedside for four days, and Elizabeth sat with her throughout Sunday and visited each morning before rounds and each evening after. Estella came as well sometimes. On the afternoon of the fourth day, Wednesday, Sophie regained consciousness. She suffered a concussion and numerous bruises the doctors said, but the baby was unharmed. The police apprehended the suspects on Tuesday night, the fools returning to the tavern where they met Sophie and Mary Bette. Mary Bette Flynn of County Mayo's funeral mass was on Tuesday, attended by Mrs. Flanagan and several others who lived at her boarding house, and her body was buried in a Catholic cemetery in Queens, across the East River.

Róisín escorted Sophie, shaken terribly by what happened to her companion, around the ward when she could walk, and the doctors monitored her pregnancy. They expected that the trauma would make the birth premature, and they were right. Sophie went into labor barely a week after the beating. She was strong enough to give birth to a baby son. But she was not strong enough to survive herself, and so her funeral mass was held just over a week after Mary Bette's and her body, too, was taken across the river to Queens where it was laid to rest beside the girl from County Mayo and not far from the larger plot in which her baby and too many others not yet baptized had been laid to rest.

Although everyone knew who the baby boy's father was, no one dared include it on the birth certificate. Instead, Diarmaid Campbell Cassidy was given the name of Sophie's only love (other than her first baby) and that of a man she grew, without reason, to despise.

Baby Diarmaid was at Bellevue for only a few days, his mother still above ground, when Sister Taylor sat with Róisín. Róisín was sitting with the baby, refusing to leave as a wet nurse was found to feed him.

"They will come for him soon," the nurse said. She was talking about the Sisters of Charity. They had taken charge of seeing to the care and ultimate adoption of Catholic babies, usually Irish ones, who were abandoned, abused, or left orphaned by their parents. Róisín went to Cassidy on Tuesday, telling him of Sophie, the baby, and the death. He deigned to speak with her at the door after he was summoned by his man but declined to participate in any way with the matters that, he said, were no longer of any concern of his. He closed the door, and Róisín stared at its ornate doorknocker before turning and starting back to Bellevue.

Before she arrived, though, she changed course and walked to Mr. Henry's. They still strolled frequently, though not so often as they had in earlier days. It was late, perhaps ten, when she knocked on his door, and his man immediately showed her to the sitting-room. Mr. Henry knew about Sophie but was unaware of the beating or the birth of the boy or about what happened to Mary Bette, who Róisín mentioned to him once before. He asked her in and gave her some whiskey to calm her nerves.

They spoke at length, and when the clock struck eleven, they left. Mr. Henry hailed a cab on the avenue and accompanied her back to Bellevue, where she would sleep near Baby Diarmaid. He assured her that he would do all in his power to see to the well-being of the baby and begged that she maintain her spirit, the loss of which would be of no service to her nephew.

They spoke again after Sophie's funeral mass the next morning. It was a small gathering, again with Mrs. Flanagan but also Róisín, Elizabeth, and Estella as well as Doctor Doyle and Nurse Evans and Sister Taylor, who walked to the church with her two students. Cassidy allowed Sally to be there, and she stood alone to the side after crying into

Róisín's shoulder. Mr. Henry stood to Róisín's right and Elizabeth to her left. Jimmy Regan stood quietly at the back.

The group watched the launch carry Sophie's body to Queens and when it reached the far shore, Róisín and Elizabeth walked with Mr. Henry, the women on either side of him.

"I have not as yet had the opportunity to make inquiries, but I shall do so presently. I am glad that Sister Taylor came today. Her support will be important in convincing the authorities to allow you to keep the child."

Róisín stopped. It was an inevitable and necessary question, but she had not asked, let alone answered, it. She expected that when Sophie had the baby, she would care for it. With Sophie gone, who would? It was foolish to think Cassidy would have anything to do with the boy, let alone that Meade would. Last she heard of him—and she was not particularly in a line of those who regularly received word about the comings and goings of Edward Meade—he was continuing to flaunt decency and propriety by sharing his bed with another younger woman. He might need to be approached eventually. But he could not participate with the child if it could be helped.

"You know, of course, of the orphan trains, where groups of orphans are shipped to farms in the Midwest, farmhands in the making. Some do well, but they're all gone from New York. But that's mostly for the Protestants. No, more likely for a Catholic is the Foundling Asylum."

The women knew about both. The Asylum sent Catholic orphans chiefly to the homes of Catholics who applied for them. Children at times remained at the Asylum for years, but an infant like Diarmaid would surely go quickly. If he survived. At that point, it was too early to say. After all, Sophie's first baby did not make it much past a month before succumbing. But, Sister Taylor told Róisín, Baby

Diarmaid seemed healthy. He was gaining weight and would, God willing, thrive.

"I fear you must decide quickly what is to be done," Mr. Henry continued. "The authorities will be informed shortly if they have not yet been told about the birth and the mother's death. They will soon be advised that the father will refuse to care for the infant, whatever his obligations under the law, and that the infant is for all intents and purposes an orphan."

They resumed walking, with the others who had been with them well out of sight.

"I am sorry, my dear Róisín, but you must decide quickly whether you will step forward to care for the child. I cannot even say that if you do so you will succeed. I will make inquiries if you wish me to. But you cannot be blamed were you to release the child and have him get an opportunity that you might never be able to give him."

"Mr. Henry." Róisín's arm was tightly through his and the wind had eased since they left the river. "I beg you give me time to think on it. I should be eternally grateful, moreover, if you could make inquiries as to whether I might succeed in securing the child should it be my wish."

Mr. Henry said he would do both but again warned her that it was likely best to avoid Diarmaid's coming too much to the attention of the authorities while she waited. When the three reached the avenue, Mr. Henry excused himself, promising both that he would return as soon as he had news, good or not. When he was gone, the two women turned towards Bellevue.

They were silent for several blocks. Róisín broke it.

"What shall I do, my sweet Elizabeth?"

Elizabeth waited several steps to respond.

"Will you please allow me to think about it? My heart is too raw right now for all you endured. He is a lovely child, I think. I believe it would be best if he were to be with you."

She stopped, pulling her arm from Róisín's and using both hands to turn Róisín to face her.

Róisín seemed so much older and more vulnerable than she was when they spent happier days together, and Elizabeth wondered that she might fall were she to be let go. Her eyes were downcast, and Elizabeth waited until they looked into hers. Then she said, "I promise you, whatever you decide, I will be with you."

Elizabeth released Róisín and turned to resume the walk back, and Róisín was quickly beside her, putting her arm through Elizabeth's and they were silent until they reached the hospital, where Elizabeth went to her room and Róisín went to Diarmaid's.

53.

"**I** do not give a whit for your mistress's instructions. I have no desire, I assure you, to cross the threshold of this place. I merely wish to see my mother."

The McNabbs' butler, Bradley, advised Elizabeth upon seeing her at the door that he was instructed that she herself was not permitted other than to see his mistress. Elizabeth had no interest in groveling her way back into the house. She simply needed to see her mother.

"Mrs. Geherty has retired for the evening, I am afraid, Miss Elizabeth. When she rises, I shall be pleased to inform her, and the mistress, of your appearance."

"I do not care that she has retired. I do not care if you tell the world that I am here as long as you inform my mother. It is a matter of life or death, and I will not leave until she appears. I will not soil the house by entering."

Bradley weighed the fury that would be unleashed should he comply with Elizabeth's wishes but he was not so hard a man as to ignore a matter of "life or death." He asked Elizabeth to enter, but she insisted on remaining on the steps as he closed the door after saying, "I shall be but a moment."

Elizabeth turned towards the street and stayed glued to the marble on which she stood. She had seen her mother several times each month, when Mary was out and about, since she fled the McNabb House on the evening of her arrival. They often strolled, when the weather allowed it, along the Ladies' Mile where the stores, Lord & Taylor among them, were closed but the sidewalks were rich with people for whom Sunday was their only day off and their only opportunity to take in the lavish window displays.

On these walks, after Elizabeth reported on her progress at Bellevue since she began training, Mrs. Geherty had the chance to vent of the life she and Elizabeth's father had fallen into under the dictates of her eldest daughter. She offered gossip about the goings-on of Michael and his wife and daughter but avoided any but the necessary mention of Mary and Peter McNabb, who they thought very little of, or Róisín, of whom they thought a great deal.

It was maybe five minutes before Elizabeth heard the door start to open and she turned. Her mother stood there in a dressing gown. Neither knew what to say, but Mrs. Geherty stepped out to hug her child.

"Oh, mother. I do not know what to do."

Mrs. Geherty insisted that Elizabeth come inside, saying that it was improper for her, Mrs. Geherty, to be outside in a gown.

"We will go into the small room to the back. I have told Bradley not to mention that you are here if he can avoid it. He is a good man, if bound by the strictures of your sister."

When the door was shut in the room and the gaslights lit, Elizabeth explained the reason for her visit.

"I want to help her, mother."

Mrs. Geherty was slapped with guilt for making Róisín promise to abandon her daughter because of Sophie. She explained that it was she who visited Róisín and asked her not to destroy what reputation Elizabeth had by continuing their association.

"I thought as much," Elizabeth replied. "I do not blame either of you."

The room was rarely used. It was paneled in knotted wood and had a bookshelf along one wall, lined with books never read or even opened. There were a small desk and a small desk chair and a pair of wooden chairs that faced it. It might have been used by the house's prior owner, but if anyone sat at that desk since and drafted a note on it that fact was lost to history.

The mother and daughter sat in the chairs, which they moved so they faced each other, and the women could hold each other's hands and look into each other's eyes.

Elizabeth told of what happened since discovering Róisín's sister during rounds at Bellevue, flooding wildly from the beating to the reunion to the poor mother's death. The boat carrying the body away, much as one did the same for Charlie. The growing hope and belief that the baby could and would survive. Her dilemma about Róisín. Ending with the conversation with Mr. Henry and the words exchanged with Róisín as they headed to the hospital. Mrs. Geherty listened quietly, aware of the unconscious tightening and loosening of Elizabeth's grip in rhythm with her words.

Elizabeth ended by saying she knew she must help Róisín but did not know how.

Mrs. Geherty confessed that she did not know either. Elizabeth—Lizzie—was the strong and independent one. Charles was weak, and Mary let her vanity and insecurity entrap her. Michael was sweet and compliant. Lizzie was different. She had, after all, stormed out when her sister set out conditions she could and would not accept. They were unacceptable, too, to Abigail Geherty and her husband, but they had no alternative to acquiescing. Indeed, a part of Mrs. Geherty feared what would happen should Mary become aware of this little meeting with her own daughter.

That could not be helped.

"What kind of support can you provide?" she asked.

"I do not know. I need you to help me. To *tell* me."

"If you go too far, Lizzie, you will be forever ruined and will not find a husband."

Elizabeth pulled back. "When I entered the training program, I knew it meant it was unlikely that I would marry. I'd have to leave should that happen."

"Surely not after you became a nurse."

"Mother. I made that decision anyway. I am lucky to have avoided Edward."

"I never told you, but I was relieved when that foolishness ended."

Elizabeth was surprised and a little angry. "Then why did you allow me to continue with him?"

"Lizzie." She reached to again hold her daughter's hands. "I thought it necessary. I did not like him, but your father believed the alliance with the Meades was important. And I did not disagree. Perhaps I should have. But I did not. It was another way I wronged you."

Elizabeth was unsure of how to respond. Given the realities of fashionable society and that no other appropriate man had expressed the slightest interest in an alliance with the Gehertys through Elizabeth, she escaped that fate and was relieved that her mother, too, was relieved. So now Elizabeth was a free and independent and poor woman. She was older and her looks, never as grand as her sister's, were fading. Both women knew that if there was to be an alliance, it would likely be based on affection at least and love at best.

That Elizabeth exiled herself from Mary's house reduced her opportunities to simply meet an eligible man was understood by Elizabeth and her mother, but both also understood that the chance of such a meeting maturing into love was already slim. For love in such precincts was well down on the list of qualities that one looked for in a spouse. Money remained, as it likely always would, the primary—and to some eyes the sole—basis for marriage.

Mrs. Geherty held out the hope that a close proximity with a doctor at Bellevue would lead Elizabeth to an acceptable marriage. A young doctor was unlikely to be fashionable unless he was the son of a doctor within a social circle. Elizabeth made it clear, though, that she had no interest in a fashionable life and while she could never admit it, she'd had no interest in any of the men she had come across in her twenty-one years. Mrs. Geherty was a lawyer's daughter and sometimes wished she and her husband shared the same indifference to society. But it was New York and in their class seeking to rise in the fashionable world was as natural and unavoidable as breathing.

Mary still trotted her parents out at the appropriate times. If she had an event at the McNabb House, they were directed to appear in the latest and finest outfits ordered and paid for by their daughter (or more truly by their daughter's husband) and to display the solicitousness appropriate to a child that had ascended well beyond where they had been and infinitely above where they ended up.

These thoughts had long occupied Mrs. Geherty about her second daughter. She, fortunately, had a high opinion of Róisín Campbell. As that woman said when they sat together at the café , one may carry the weight of one's family but is not defined by it. Elizabeth was pleading with her about what to do about a newly arrived member of Róisín's family. The bastard of a man to whom Elizabeth was once engaged.

Mrs. Geherty had a moment's fear that any association with that "bastard" would destroy not only Elizabeth but all her family. Up to and including Mary McNabb. Money and wealth were the primary currency of this world, but they were not the only ones. Were not the pauper descendants of the original Dutch families, the group known as the Knickerbockers, held in the highest regard though they could not entertain more than a handful of guests at a time? Were not the most boorish of families welcomed into the fashionable world simply for having made a random killing in an oil field in Pennsylvania who if they spoke English did so in a manner that was indecipherable to those who appreciated it as the Queen's tongue?

For her part, Mary McNabb survived the fall of her parents. She did so based on the *bona fides* of her husband and, more particularly, his parents and grandparents who were in society entirely based upon Grandfather McNabb's investment in Robert Fulton's adventure in building the Erie Canal that brought forth riches to all those who entered the venture with him. So, the McNabbs had the patina of relatively old money, and that went far in New York Society.

Mrs. Geherty reached across to Elizabeth and held her hands.

"If you commit to this woman, you will be ruined forever. It is a good deed, but the child is still a bastard, the bastard of a woman of no repute, and that reputation inevitably must fall on Miss Campbell and thus on you. You will surrender your position in the training. You will lose all of your friends—"

"Mother, I have no friends from this world. Only my fellow students and a few I know otherwise. And, I hope, Róisín."

Mrs. Geherty shook her head and tightened her grip.

"I know you have decided. If you came for my blessing, I give it to you. If I, too, am cast out by Mary, I may have to live with you. But as nothing will come of nothing, something will come of this."

The two women reached over and embraced. As they separated the door flung open.

"What in the name of God is the meaning of this? I left explicit instructions that she"—and she pointed at Elizabeth—"was not to be allowed admittance to this house unless I gave permission and I assure you that I didn't give it."

Bradley stood uncomfortably by the door. Mrs. Geherty immediately said that Bradley did not allow Elizabeth in, but that she, her mother, insisted.

"And, Mary, I am sorry you have been disturbed by this little meeting between a mother and her daughter."

"Disturbed? You defy my instructions and you regret my being 'disturbed.' That's what you have to say? I'd have thought you'd be on your knees right now begging for my forgiveness for this grotesque disregard of my wishes and my instructions."

Her venom directed at her mother being spent, Mary turned to Elizabeth, who by now was standing, though her mother was sinking into her chair.

"And you. How dare you come to this house without my permission?"

"I came to your house because I wanted to see my dear mother. The one you keep captive to your imperious nature."

Mary stepped deeper into the room, and Elizabeth moved towards her.

"I assume what you needed to say to mother has been said and you are to leave, never to return to my home. Do you hear? MY home."

Elizabeth looked back at her, *their,* shivering mother, whose eyes were cast the ground. She loved her and now more than perhaps ever and vowed to rescue her someday. But that day was not the one they occupied.

"I have spoken to our mother. She has provided me with the guidance I sought. I hope never to have to darken these halls again."

Mary was immobile, her feet solidly planted. Her day dress was askew, and her hair was undone as Elizabeth passed her.

"I will thank you never to return."

As Elizabeth was out the door of the room and heading towards the door of the house, Mary shot into the hall.

"It's about her, isn't it?"

Elizabeth ignored the question, more an accusation, and walked out into the city air.

* * * *

RÓISÍN, WHO DID not know what Elizabeth was doing, sat in a hallway in Bellevue. She held her nephew, lightly rocking him and murmuring noises she hoped were of comfort. She prayed that Diarmaid was strong and would survive and she swore at that moment that she would never abandon him. It was late when a nurse took the baby from her for a feeding with the wet nurse and Róisín fell asleep on the bench for another night.

54.

Nurse Evans brought a change of clothes to Bellevue for Róisín. Sister Bowdin gave Elizabeth leave to sit with her for several hours each day, including when her training was ended. Others, fellow trainees and otherwise, brought meals to her as she slept in a bed beside the boy's cradle. When he slept, Róisín often assisted the nurses on the ward, well familiar with procedures from her days at the German Hospital. Indeed, several times her particular experience at the clinic proved of use with a patient rushed in after being brought in from a tenement with maladies not often encountered at Bellevue.

On the fifth day, Sister Taylor arrived with the doctor who had undertaken the care of Diarmaid. He examined the infant and, satisfied with the baby's condition, he allowed Róisín to take him to her room at the clinic. He wrote detailed instructions for his friend Callum Doyle. Diarmaid was wrapped tightly, and Elizabeth was permitted to walk the two of them to the clinic, it being a warm but not hot day.

While Róisín was away, Nurse Evans had rearranged her rooms. A bassinet was now beside the bed. She also made up a small room where the wet nurse could stay while she fed the baby. When the girls and the baby reached the clinic, Nurse Evans took Róisín to her rooms and the temporary wet nurse from the hospital to hers and when the latter took the child, Róisín fell asleep exhausted.

When she realized that Róisín would be coming home with the infant, Nurse Evans went to a neighborhood filled with mothers who'd lost their children in childbirth, sometimes at the clinic, often in the middle of the night. She had in mind one, a girl really, who came to New York not long after Sophie did. She fell pregnant by someone soon after she arrived, though she would never say by whom.

Only that he was married. She carried the baby to term, but when she had horrible pains as she went into labor she was rushed to the clinic. Nurse Evans held her hand as she gave birth to a little girl who did not survive the night.

The mother, Nora Brady, was living with an aunt and uncle, too desolate and delicate to seek work. Now, a month after losing her own daughter, Nurse Evans navigated the dark stairs to the flat on the fourth floor of a mid-block tenement. With her aunt and uncle out at work, Nora was alone, tidying as best she could in the filthy, stinking conditions. She, of course, remembered Nurse Evans, and she offered to make her some tea.

Nurse Evans did not have much to offer Nora in terms of money. But it was more than she would get being a wet nurse for a child in the tenements. Nora would also have the chance to keep her days busy by helping in the clinic. She worked as a seamstress before she got too heavy to continue and dreaded returning to that life of piecework and missed pay. Nurse Evans told Nora that it was the nephew of Róisín to whom she would provide nourishment, and Nora recalled and admired Róisín from her visits to the clinic and how she cared for so many bereaved mothers.

In the end, it was not much of a decision, and Nurse Evans returned to the clinic with Nora, who was eager to meet her new mistress and, more, the infant she would sustain.

Nora was young and naïve, and so she reminded Róisín of Sophie. More important, Diarmaid took to her teats immediately, and Róisín took to watching the two, Nora humming and going back-and-forth slightly in a rocking chair Nurse Evans procured for her room and Diarmaid suckling on her breast.

* * * *

SISTER BOWDIN AND SISTER Taylor were solicitous of Elizabeth while Róisín was at Bellevue, but they required her to return to her regular duties when her friend and the baby were gone. To Elizabeth, the time had been something of a vacation, but she was abruptly returned when the other trainees made sure she made up for the increased duties they felt while she was spending time with her friend.

She was pleased to be back, busy as she was, and on the first Sunday, she and Estella walked to the clinic to visit their friend after mass. Róisín was only just recovering from her lack of sleep at Bellevue, and she sat with the girls in the sitting-room on the ground floor. Nurse Evans and Dr. Doyle were out, and Nora was feeding Diarmaid, promising to join the others with the baby when they were done.

The three were not there long when Nora came down with the infant. After sincere fawning over the boy, Estella suggested a walk, but much as Nora liked the idea, she agreed it was too soon for Diarmaid to be exposed to what was turning into a hot day. She remained in the room while the other three headed to the avenue in their Sunday best.

Róisín was in the middle as the others put their arms through hers. They did not speak much. Or they spoke much but not of anything of any significance. They soon reached the avenue and continued to the river. There they found numerous couples leaning against the railing, watching the occasional boat pass by and exchanging waves with its occupants.

The three were tired and warm and found a bench looking out that was recently vacated. They sat, again with Róisín in the middle. Elizabeth saw an Italian man selling ices and went to get each of them one so they could cool down a bit. While she did, Estella told Róisín how their friend would not stop talking about Diarmaid when they were together.

"I fear she was always destined to be a good mother but has had her chances ruined."

Róisín looked over at Elizabeth, fumbling with her purse to pay the man and then awkwardly trying to hold the three ices without them falling to the ground. She jumped up to help.

Estella did not continue the train of thought she started, but as they walked back, she squeezed Róisín's hand whenever Elizabeth mentioned the baby. Their talk was more concrete as they returned than it was as they headed to the river, and Róisín, too, noticed how Elizabeth's tone changed when she mentioned the child. It was not louder or quieter. Yet it was somehow different.

Róisín would not hear of the girls leaving so soon when they returned to the clinic and made them promise to go with her to the avenue to get tea and pastries.

After she looked in on Nora and Diarmaid.

55.

Thomas Fleming was a man of indeterminate age but surely closer to sixty than forty. He was portly with a double chin and much of his hair had long since abandoned him. He had risen through the court system to become the chief clerk of the Surrogate's Court of the City of New York. While the chief responsibility of the court was to deal with wills and disputes as to how a rich person wished his estate to be allocated, it also was responsible for approving or disapproving the adoption of children.

It was in this latter capacity that brought Róisín to Mr. Fleming's cluttered office in a courthouse near City Hall. Work on a replacement courthouse had halted in a wave of corruption inquiries, and this one was dark and heavily paneled. She climbed a narrow flight of stairs to the third floor and room 306. On the door was a small brass plaque barely visible in the darkness of the hallway: "Thomas Fleming, Clerk of the Surrogate's Court." She looked at it for a moment or two before knocking.

Róisín was given his name by Mr. Henry, who obtained it after several inquiries. Shortly following their walk after Sophie's funeral, and after Elizabeth made her vow to Róisín, Róisín told Mr. Henry that she was desperate to care for Diarmaid Cassidy. Mr. Henry returned with the knowledge that Mr. Fleming was the man to see for the purpose.

It was the Monday of the week following Sophie's funeral, the day after her walk with her two friends. Through associates of Mr. Henry, Mr. Fleming was given word that a woman would visit him to discuss what she had to do to formally adopt her nephew. Mr. Fleming went to the door when Róisín knocked and led her to a leather chair in front of his desk. After closing the door, he removed a pile of papers and scrolls from a matching chair and placed them atop a similar stack against the window. He adjusted that chair so it was close to its twin and sat.

Róisín told the story of her sister. Of the first, lost child of a boy in Ireland and the sham marriage to Cassidy to provide respectability. Of the second child—the one in question—by another, known man whose identity she refused to divulge and who was not her sister's husband. Of how the titular husband refused to have anything to do with another man's child. Of how Róisín was respectable and had a respectable job acting as a nurse at the clinic caring for the poor and the more general at the hospital.

When Mr. Fleming asked how she proposed to care for the infant while she was working as a nurse, she assured him that she would limit her work to the clinic where she had an apartment and would retain a nurse to care for the baby. She added that she had a friend who was training to be a nurse in Sister Bowdin's program who offered to do whatever was necessary for the care and protection of Diarmaid.

Mr. Fleming said he was skeptical.

"Will the husband, who I am to understand is *not* the father, cooperate?"

"Cooperate, sir?"

"Yes. By signing an affidavit disavowing his paternity and any claims he has to the care and protection of the child."

"I do not know."

"Well, you had better find out, hadn't you? Perhaps if you tell him that you, if you are the child's adopted mother, will terminate any legal obligations he has to participate in the growth of a child who is, after all, undeniably the product of the woman to whom he was married when she died, he will, as I say, cooperate." The final word was elongated.

As Róisín contemplated the likelihood of such an arrangement, she felt Mr. Fleming's hand brush across her dress at the knee. He turned his chair slightly so it better faced hers.

"I may be able to provide some assistance in ensuring that your petition is granted."

He was looking up at her widening eyes.

"The surrogate relies heavily on my recommendations in matters such as this."

He had both hands on her dress and both began moving up, pushing the dress's material with them. Róisín was stunned, but only for a moment, and she slapped the man's left hand, and Mr. Fleming quickly pulled them both from her. He sat back in his chair, his hands dangling harmlessly in his lap.

"I say this only as a means of providing assistance to you, comfort to you. I have only your interest, and that of the poor orphan, in mind. Thank you for stopping by, Miss Campbell."

With that, he stood and stepped to the door. He opened it and said "good day" to Róisín and after watching her walk unsteadily down the dark hallway and imagining how much he would like to help her, he closed the door and returned to the chair at his desk and resumed reviewing the petition of a dead banker dividing his middling estate among three of his four children, knowing that the fourth would soon be filing some sort of writ or petition to get what he deemed to be his fair share of the rest and residue of his father's material life.

It took several blocks for the unsteadiness of Róisín's walk and the echo of Mr. Fleming's elongated final "Miss Campbell" to dissipate. Realizing she was not too distant from Mr. Henry's office, she went south. She was never there before, but he provided the address and suggested she visit it after her interview with Thomas Fleming.

When she arrived and a clerk announced her presence, Mr. Henry saw how anxious she was and feared that her interview had not gone as they had hoped.

"I swear to you, my dear. I had no idea he would do that. I was told that he was a person whose assistance was perhaps crucial in gaining the surrogate's approval for the adoption. I should have gone with you."

Róisín, of course, believed her friend. She had not for a moment considered him a part of it but had allowed her emotions to carry her away when they met that evening. They sat in the sitting-room at his house after he insisted that she remain for dinner, and he sent a note to Dr. Doyle. She was rarely in his house; they often walked together but met near where she lived. It was a house not unlike Cassidy's but better decorated and more welcoming. His servants were attentive, perhaps to a fault for someone as unaccustomed to such treatment as was Róisín.

"I do have one other possibility."

They were both sipping brandy from snifters and Mr. Henry was savoring a cigar, the fiery tip of which he sometimes glanced at while he thought. He was doing so now.

"Fleming has extreme power. Some say even more than the surrogate himself. But his position is one based on politics. Were yours just a normal case, I would not dare try it. Given your refusal to succumb to his...charms, an attempt to supersede him via Tammany might doom the effort forever."

"Mr. Henry. I fear that he made it clear that were I not to give him some level of satisfaction—I dare not contemplate what—Diarmaid will be off to the Founding Asylum before we left the courthouse. I think we must take the chance."

Mr. Henry looked at her a moment before reaching down and placing his cigar in an ashtray. He rose. "I must take you home." It was not a long journey, and as the cab slowed in front of the clinic, he gripped her hand.

"I promise you, my dear Róisín, I will do whatever is required for you to have your child."

So assured, and doubting neither the sincerity nor the influence of Mr. Henry, Róisín was calm as she walked across the sidewalk to the clinic's front door, and when she reached it she turned to give him a smile and a nod and in that moment wondered not for the first time what would become of her were he not her dear friend.

In that comfort, she slept well, something she feared she would never again do as she walked down the halls of the courthouse after her interview with Mr. Thomas Fleming, Chief Clerk of the Surrogate's Court of the City of New York.

56.

Some days later, as she returned with Mr. Henry in a cab after another late meeting, Róisín saw a grand carriage lit by the glare of a gaslight in front of the clinic. The barouche's top was down, and its occupants were elsewhere, with a coachman and a footman sitting on the outside seat. Its body was a shiny ebony with a trim of the sort that would have been frequently seen on the block in the past, but the fashionable had long since moved north. Its stark-red wheels stood out. She could see the lamps in the front room where patients waited were lit, which was unusual. Mr. Henry asked if he should accompany her inside, but she declined the offer and wished him a good night. He waited until she was through the door before having the cabbie drive him home.

When she was through the front door, Róisín saw that Nurse Evans was attempting to converse with a lady and a gentleman who were formally dressed. Dr. Doyle entered, carrying a pot of tea. It took a moment, but she recognized the couple as the two who ignored her when she was with Elizabeth on the day of the gig accident. The Meades.

Mr. Meade rose when he noticed Róisín, but Mrs. Meade did not.

"You must be Miss Campbell," she said with barely a glance in Róisín's direction.

"Yes, I am. And I believe you to be Mr. and Mrs. Meade."

This startled the pair, the female part saying, "I do not believe we know you."

"I was with Elizabeth Geherty at the hospital after the accident with your son."

"I do not recall you, but it is of no matter. We are here on a matter of some importance. Thank you, Doc—"

"Doctor Doyle, ma'am. And this is Nurse Evans."

"Well, yes. Thank you both. We have no further need of your services. You may go."

Róisín saw, though the Meades did not, a reddening of Dr. Doyle's cheeks and Margaret Evans's hand reaching around to guide her lover from the room. When the door was shut, Róisín sat facing Mrs. Meade, and Mrs. Meade looked pained by the blithe manner in which she did so. Mr. Meade was noticing Róisín.

"Miss Campbell, I have had some disturbing news. We came directly from dinner to discuss it with you, only to find that you were not home. We have waited fully two hours for you to be here."

"I am sorry, Mrs. Meade. I had no reason to expect that you would be visiting. But I am here now. Please, I am tired. What is your business?"

Mr. Meade put a hand on his wife's wrist and her growing hardness eased slightly.

"My, you are direct. It has come to our attention that your late sister may, and I emphasize *may*, have given birth to a child of which our son is the father."

"Mrs. Meade. Mr. Meade. There is no question that your son is the father of Diarmaid."

"Diarmaid? A peasant name. Like yours. Is that what it is called?"

"That is what he is called by those who love him. How others may refer to him is of no moment. But I am sure you are not here to speak of his name."

"No, we are not. We have been further and more recently advised that you have given thought to attempting to adopt the child. Whether you will be able to do so, we have been told, is in serious doubt. But having now met you, I say that we will challenge any such attempt on your part. He is our blood, and if anyone is to raise him, it shall be his grandparents. To be clear, his grandparents in America."

With that, Mr. Meade rose, and Mrs. Meade began to get up.

"He is as much my blood as yours." She paused. "And you are wrong."

Mrs. Meade now stood, and the women considered each other.

"Yes, having met you I tell *you* that I have not merely given thought to adopting him. I fully intend to."

Mrs. Meade considered the insolent girl. "Then you shall fail." She turned to her husband.

"We will go."

When Róisín heard the front door shut, she went to the window. Ensuring she could not be seen, she watched the old couple get into their carriage and watched until she could see it no more, trying to control the shaking that enveloped her the instant they left the building as she slowly melted to the floor.

Though this was always a possibility, she did not think the Meades would become involved if only to avoid confirming the well-known fact that Edward Meade was the father of Diarmaid Cassidy. Now, they did not appear to care about that. Were they to get an affidavit from Meade confirming his paternity, all would surely be lost.

She finally rose and climbed to her room, though not before knocking on the door of Doctor Doyle and Nurse Evans and telling them that the visit was unpleasant but fortunately over and that she would tell them more in the morning, and she tossed and turned until finally falling into a disturbed sleep.

"This is, indeed, a problem," Mr. Henry told Róisín in the morning. She was at his house early, and he was getting dressed before going to his office when she appeared. "We will have to think about it. I shall speak to some people, and I will visit you at the clinic this evening. In the meantime, concentrate on your work. It will keep your mind off it."

Her work did not, of course, keep Roisin's mind off it. It gnawed at her until she was raw inside. She soldiered on. Before the clinic's doors opened, she detailed Doctor Doyle and Nurse Evans about her encounter with the Meades, chiefly with Mrs. Meade.

She went about her tasks until she entered the front room in the early afternoon and saw the Meades' barouche out front. She did not know for how long it had been there, but she removed her apron and walked out. The top was down as it was warm, and she saw that it was Mr. Meade and Mr. Meade alone who sat in it. As she approached, a footman jumped down and opened the door for his master, and Mr. Meade stepped out. He put on a top hat and reached for a walking stick.

"Miss Campbell. Might you join me for a short stroll?" He held out his free arm.

Róisín looked at the clinic, and Nurse Evans was in the window, gesturing for Róisín to go with him. Róisín nodded, and the two walked west.

"I fear that last evening did not go as Mrs. Meade and I intended. It was nobody's fault, mind you, but I think, and please do not be offended, I think you both were too harsh with each other. We have long shared the concern expressed in the community about our son's behavior since his accident. He has not quite recovered from the loss of Miss Geherty. The girl you were with at the hospital. She was my son's fiancée but after her family had some, er, difficulties, the engagement could not be sustained, and they separated."

Róisín remained silent on this, knowing far more than Mr. Meade could suspect.

"I do not know the circumstances of how Edward came to meet your sister, but I do know that he sometimes rebelled against what he saw as the vacuity of our set and railed against fellows whom he knew mocked him for his injuries when he was out of the room.

"He may have met your sister in such a foray. Probably. I do think his intentions initially were honorable. I cannot speak to the truth of what she told him, but he genuinely was concerned for her well-being based upon what she told him about her husband."

"You knew she was married?"

"Of course. He told us that the first day we met her. He sat with Mrs. Meade and me and told of the good deed he was doing. We believed him, hoping it was a signal that he had moved away from Miss Geherty. We knew nothing could come of being with your sister, of course, but if she could stabilize him, he might be able to find an appropriate wife.

"We had no idea, I assure you, Miss Campbell, that he had...relations with her. She was in a separate small room down the hall from his. We never saw anything inappropriate between them, though I confess we did not look hard to see what he was up to with her. I feared that she was becoming obsessed with him and that he was dangling her along, but when it was mentioned to him, he angrily rejected the accusation."

The pair reached the avenue, Mr. Meade at his most dapper and Róisín in her work clothes without her apron, and more than a few of those they passed noticed the incongruity. They turned south, into a blinding sun in a crystal-clear sky.

"Mrs. Meade and I were shocked when one morning your sister was gone. Vanished in the night. We were relieved. Nothing could come of it and the sooner it was terminated the better. Only some days later did we learn that she was likely with child. Mrs. Meade and I berated him for the act and for forcing her to leave."

Mr. Meade huffed and pulled a handkerchief from his pocket. After he used it to blow his nose, he returned it to his pocket and resumed.

"Edward proclaimed that he loved her, but he would not know the meaning of such a thing. And, of course, he could not have remained in our house had she given birth. Our reputation was already damaged enough. That would be a death blow.

"We would have set them up somewhere, assuming affairs could be resolved with her husband. Edward said he acted foolishly when she told him of her condition. That he lashed out at her, verbally only, he swore. Yet that only lasted a few days as he returned shortly with another young Irish woman he found we know not where. And now she occupies the room once used by your sister and we do not know what is to be done about it."

Much of what Róisín heard made sense to her. Edward Meade may have genuinely had affection for Sophie, but he disproved any good intentions when he took up with another lass. She was at a loss for why Mr. Meade was telling her this, the memory of the last evening's encounter with his wife still foremost in her mind.

At some point, likely out of habit, Mr. Meade put his arm through Róisín's as he walked to her right towards the curb. He noticed her beauty the night before and again when they met in front of the clinic. Now, as they walked to the south on the avenue, his stiffness was gone, and she felt comfortable enough to raise no objection.

"Ah, Miss Campbell."

"Please, sir. You may call me 'Róisín.'"

"'Tis a lovely name," he said with a slight lilt, before adding a whispered "just between us," and he roared at his little repulse of his wife's observation of the night before.

Resuming his serious tone, he continued. "Well, Róisín. I daresay you are curious about where I am going. I just want you to understand what I believe happened between my son and your sister. It is a sad story, far sadder for you. But we do not doubt that the child is my son's. We cannot, however, put our imprimatur on it. I am sorry. It is one thing for people to suspect. It is another for them to *know*. One thing to accept the sins of a child. Another to accept parents who endorse those sins, whatever the motive.

"No, Mrs. Meade and I had and have no intention of interfering with you and the child. We agreed to that before we met you last evening, but, as I say, things began badly and turned worse. We will not acknowledge our relationship with the child to the world. But he is our grandson, and we must account for that. Financially and emotionally."

"And discreetly?"

"Yes, Róisín. You are right. Very discreetly."

As the two turned east to continue their journey around the block, he explained their intentions. It would have nothing to do with their son. He, they knew, might be all enthusiasm in one moment and all distance the next and while eventually it would prove helpful for him to have dealings with Diarmaid, it would not be for some time.

No, they would provide money enough for Róisín, should she win custody of the child, to find an appropriate apartment and hire a competent nursemaid for him. In time, a governess. Their attorney would arrange for some type of vehicle that would provide for him when he came of age. Perhaps to pay for higher education. It was long off, and they knew such a bastard would never be fully accepted in society. Even so, he could become educated and find himself blossom in one or another profession. Perhaps in medicine?

In exchange, Róisín would allow his grandparents to see him.

"Discreetly?" she said with a smile.

He echoed, "Discreetly."

By the time they turned north, they understood each other and liked each other.

When they again walked west to return to where they began, Mr. Meade said, "Mrs. Meade can be a harsh woman. But she is in truth a kind one. We have always regretted how Edward turned out. We do not presume to interfere with you. But I do hope you can get to know and understand Mrs. Meade. As I saw last evening, the two of you are not as unlike as either of you would like to believe."

As they neared the clinic, Róisín stopped and turned her companion to see him.

"There is one thing you and Mrs. Meade must know, sir. To not tell you would be to act under false pretenses. You spoke of Miss Geherty. You should know that while that day you saw us in the hospital was the day I met her, I have come to know her well since and she is my dearest friend. I know her background and that of her family."

He thought for a moment. "Were you the one who found poor Charlie?"

"Yes, sir. That was me. I was, am, the reason she fled her family though it is inappropriate for me to say more. I wish you, and Mrs. Meade, to know that it is likely if not probable that Miss Geherty will have a role in Diarmaid's life, perhaps a very large one, and that it is quite likely that you will encounter her in the course of your dealings with the boy."

She stopped and he thought. Then he laughed.

"Oh, that would be ironic. We always liked her, so unlike her sister. We regretted losing her not only for what a loss it was for our son but because we had hoped that she would be in our company frequently after they married. Oh, this is irony indeed. You need not wonder, Miss Campbell. Her appearance shall not but enhance the arrangement we have made."

They resumed the walk over the final yards, to the clinic for her and the carriage for him.

"Oh, I do miss playing cards with her on an evening. Though she lacks the caustic wit that you displayed so well last evening. Well, I must leave you, my dear. I am delighted to get to know you, and I know Mrs. Meade shall be too."

As he turned into the carriage he smiled. "Lizzie Geherty. I shall be pleased to see her again. Good day, Miss Campbell."

With that, the footman closed the door and when he was aboard with his top hat secured to his head, the barouche headed west for its return to the greater precincts where the Meades lived.

Róisín was quite amazed as she watched it disappear at the avenue. She could never have imagined such a resolution of what just hours before seemed impossible to solve.

"It is all good," was all she said when she met Nurse Evans in the clinic before resuming her duties.

57.

Although the work was becoming strained at the clinic in her absence, Dr. Doyle insisted that Róisín take care of issues related to Diarmaid before anything.

"You are of little use to us while your mind is elsewhere," he told her. This day she was taking advantage of this license and sat again in a cab with Mr. Henry who, too, had largely put his other affairs to the side in favor of helping his friend. In light of *l'affaire Fleming*, he would not again allow her to enter a potential lion's den alone.

It was not long before they reached a broad three-story building, and a doorman directed them to an office on the second floor that overlooked Fourteenth Street. The door, with "John O'Neal" scrolled across the glass, was open and when Mr. Henry knocked on the frame, the large man sitting behind the desk jumped up, rushing to shake Mr. Henry's hand and then Róisín's, saying, "You must be Miss Campbell. Come in, come in."

As the visitors sat, he closed the door and was quickly back in his seat.

"Miss Campbell, Mr. Henry here has told me of your predicament. It is a sad thing you are going through, but I have heard that you have done very good things for our community, especially the younger women in the community, and I wish to help you so far as I can."

She thanked him and told of her experience several days earlier with Mr. Fleming. He well knew of Fleming's peccadilloes, and he knew by looking at her what he did. Nothing needed to be said on that front. He leaned across the desk in her direction. He knew a good story when he saw it and even more a bad one when he heard it. He heard about "Meade's Whore" because everyone remotely Irish had. He was hardened to the frailties of the Irish in New York, high and low, and it did not matter.

John O'Neal knew there would be the moralizers, the priests manning the barricades. Far more were the people who mattered, the hordes of voters living in squalor—the well-off largely abdicated a role in local elections—and thrilled by the celebrity of a farmgirl taking up with a dandy and the story of a boy being adopted by his aunt, a nurse. And not just any nurse. No. A nurse who'd tended to nearly all of the community, especially the young mothers, on the lower east side since shortly after she arrived from County Limerick.

"Oh, Miss Campbell. You are a guardian angel. The girls and the women want to beatify you, and the men and the boys want...Well, let us say you are admired all around. Yes, all around. Still, the rules of the surrogate's court, I fear, are stringent. Yes, Fleming has a large influence, but we must abide by what we must abide by."

John O'Neal was now leaning back, looking alternately at Róisín and Mr. Henry, both of whom nodded in agreement with what they were being told. He rose and walked to the window. He reached back and opened a drawer and pulled out two cigars, offering one to Mr. Henry, who declined with a wave and a "Thank you, no." He took the other and cut it, and he then lit it methodically on a drunkard's match he held in front of his mouth until a cloud of smoke created a halo about his face. He took a long drag and he held the cigar to his side as he again looked out to the street, and with the window open the sounds and smells of the carriages and wagons floated in.

"Yes, we must abide by what we must abide by."

Tammany was under great scrutiny and only recently regained power against some reformer nonsense. Hence, taking up this cause, if done delicately, could not but help its reputation. O'Neal turned abruptly. "You say that this Cassidy refuses to have anything to do with it?"

Mr. Henry nodded. "I have known him for a while, but even I could not persuade him to take the slightest interest."

O'Neal returned to his view of the street. "That may be the easiest route, for him to provide an affidavit. But there may be alternatives."

He again turned and after placing his cigar in an ashtray he lifted his hands, and his visitors stood. He came around the desk and reached for Róisín's hand.

"I shall ponder it, Miss Campbell. I shall ponder it indeed. Mr. Henry," he said as he turned to him, "can you please provide Mr. Cassidy's address? I might have a word with him." He handed Mr. Henry a small sheet of paper and a fountain pen, and Mr. Henry provided the information.

While he was doing that, O'Neal gripped Róisín's hand. "I promise you, Miss Campbell, if there is a way we can keep your family together, we shall find it. Yes, we shall find it," and he shook the hand vigorously before releasing it and doing, albeit not quite so enthusiastically, the same with Mr. Henry.

The two elected to walk to the clinic, it being well less than a mile, saying barely a word as they did.

58.

After an anxious week following their meeting with John O'Neal from Tammany Hall, Róisín and Mr. Henry were summoned back. When Mr. Henry rapped on the door, the two were again welcomed into the politician's office. When he turned and sat back in his chair, he lifted some sheets from his desk and handed them to his visitors.

It was an affidavit sworn to the day before by Stephen Cassidy in the precise hand of a scrivener and with a large seal impressed on it and a red ribbon draped over it.

State of New York   )
*   ) ss.:*
County of New York   )

STEPHEN CASSIDY, being duly sworn, says:

1. I was the husband of the late Sophie Cassidy, née Campbell.

2. I became estranged from her on February 15, 1874, and did not speak or communicate with her after that. In particular, I did not have relations with her after that date and therefore I could not have been the instrument of her becoming pregnant with the child I understand was born on or about April 4, 1875.

3. I have no interest in that child or in any other matter concerning my late wife. I disavow any future interest in that child and hereby relinquish any and all rights I might otherwise have as the husband of a woman who had a child by another man.

4. I will not object and indeed support the petition of my sister-in-law, Róisín Campbell, of whom I have personal knowledge which leads me to believe she would be a fine parent to the child, to adopt the infant as her own and I wish her Godspeed in doing so.

<u>*Stephen Cassidy*</u>

Sworn to before me this
eighteenth day June in
the year of our Lord 1875

<u>*John L. O'Neal*</u>

Notary Public of the
State of New York

When done, with Mr. Henry reading it too, Róisín handed it back to Mr. O'Neal.

"What it means, my dear, is that this major obstacle is swept away. And as I understand that the true father and his family will have nothing to do with this, we have a good chance, a very good chance indeed, of convincing the surrogate to allow you to adopt the boy."

Róisín and Mr. Henry looked at one another.

"Now, Miss Campbell, I must tell you that it is not assured. You will need to find an attorney to prepare your petition, and I believe I have just the man for you, and you must meet with the surrogate himself because it is for him to decide, as they say, that the moral and temperate interests of the child shall be advanced by your adoption. But, again, I cannot assure you."

"What could interfere with such a result?" Mr. Henry asked.

Mr. O'Neal frowned. "I fear the one remaining obstacle is the good Sisters of Charity and meddling priests. They may...I do not say they *will,* but they *may* seek to obtain the child for themselves, to be farmed out to what they consider to be a good Catholic family. They may argue that a child with a mother and father with whom he shares no blood is preferable to an unmarried aunt with whom he does.

"It would be easier, Miss Campbell, if you were married, but I daresay that is not likely to happen now, is it?"

Róisín shook her head.

"I thought not. And it could strike the surrogate as a subterfuge and harm your case. That being so, it is my suggestion that you consider heading up to the Foundling Asylum to plead your case and perhaps convince the good sisters to support you or at least not to oppose you. Even if some parish priest got on his high horse about the immorality of it all, he would be given no weight unless the Asylum agreed."

Róisín and Mr. Henry left the building again clad in the fear that their efforts would be for naught.

       59.

All who knew of the Sisters of Charity and the work they did admired them. For Catholics, they had a tremendous influence when it came to questions of adoption as the relatively new Children's Aid Society had for Protestant orphans, who were frequently designated to travel by orphan train to a farm somewhere in the Midwest, maybe Iowa or Kansas.

The Sisters, too, had the support of Tammany in the byzantine world of New York City politics, and this and the nature of their work was what gave them their influence. Even Tammany's John O'Neal could not deny it.

So, on the Saturday after they met with Mr. O'Neal for the second time, Róisín and Mr. Henry took a cab uptown to the Asylum. Upon entering and telling their business, a young novitiate led them to a large office in the rear of the building, with the sounds of children playing and crying echoing through the dark halls.

Sister Margaret Ryan was the eldest daughter of an affluent New Jersey family. She felt a calling to the Sisters of Charity and was one of the earliest to understand the need for them to undertake the care of Catholic, chiefly Irish, orphans in light of an increasing Protestant movement to remove them to what were claimed to be less dangerous homes than a poor Irish family in the city could possibly provide.

She knew of Diarmaid Cassidy. She was preparing to intervene on behalf of the Asylum once the matter came before the surrogate. Her understanding was vague but largely accurate. A woman from Ireland lost her first baby and abandoned her husband to another man. She was pregnant and cast out by him and was in part supported by her sister. She survived a vicious attack, which a companion did not, and died giving birth to the boy.

She knew nothing about the girl's sister. She assumed she had been neglectful and careless in allowing the mother to put herself in a way that she could be with yet a second child. Now that sister sat before her. She was a pretty girl, and while her features were soft in some respects, they were hard in others. It was clear that she was not in service but also that she was not from one of the proper homes.

Mr. Henry deferred to his friend, and Sister Ryan was impressed. Róisín's intelligence was clear as was her strength and intensity and, most of all, her complete dedication to the child. She was there on a mission, to convince Sister Ryan that hers was the best place for her nephew to go. She explained her inability to control Sophie's wanderings.

After she laid out her situation and her plans for the child, down to where he would be baptized (though not mentioning the help she expected from Diarmaid's grandparents because she promised the Meades that she would not) she stopped and waited.

"You make a strong argument, Miss Campbell. But it is quite impossible. You must see that. You are unmarried. You propose to live in a medical building in which you admit that the doctor and head nurse are in a relationship while one of them is married to another."

"But sister—"

"Do not interrupt, my child. It is hardly an appropriate place to raise a boy. Your sister, I must say, has been a harlot on two continents, and this is too much a burden to place on any child without adding being brought up, however well you might do it, by an unmarried if intelligent and well-intentioned woman in an unsuitable environment.

"I am sorry, Miss Campbell, Mr. Henry, but the Asylum will seek to take responsibility for this baby. I am confident that for all of your good intentions he will be better off sent elsewhere."

60.

"**P**erhaps Mr. Henry can explain it to you."

"Mr. Neally. I can assure you. I am fully capable of understanding what you have to say."

"I am glad to hear it, my dear." He was genuinely pleased by the intelligence and intensity of his client. "Very glad. It is uppermost that you convince the surrogate you are intelligent and capable and able to care for the needs of the boy. This is excellent."

He shifted some papers on his desk.

"Now there is no time to lose. Since the Foundling Asylum knows about the situation, we can expect it to file an emergency petition with the surrogate."

"An emergency petition for what?" Mr. Henry asked.

"Well, sir, to gain immediate custody of the child. And if they succeed, it may be hard to get him out of their clutches."

He turned to an aghast Róisín. "Our first order of business, then, is to make the living arrangements for the boy as fine as we can do. There is no time to lose, but there are several major issues."

Without seeming to take a breath, he continued. "First, is that he will be living above sick people. Yes, it is all well and good to care for such people, but he will be living above them.

"Second is the well-known fact that Doctor Doyle and Nurse Evans share a bed though they are not married to one another."

"Why should that matter?" asked Róisín.

"Oh, Miss Campbell. It can matter a great deal. The Sisters are going to say that it is a situation fraught with moral difficulties."

"But he is not a month old," the aunt said.

"It does not matter very much. He is in, they will say, a bad environment and must be removed as quickly as possible. This will be the argument. I fear that you must immediately convince the good doctor and nurse to maintain separate living quarters for at least the time being."

"But everyone knows."

"Yes, Miss Campbell. But in the law, it is one thing to *know* and quite another to *prove*. No time may be lost."

"I know they will comply."

"Very good. I'll be honest. This will be difficult. A difficult case."

"But Mr. O'Neal said or at least suggested that it was not insurmountable."

"Ah, Mr. Henry. John O'Neal is a wonderful politician, but he is not a lawyer and he does not know the intricacies of surrogate's court. His political skills may prove of use. Indeed, I think they may prove indispensable. But on this, you must rely on me. This is your immediate task. To separate the two love birds with whom you live."

The two visitors looked at one another.

"Oh, do not be despondent. If it can be done it will be done. You must understand, though, that you are dealing with an opponent not motivated by malice. The Sisters have dedicated their lives to caring for lost children and they are rightly and widely admired for it. We must establish not that they are wrong but that they are wrong *in this case*." His right index finger hit the desk in time with each of the final three words. "We must convince the surrogate that remaining with his aunt is the best way for the boy to thrive.

"This means, Miss Campbell, that there will have to be some adjustments in your life. You must create a stable place for the boy to live and grow. It is not enough that you say you will make it so. You must do something now. I do not know what. But something must be done.

"I daresay you have little money?"

"Yes, sir, very little."

"I shall be generous in my support," Mr. Henry said.

"That is very, very good, sir. We, both Miss Campbell and I, shall need and shall be much in your debt. Now, Miss Campbell, I believe the first thing is for you to find another place to live. With Mr. Henry's support, I hope you'll be able to settle into an apartment or flat for you and the baby and the wet nurse. Perhaps you can find another woman to share the expense and to enhance the stability. I leave that to you, but you should contemplate it.

"As I said, there is no time to lose, none at all. I will write to Mr. Fleming, who I understand you, Miss Campbell, have met, and direct him to contact me immediately should the Asylum file any papers in this matter. You must also be prepared for someone, perhaps a sister, perhaps not, to visit the clinic to examine where the baby and you live. Thus, make sure that Dr. Doyle and Nurse," he looked to his paper, "Evans are well established with beds of their own.

"I will contact you both should I have any news, and your job now is to follow my instructions. Again, there is no time to lose."

When they were on the sidewalk, both were somewhat stunned by the rapidity of their lawyer and his insistence that there was no time to lose.

61.

"**I** am sorry, miss, but the trade entrance is to the side."

Róisín drilled into the tall man blocking the door.

"I'm sure it is. I am here to see Mrs. Meade. It is a personal matter of some delicacy."

"Whom shall I say is calling?"

"Tell her it is Miss Campbell. She will know me," not vocalizing her "I hope." He waited a moment. "I am sorry. I do not have a card."

The butler nodded and moved aside and then directed her into the sitting-room. As he left, he turned and advised Róisín that he would see if madam were available.

He returned presently.

"She will see you in her study," and she followed him up the staircase, which, unlike the McNabb's, was lined with portraits of real or feigned ancestors and one each of Mr. and Mrs. Meade, to the second floor. There he knocked on the study door, and Mrs. Meade said, "Come in." Róisín found herself standing across the desk from Mrs. Meade, who was writing notes on a Louis XIV desk, much like the one she saw when she was interviewed by, and later dismissed by, Mrs. Geherty.

"I shall be right with you, my dear. Jenkins, you may leave."

When he was gone, his mistress rose and directed Róisín to a love seat that was along the right wall, where she joined her. Róisín declined her offer of tea.

"I have spoken to Mr. Meade, and I agree with him. But why are you here?"

"I need your help, Mrs. Meade."

"*Now* you need my help?"

"Please, Mrs. Meade. I hope that we may be able to tolerate one another. Yes. I need your help. Without it, our cause will be lost, and Diarmaid will be taken by the Sisters and shipped off to who knows where and neither of us will see him again."

Mrs. Meade looked at the girl. And smiled.

"We are too much alike, I think. Tell me, Miss Campbell, what is it that you need?"

Róisín explained what was happening and the likelihood that the Sisters of Charity would seek to take the child to the Foundling Asylum. It was some time before Róisín was again on the sidewalk, but she was well satisfied with her conversation.

62

Thankfully, Dr. Doyle granted Róisín leave to avoid work so she could see to what needed to be done regarding Diarmaid. So once her meeting with Mrs. Meade was over, a tired and hungry Róisín Campbell returned to her apartment, looking forward to seeing her nephew.

Several days later, as she approached the door to the building after running errands, she heard, "Róisín."

She turned and saw Elizabeth. Elizabeth Geherty. Who should have been at Bellevue.

"I left the program."

It took a moment, or three, for Róisín to understand. She could not believe it.

"I want to help you."

"Of course, you cannot do it."

"Of course, I can, and I have."

"My love. You'd be throwing everything you have worked for away."

"I can be a nurse at the clinic. You've learned more there than I ever could at Bellevue. I'm more of a nursemaid than a nurse, much as I love my friends and Sister Bowdin and Sister Taylor."

"But it probably won't work." The two went to Róisín's room and sat. Róisín told Elizabeth that she had obtained a lease on a two-bedroom apartment with servants' quarters in a new apartment building in the twenties. She was pretending it was all thanks to Mr. Henry, but the bulk of the rent was agreed to by the Meades, who happened to live on the same block and who happened to share access to a private park on the corner. Róisín did not care that her living there would rely on their continued kindness. They were his grandparents, likely the only ones he would ever have the chance to know. Her parents knew of what happened with Sophie and Diarmaid from Róisín's letters, and her mother sent her sympathies and prayers. But they were thousands of miles away and always would be.

Elizabeth, after noting she liked Meade's parents infinitely more than she liked Meade, pursued her argument.

"Being with you accomplishes several things. First, it gives you more stability in the apartment. The Gehertys may not be what they once were, but they are still respectable, in part, unfortunately, thanks to my sister. But there is a second reason. If it is known that I am your flatmate, how would it look for Mrs. McNabb to try to upset the apple cart? Even she couldn't be so vindictive. Besides from what I hear Mr. McNabb has long since found other woman on whom to shower his lusts."

Róisín did not know this and did not care to know this. Mary had long needed no justification for her hatred.

"It may not work. The Meades may withdraw their support and you may have to vacate these premises childless and return to the clinic. But I could move there with you. Don't you see? I could be with you."

The two looked at one another. Róisín did not realize it, but she had no answer to Elizabeth's final point.

So, a nervous Elizabeth gave up at Bellevue. The other girls and Sisters Bowdin and Taylor understood, and all were sad to see Elizabeth Geherty leave. But leave she did, just in time to move her things into the second bedroom in the new apartment.

63.

For several days, Mary McNabb spent a part of her morning sitting in a window seat in her room looking out onto the street. She was awaiting the arrival of the postman, and when he was gone, she nonchalantly walked down the main staircase to inquire of Bradley whether an invitation arrived.

"Not today, ma'am," he said on each of those. "Is there any in particular that you are expecting?"

She insisted there was not and climbed back to her room.

It was dawning upon her that it would not come. She did not care whether she went to the Meades' annual dinner and had declined the invitation in an earlier year when she had something better to do. But it was nearly a week since the first of her circle received her invitation and within three days so had all of the others. She had not.

That evening, she spoke to her husband after dinner.

"I'm sure it's just an oversight," McNabb assured his wife. "I shall call upon Edward Meade in the morning and get it straightened out." And that afternoon when he returned from luncheon at his club, he found his wife waiting for him and he told her that he learned that it was no oversight. The McNabbs were not invited to the event.

"Their son is a whore monger, and they presume not to invite us to their little party? Well, we shall see. I would not have gone anyway, but now I will insist that no one we know shall attend either. The impudence."

64.

The courtroom was cavernous and very dark. The rows of gaslights on the walls did little to supplement the light that managed to find its way in through the small windows near the high ceiling. The surrogate's bench—in truth a large and imposing desk—was raised. Rows of simple wooden benches for spectators to sit on stretched to the rear wall. As one neared the bench, there was a long wooden rail—known as the "bar"—with a swinging gate to allow entry into the hallowed space. In front of the bar were two long tables for the lawyers and their clients, with chairs facing the surrogate's bench, and to the left two rows of chairs, twelve in all, were on an elevated platform for use by a jury.

Normally, the room was nearly empty except for lawyers and sometimes parties who had business with the surrogate and who left quickly when their particular matter was concluded. The proceedings were slow and as lugubrious as anything in any courtroom, and the lawyers had learned to shout to be heard. The whole scene suggested something from Mr. Dickens more than anything else.

But this was not a normal morning. The Asylum had run to the court with an initial petition seeking the immediate custody of *"Baby Diarmaid Cassidy, currently in the possession of Róisín Campbell and residing at 212 East 19th Street."* The room was full of reporters and gadflies and interested people from the Irish community, and many who could not enter the courtroom mingled noisily in the hallway outside it.

Sitting at one of the tables facing the bench, the one closest to the jury box, was the Asylum's lawyer and beside him was Sister Margaret Ryan in full habit, the representative of the Foundling Asylum, the petitioner.

At the other table sat Francis Neally and Róisín Campbell. Róisín was the respondent and would soon file her cross-petition in which she sought to adopt Diarmaid. In the first row of spectator seats behind them were Mr. Henry and Elizabeth, and the former reached to hold the latter's hand as Róisín's proxy.

There was a rumble in the room of talking which ended abruptly when a clerk banged his hand on a door by the bench and shouted, "All rise," and the crowd rose and the surrogate entered, stepping up to the leather chair at his bench. Mr. Fleming followed, sitting at a desk facing out to the crowd with a stack of papers. When they were in position, the surrogate said, "You may be seated," and the crowd sat.

He called the room to order and said that there was only the one matter on the calendar, the Asylum's petition.

The Asylum's lawyer made a clear, impassioned argument supporting the immediate removal of Diarmaid from Róisín for the infant's safety pending a determination of who would ultimately have custody of him. He spoke in detail about the conditions at the clinic and the inadequate quarters for the baby, his wet nurse, and Róisín.

The surrogate, with his chin resting on his fists and occasionally looking at one of the papers before him, sat silently as he listened to the concerns of the Asylum, as did the crowd, murmuring now and then in agreement or disagreement with something the lawyer said.

The Asylum's lawyer described Róisín as being "no doubt a fine young lady" but one who was unmarried and had no choice but to work, though for a good cause, and who left the infant alone during the day.

He ended with, "Thank you, Your Honor, I have nothing further to say," and when he sat, Mr. Neally was on his feet.

"Your Honor. We appreciate the Asylum's position, but it is out of date. In light of the presence of the child, Miss

Campbell has removed herself from the apartment she had at the clinic. She has moved to a two-bedroom apartment on East Twenty-Fourth Street. There she has sufficient room for herself, the boy, and the wet nurse. The child will be safe and secure, and there is no reason for him to be removed to the Asylum. Surely it is better that he remain close to his aunt while this proceeding goes forward."

"But, Mr. Neally, what is to happen during the day? Miss Campbell is working, is she not?"

"She is, Your Honor. She has engaged the services of a nursemaid as well to see to the care of the boy throughout the day. She is with the child as we speak. Miss Campbell will return from her work, which I believe we can all agree is important work at the clinic, at least once during the day. It is not far. This will provide more than adequate protection for the baby while you decide the important issue of what is to become of him. I should also like to advise the Court that Miss Campbell has the further support of a Miss Elizabeth Geherty, late of the Bellevue Nursing School, who is also training to be a nurse and also working at the clinic. Miss Geherty, who is sitting in the courtroom"—and Mr. Neally pointed to her and the crowd gawked to see her as she reddened—"has made her residence with Miss Campbell and is fully committed to providing whatever assistance Miss Campbell requires to care for the child.

"In sum, Your Honor, we believe that to take baby Diarmaid and put him in a group, institutional setting, however caring we know the Sisters will be to him"—and he nodded to Sister Ryan—"can be no substitute for the individual attention he will obtain by remaining with his aunt and those who have pledged to support her."

Mr. Neally concluded by telling the surrogate that the rent for the apartment and the wages of the nursemaid were taken care of by a third-party benefactor (everyone assuming it was her friend, Mr. Henry) and that she would be financially secure in the premises.

The surrogate said he'd heard enough. He rose, and the room rose with him, and went into his chambers followed by Mr. Fleming. The moment the door closed the crowd resumed the roar that the surrogate had gaveled quiet earlier, much animated by what it had heard.

Róisín could barely breathe as she paced next to Mr. Henry, and Elizabeth massaged her left arm. An eternity seemed to pass before the surrogate retook the bench, at which point the same "all rise" and "be seated" was repeated.

He ruled that given the unusual nature of the proceeding and notwithstanding the Asylum's concern the immediate well-being of the baby, Róisín had sufficiently presented evidence that satisfied him that the current situation—the *status quo*—should remain until he could hear and decide the adoption petition itself.

With that, the court adjourned. Mr. Neally said it was a victory, and a crucial one, but that the larger battle lay ahead and that they would need to work diligently to convince the surrogate to maintain Róisín in custody of the infant.

The surrogate set the matter down for a further hearing only two weeks later. He issued an order appointing a lawyer to act for Diarmaid, as a way to have someone express what Diarmaid might think of the goings-on.

65.

After the victory, Mr. Neally sat with Róisín, Elizabeth, and Mr. Henry in his office.

"This is only the beginning. The Asylum is revered, including by the surrogate. We will not succeed by attacking it and its motives."

"I would never attack its motives," Róisín said.

"No, Miss Campbell, I would not think you would." After offering one to Mr. Henry, who declined, he lit his cigar, much the way Mr. O'Neal had. "It is very delicate what we must do, but we must do it."

The others waited.

"Our hope is to gain the support of the community. The surrogate is a good, honest man, no matter what Fleming may think, and he will do what he thinks is best for the boy. But he is not immune from community or political pressure." He took a long drag on his cigar, watching the cloud of smoke he generated rise. He leaned on his arms, bent on the desktop.

"The best way for you, Miss Campbell, is to get married. I know Mr. O'Neal believes it might be considered a subterfuge, but now I believe we must seriously consider it."

He looked from her to Mr. Henry and back.

"Mr. Neally," she said, "Mr. Henry and I have discussed that prospect and agree that it is quite impossible."

Mr. Neally again looked from one to another.

"As a last resort?" he asked.

The two others looked at one another. Mr. Henry touched Róisín's hand and said, "Perhaps. As a last resort."

"Well, then, we must work in a different direction." He sent them to again see Mr. O'Neal at Tammany Hall.

66

Róisín and Neally and the rest seeking to allow her to adopt the baby were against a formidable obstacle from the start, the Catholic Church. As with the Sisters of Charity, there was no question that the Church was acting in what it believed was the best interests of the child. In New York the influence of the Catholic Church when it came to the Irish community was immense. It went from John McCloskey, who months earlier became America's first cardinal, to the parish priest to the congregations that celebrated mass throughout the city each Sunday and on the Church's many Holy Days of Obligation.

They would insist that the only appropriate place for a child such as Diarmaid to be raised was the home of a strict Catholic family with at least a mother and a father and, even better, some children. And were Róisín to do nothing, they would prevail and Diarmaid would be gone. O'Neal, though, thought the notoriety that had led the Church to become involved could be used to Róisín's advantage.

It was the peculiarity of Róisín's position that made this possible. She cared for the aches and illnesses of thousands of lower east side Irish Catholics. She cared for her poor sister having come from Ireland, who might have been a wayward girl but was an Irish one, who lost one little boy shortly after he was born and who died while giving birth to a second, Diarmaid Cassidy. Róisín came forward to undertake the care for the boy, surrendering her plans and ambitions to do so.

The Irish in New York were accustomed to the self-sacrificing Irish farmgirls, who came and would forego marriage so they could earn money to send home so that a brother or a sister or a cousin could join them in New York or elsewhere in America. Róisín had sacrificed finding a husband so she might care for them at the clinic. She was willing to do the same for Diarmaid.

O'Neal well understood that while the womenfolk could not vote and votes were the lifeblood of Tammany, the menfolk would never turn on an issue their wives and mothers and even daughters thought important. He knew he had to make the politics normally within the grasp of the Church shift to Róisín Campbell. The surrogate did not act based on the politics—he was indeed a good man—but he was a product of politics and could be swayed. To O'Neal, he was not putting a thumb on the surrogate's scale beyond matching the one, or two or three, that the Church put on the other side.

He knew well enough not to speak to Róisín of such sausage-making, though he did know she would soon figure it out, as Mr. Henry would. He needed her to understand just enough from the start the reality of the politics of the case.

In this, O'Neal was mistaken. Róisín immediately understood. Her time in New York was spent moving between the various strata of New York society, from the most dank tenement to the most glorious mansion. Her encounter with Sister Margaret Ryan at the Asylum also convinced her that she could not be passive.

Since her new apartment was on the same block as the Meades' house, it was a short walk for Róisín. She rang the bell and the Meades' butler quickly recognized her and his haughtiness was gone. He led Róisín into the sitting-room while he fetched Mrs. Meade.

Róisín gave her a report on the events at the surrogate's court and her conversation with Neally and later with O'Neal.

"Why do you not simply marry Henry? Will that not put an end to it?"

Mrs. Meade seemed at least half-satisfied by the answer and asked Róisín what she wanted. The idea and then the prospect of having her grandson nearby was now deep in her heart, and Róisín hoped, rightly, that she would do whatever she could to continue the arrangement.

67

"Fiona Meade, as I live and breathe."

"Yes, Abigail. It has been too long."

The two, Fiona Meade and Abigail Geherty, knew each other from even before the latter's daughter was engaged to marry the former's son. But with the reversals that led to the Gehertys' disappearance from society, there was no reason for their paths to cross and they never in fact did. When the McNabbs' butler, the long-suffering Bradley, handed Mrs. Geherty the card that read "Mrs. Fiona Meade," she was more stunned than she had been in years.

Now the woman herself was in her sitting-room. More precisely and as Mrs. Geherty was frequently reminded, the McNabbs' sitting-room. They sat, and Mrs. Meade declined the offer of refreshments.

"I am sent by your daughter."

"Mary?"

"No, dear. Elizabeth. The one I always liked."

Mrs. Geherty's confusion ratcheted up.

"I will not delay. I am ultimately here for Róisín Campbell. I believe you know her."

Mrs. Geherty nodded.

"She is a very good friend of Elizabeth's. Miss Campbell has solicited me to assist her in the business of her nephew, which I am certain you have heard of."

Mrs. Geherty said of course she had but wondered what that had to do with her.

"It is simple. It concerns the daughter I do not like...so much. Mrs. McNabb. Elizabeth told me that much of her differences with her sister revolves around Elizabeth's friendship with Miss Campbell. Now, you may understand my delicate position in the matter"—which Mrs. Geherty did but neither woman would speak of—"and, frankly, I desire that the court award custody of the child to his aunt. That is, to Miss Campbell."

Mrs. Geherty had no sense of where her former friend was going. When she did, when she understood Mrs. Meade wished her to keep her informed so much as she could about whether Mrs. McNabb intended to do anything to interfere with Róisín's adoption, Abigail Geherty agreed. When Mrs. Meade left, Mrs. Geherty took out a small sheet of paper and sat at the small desk in the room allotted to her by her daughter on the fourth floor where she could conduct personal business.

My Dearest Lizzie,

I have learned, I cannot say how, about your decision related to the child and to ~~Miss Campbell~~ Róisín. I regret doing anything to separate you from her. You will have my full support and blessing going forward—and I am sure your father's—but you will understand that now it is I that must cut off contact with you, at least until the matter involving the child is settled.

I fear that contact with you will be deemed contact with Róisín and that that will have repercussions for a source with which we are both familiar that we must avoid.

For now, please do not take my silence as anything but my full love and support for you and your good friend. And pray that I shall soon be able to share your joy.

Your always proud and loving, Mother

68.

When Mrs. Meade stepped from her barouche, she had the coachman move it away from the house she was visiting. She steeled herself and climbed the three steps to a single, large ebony door and she pulled the bell to its right. Soon a butler in full livery appeared. He stepped aside, and she entered the foyer. She handed him her card and asked that Mrs. Reynolds be told that she would like to have a brief word.

The butler showed her into the sitting-room and left, leaving her to gaze out the large window that overlooked the street. This was the first time she was in the house, and it was as grand a one as she'd ever entered. The divide was too far to bridge. Before long, the butler returned and said he regretted that Mrs. Reynolds was indisposed and could not see her.

Mrs. Meade asked for paper and a pen, which he fetched from a secretary in the far corner of the room. She sat and leaned across a small table to write.

My Dear Mrs. Reynolds,

> *I would not presume to disturb you were it not a matter of some personal urgency and great personal importance. I beg you accord me just a moment of your time.*

Your obedient servant,
(Mrs.) Fiona Meade

The butler bowed and took the folded message on a silver tray to his mistress.

It was not long before Hyacinth Reynolds floated into the room, and Mrs. Meade turned to see her, hands outstretched as if they had met thousands of times when it was perhaps four.

"Dempsey. Please get us some tea," she said as she directed Mrs. Meade to one of two armless chairs that offered a view to the street.

"I am so sorry I was detained, and I apologize for keeping you waiting so long. We must meet together more often, my dear. I see so little of you."

"Mrs. Reynolds—"

"Hyacinth, my dear Fiona, Hyacinth."

"Yes, Hyacinth. You have likely heard about some unpleasant business involving an Irish girl who died giving birth."

"Oh, yes. Dreadful news. Dreadful. But what can that have to do with you?"

"Yes. You may have heard other news suggesting that my family is connected with the child."

"Oh, Fiona. I may have heard such, but I never put any credence in rumors. Good God, what do people say of me? I neither know nor care. So, while I may have heard a thing or two, I pay it no mind."

"That is very good of you. But without regard to whether the rumors are true, the fact remains that the child is viewed by at least some, lesser people as having a connection with...my son."

Dempsey interrupted with his tray of tea and biscuits, which he placed on the small table Mrs. Meade recently used when she wrote her plea to her host. He poured the tea and was gone with the closing of the door.

"Hyacinth. I must be honest. The poor girl's sister is seeking custody of the child. You may not know this, but she once worked for you, Róisín Campbell."

This surprised Mrs. Reynolds.

"Campbell? A pretty Irish girl? My Marilyn liked her, and I never understood why she insisted that the girl be dismissed. But it was long ago, and we are sometimes overly solicitous of the wishes of our children, are we not?"

She took a sip of her tea, and her guest did the same.

"But the girl. I never connected her with the baby. Are you sure?"

"I have met with her."

"Why would you have met with her?"

"It is a complicated story, but ultimately she and my son's former fiancée became good friends. Miss Campbell, fearful that my family might seek to adopt the child, spoke to Mr. Meade and myself and implored us not to do so, to keep the field free so she could adopt."

"I fear, Fiona, that I still do not understand what I can have to do with this."

"I come to ask that the Children's Aid Society not seek the baby."

"It is a Catholic baby. Why would we interfere?"

"I do not think the Society would, but I merely ask for your assurance, as a member of the board, that it not."

"No, Fiona." She shook her head. "It is for the Foundling Asylum to get involved. We stay clear when it appears for such a child. And it has become involved, if I understand correctly."

"Yes, it has."

"Although the natural aunt seeks custody. This Miss Campbell is not married, as I understand it."

"No, she is not. She is working as a nurse."

"A nurse. She did well after I dismissed her. Perhaps she should thank me...I joke."

"So, you will not get involved?"

"The Society will not. I do not know why the Asylum is involved. One would think that there are more than enough Irish urchins to keep the sisters busy enough without grabbing one from his aunt."

Mrs. Reynolds placed her cup down, as did Mrs. Meade. She leaned closer to the other woman.

"Fiona." She reached across to touch the other's hands. Her voice dropped low. "I know what was said of the poor mother and about the poor child. I ask you. If you wish me to do what I can as a mother to keep this little boy near you, please tell me and I will do so. I will ask you nothing more."

Mrs. Meade held tightly to the superior woman's hands as she tried to contain her tears.

"Hyacinth. He is my grandson. I cannot lose my grandson. I have no right to ask anything of you. But I beg you. I—"

Mrs. Reynolds pulled her hands away and before Mrs. Meade knew it, she felt a gentle touch on her left cheek and a finger removed a tear that escaped.

The moment passed. Mrs. Reynolds stood, and her guest followed. The host rang a bell, and Dempsey entered.

"Mrs. Meade, it was so nice of you to visit. We must do it again. I give your husband and dear son my regards, and I assure you that you, and others, will be in my thoughts."

Mrs. Meade was shortly on the sidewalk, walking towards her carriage, praying that Mrs. Reynolds did more than just think about her Diarmaid.

69.

"Marilyn Anne Reynolds."

Mary McNabb stared at the card she just lifted from the tray brought to her by Bradley. She was in the rear of the house and hadn't noticed the very fine carriage or the regal woman who'd walked to her front door.

Marilyn Anne long regretted having Róisín dismissed. She never had a maid before and had not had one since with whom she felt as comfortable. Róisín was, of course, gorgeous, but never gave the slightest indication of caring about that one way or the other, and Marilyn never considered her a threat to her own prospects. She would have liked to have spent her first hours in the morning and her last ones at night talking about her dreams and prospects as she did when Róisín worked in her house. She had yet to marry though her brothers had. When her mother told her the news she received from Mrs. Meade, she was glad to learn how well things had gone for Róisín, however difficult the journey. With her mother, she agreed Róisín's dismissal, in the end, proved a blessing.

Her mother had not asked Marilyn Anne to visit Mrs. McNabb. Although the Reynoldses were much the superior family, Mrs. McNabb long treated Marilyn Anne as if it were the other way round and being the sweet thing she was Marilyn Anne accepted it and took it in stride. The unpleasantness with Róisín at the ball, though, weighed on her. When they came upon one another after, Marilyn was as cold to Mrs. McNabb as was socially acceptable, and she found this met with some success as Mrs. McNabb rarely ventured to engage with her on any but the most superficial basis.

She now stood in the McNabbs' sitting-room, looking out the window at the traffic passing. It felt like an unhappy house, starting with Bradley, the butler. She knew that Mrs. McNabb's parents were nearly prisoners and that her sister had abandoned it for Róisín. She knew *of* Elizabeth more than she knew her. Perhaps that would change when the awful business about the child was resolved. Which is one reason she was standing in the McNabbs' sitting-room.

The door suddenly opened, and Mary McNabb entered with the emptiest of smiles.

"Oh, my dearest Marilyn. It has been too long."

Marilyn offered the least civility she could and took Mary's hands in her own.

"Yes, Mary. It is good to see you."

"To what do I owe the pleasure?"

Marilyn declined Mary's offer to sit with a brusque, "I must be brief as I have an appointment for which I must not be late."

If Mary could direct Bradley to toss the pretentious spinster whence she came she would do so. But she could do nothing but hold her feigned smile.

"I will be direct with you, Mrs. McNabb. You once bade me do something that I came to regret. It has turned out for the best at least."

Mrs. McNabb racked her brain to understand what the other woman was talking about but did not get far when Marilyn Anne told her.

"If you do anything to interfere with Róisín Campbell's adoption of her nephew, it will be made known far and wide."

With that, she left a stunned Mrs. McNabb in her wake as she opened the door to the sitting-room and walked through the door poor Bradley opened for her and walked to her carriage. Mrs. McNabb watched Marilyn Anne Reynolds get in the very fine brougham and the very fine brougham disappear down the block.

70.

Late on the afternoon on the day before the final hearing at which Diarmaid's fate would be decided, Róisín, Mr. Henry, and Elizabeth sat in Mr. Neally's office. One of the lawyer's colleagues made room for himself on a windowsill by plopping a pile of tied papers on the floor, and his lower legs were rocking front-and-rear.

"I cannot say what will happen. Usually, I can. But this matter has many twists and turns," Mr. Neally said.

His colleague echoed him. "I stopped by with Fleming this morning, and he gave me no hint. I do not think he knew, but, of course, he pretended that he did."

"Miss Campbell," Mr. Neally resumed after he nodded. "We have done what we can do. We will find many allies in the courtroom, word having spread far and wide about you and the baby. For this, they will defy Cardinal McCloskey himself. But we can never know." He paused for both effect and because he was genuinely nervous about the child's fate. "We can never know."

The group fell quiet except for the unremitting street noise, a silence smacked away by Mr. Henry.

"Mr. Neally, sir. If it will matter, I will marry my dear Miss Campbell."

Róisín's head shot to look at her friend.

"Oh, Mr. Henry. You must not do that," she said.

He shook his head and addressed the lawyer.

"I said that I would if we must, and I stand by it."

Mr. Neally put up a hand.

"Are you certain of this, Mr. Henry?" though he was looking at Róisín.

"I am."

"Miss Campbell?"

She paused. "If it means keeping Diarmaid, I'll do it." She turned to Mr. Henry. "I do love you, of course. But we, neither of us, will love in the way a husband and a wife should. It must, however, be enough."

Mr. Henry broke into a spontaneous smile and reached for her hand. "I know it will be enough."

Mr. Neally looked at his colleague, and then back at the three, including a confused Elizabeth Geherty.

"Well, as you know, we cannot say how the surrogate will rule. I think there's a good, a very good chance that he shall rule in our favor though it is a near-run thing. If I determine that we are losing, Miss Campbell, I will touch your shoulder. If you nod, I will advise the surrogate that you and Mr. Henry intend to marry. I will tell him that you shall be married promptly and request a brief adjournment of the hearing so that such a joining may occur.

"It would be, I daresay, quite unusual, but under the circumstances, I believe it shall be enough. If I make the proposal to the surrogate, I don't believe that the surrogate will deny us the adjournment."

He looked at his colleague, who volunteered, "I must agree with Mr. Neally. I think, if you are willing, that this is the course we must take."

Róisín had not expected it but hoped that Mr. Henry would do what he did. He had his own life and his friends, as she did hers. They enjoyed each other's company immensely. It was, however, a particular kind of intimacy that a change such as marriage might well destroy. That it could be used in a last-ditch attempt only when all was otherwise lost made it palatable to them both. With a squeeze to Elizabeth's hand, Róisín hoped her dearest friend would understand.

As Mr. Neally made some final comments to them all, particularly imploring Róisín to attempt to get a good night's sleep and to have something easy to digest in the morning before coming to court, there was a knock on the door and five sets of eyes turned to it as one.

"Enter," Mr. Neally barked.

In came a message boy, holding a cap in one hand and an envelope in the other. Never the subject of so much interest, he blanched slightly before stuttering that he had an envelope for Francis Neally, Esq.

"I'm Neally," the man himself said, and the boy handed the envelope over, with Mr. Neally's colleague fishing a coin from his vest pocket to give the boy, who took it and turned to go in a single motion.

The room was still as Mr. Neally read.

"I do not believe it," and a smile shot across his face. "They are withdrawing the petition and asking the surrogate to award custody to you, Miss Campbell. See for yourself," and he handed the paper to his client.

She did not understand. She looked up at Neally and back at the paper, recognizing the signature as that from the Asylum's attorney.

"What does it mean?"

"It means that they have surrendered. Diarmaid will be yours upon the satisfaction of certain formalities with the surrogate."

With the words still echoing in the room, his colleague was off the windowsill and rushing from the room.

"Fleming will surely still be there. I shall speak to him to confirm this news." With that, he was gone.

"I do not doubt the news. It is clear as day," Neally told the stunned trio before him.

71

The hearing was on in the morning, and Róisín did not know whether she should believe what happened hours before. She awoke in the night, soothed by the gentle breathing of Elizabeth beside her, and turned onto her back. More and more, her friend remained with her instead of going to her own room, and the two often drifted off together. It was a reminder of Sophie's sleep (which she'd never again know), and she hoped she would hear Elizabeth's forever.

Róisín thought of that last night in her bedroom in Hospital, the fear and the excitement for the future, and felt much the same in the eerie silence the city briefly fell into in the nighttime. As then, her life was about to change irrevocably. She knew she was not prepared but prayed that if she were given the chance, she would learn to be at least a capable mother to Diarmaid as she learned to be at least a capable woman in America. Aware of who was beside her, she knew she would not be alone in it, and with that she turned to her side and fell into a sleep that was more peaceful than it had been perhaps since her sister's death.

She was surprisingly calm in the morning, though barely able to eat, when Mr. Henry appeared and took Elizabeth and her to the courthouse in a waiting cab. There was a crowd milling around on the sidewalk and many recognized Róisín from her prior appearance. Several said the building was not yet open.

It was not long, though, before Neally and his colleague hopped from a cab.

"They will let us in," he said, and as they started up the courthouse steps Róisín saw Mrs. Geherty on the side and bade her join them. The group was allowed entry, and their words echoed through the empty hall when they were through the doors. When Elizabeth noticed her mother, they exchanged hugs. She introduced her to Mr. Henry, who introduced himself to Abigail with a light peck on her right hand.

Neally's colleague told the group it was true. Fleming confirmed it. The hearing would be limited to the question of Róisín's fitness to act as Diarmaid's "mother," and it was likely to be held in the surrogate's chambers, his office just off the courtroom where things could remain confidential. The lawyer appointed to act on behalf of Diarmaid had, Neally's colleague said, agreed to the arrangement.

"It is a mere formality, Miss Campbell, mere formality," he said.

Mrs. Geherty pulled Róisín and Elizabeth aside, to a quiet corner where their words could not be heard by others.

"It was Mrs. Reynolds, Fiona Meade told me. She was able to convince Sister Ryan that being in the custody of his dear aunt, beloved in the community," which reddened Róisín's face, "and being seen by someone who may be his grandmother—which everyone knows Mrs. Meade is— would be far superior to any other resolution of a difficult situation.

"Mrs. Reynolds guaranteed to Sister Ryan that Mrs. Meade would be a part of the boy's family and would see to it that he was raised properly—or improperly Mrs. Reynolds good-naturedly added—as a Catholic. And that the guarantee was accompanied by the prospect of a generous financial gift to the Asylum as well."

Róisín was overwhelmed. She had little time to dwell on it, though, as they were called into court and she entered the courtroom held up in part by Elizabeth's arm and followed by Mr. Henry with his arm through Elizabeth's mother's and soon after they were in their places the courtroom was full of those who the guards finally let in off the street.

When the clerk said, "All rise," all rose and when the surrogate said, "Please be seated," they all sat.

"Thank you," the judge said to the dead silent room. "I received a letter late yesterday from counsel for the petitioner, the Foundling Asylum. It seems that it is desirous of withdrawing its petition"—which set off a wave of talking that ended only after the surrogate banged his gavel and called "Order" three or four times.

"I will have order." When he had it, he replaced his gavel on the bench. "The letter advised me that the Foundling Asylum has determined that it would be in the best interest of the child in question for his aunt, respondent and cross-petitioner Róisín Campbell, to have sole custody of baby Diarmaid Cassidy." He looked down at the lawyer for the Asylum, again sitting next to Sister Ryan who remained stoic throughout. The lawyer jumped to his feet.

"Yes, Your Honor. That is the case. My client has considered the matter in the light of the materials submitted by Miss Campbell and other information that came to its attention that I am not at liberty to disclose and concluded that Miss Campbell would be far and away the best candidate to be a mother to this little boy."

The lawyer sat; Sister Ryan still stoic.

"In light of that, does the Asylum withdraw its petition and support the cross-petition for custody of Miss Campbell?"

The lawyer jumped back up.

"Yes, Your Honor. The Asylum does just that."

The surrogate looked at Sister Ryan and saw a barely perceptible nod.

The lawyer acting for Diarmaid stood and said he, too, thought it was in the boy's best interest to be adopted by his aunt.

"Very well," the surrogate said. "Subject to my interview with Miss Campbell, the cross-petition is granted. We will adjourn to my chambers now to discuss the matter further."

The surrogate asked that Róisín, Neally, and the lawyer acting for Diarmaid join him in his chambers and banged his gavel to signal that the hearing was adjourned.

Even before he and the others were through the door with Mr. Fleming to his chambers, the courtroom burst into noise, with several reporters rushing out to file news stories on the shocking development in the matter of *Diarmaid Cassidy, infant.*

After speaking with Róisín and satisfying himself, the surrogate approved of her and her intentions for her nephew. While a crowd milled around the courtroom and the hallway outside it, the surrogate's dour expression turned to a smile.

"Well, Miss Campbell. I see no reason not to permit you to adopt your nephew. You realize that it is tantamount to you signing on as his mother, and you have told me that that is your understanding and that that is your intention and that you will have the support of others in this undertaking. Accordingly, and with the consent of counsel retained to represent Diarmaid in this proceeding"—who nodded—"I will sign an order confirming your adoption of the boy."

With that, Róisín again breathed. The surrogate said they would put something on the record, and everyone rose with him and filed out into the courtroom. When the door to the chambers opened, a sudden silence swept across. Elizabeth stood at the front, on the far side of the bar, between Mr. Henry and her mother, squeezing both of their hands until a smile directed at her from Róisín arrived and she, too, could again breathe.

It did not take long, the surrogate's putting his approval of the adoption on the record, with all of the required "are-there-any-objections?"/"no-objection-Your-Honor"s.
When the surrogate was again gone to his chambers with Mr. Fleming and the crowd resumed its buzzing, Sister Ryan approached Róisín. It was loud, so she leaned in, her lips close to Róisín's ear.

"I am happy for you, my child. It is a grave responsibility, this precious boy, and I pray that you shall be a good mother to him."

She pulled away and turned, only to have Róisín grab her arm to turn her back.

"Please, sister, tell me I can be a good mother."

It was a bit louder than the sister's whisper, but only Elizabeth also heard. Sister Ryan reached for Róisín's left hand with her right and tapped it with her left hand.

"If we did not believe that, we would not have done what we did," and with that the good sister released her grip, adding, "We will pray for you," and looking into Elizabeth's eyes and reaching her hand so Elizabeth could take it, said "for all of you." The sister again turned, and the crowd parted to allow her and the Asylum's attorney to pass.

Elizabeth stepped behind Róisín and wrapped her arms around her friend.

"You will be a wonderful mother," she whispered.

Róisín turned on her friend quickly to face her, and with the most beatific smile told her that she would be a wonderful aunt. And the crowd cleared for them and for Mr. Henry and Abigail Geherty and a line waiting for cabs deferred to the four so that Róisín could go to her son.

THE END*

* Except as continued in *A Studio on Bleecker Street*

<u>Afterward</u>

A Studio on Bleecker Street

Y ou, dear reader, may recall that in early 1874 Emily Connor abandoned her friend Elizabeth Geherty for Greenwich Village, "moving in with an unmarried friend who had artistic aspirations." (It's back on page 164.) That aspiring artist is Clara Bowman. Her story, and several interactions with Róisín, Elizabeth, and Diarmaid and others in this book, and of course Emily, are in *A Studio on Bleecker Street*, which was published in March 2021 and is available as both an ebook and a paperback.

A Studio on Bleecker Street begins on May 12, 1872, a rainy Sunday in New York. Its last chapter takes place on May 12, 1879. Clara Bowman and Emily Connor learn of the final hearing here by reading about it the next morning in the *New York Sun* newspaper while they sit at a café near their apartment the morning after. The article is entitled "Single Aunt Awarded Custody of Orphaned Nephew."

About the Author

Joseph P. Garland is a native New Yorker. He is a practicing lawyer, and lives in Westchester County, New York. This is his first novel.

In addition to *A Studio on Bleecker Street* and 2022's *A Maid's Life: Unexpected Love in New York's Gilded Age*, he has written *I Am Alex Locus*, a contemporary novel set chiefly in and around New York City.

For further information on these and other books and stories, please visit: DermodyHouse.com/books.

Acknowledgments

Thanks to the many who read my manuscript at various points along the way and who made constructive comments, nearly all of which are reflected in the final product.

My sisters Patty Garland, Clio Garland, and Liz Sauer, my brother Jimmy Garland, and my cousin Donna Vaters provided useful insights as did my mother-in-law, Teresa Grogan, who grew up in the Town of Hospital and is a retired nurse and has given me insights in many things Irish for the book. Editor Cassandra Filice (@CassandraFilice) took several looks *gratis* and provided incredibly valuable feedback, as did publicist Susan Schwartzman. From Twitter, I obtained a regular dose of photographs of clothing from the period from incomparable @WikiVictorian (Helena DiGiusti) of Andalusia. Also, the description of where Elizabeth liked to sit and read in Stockbridge when the weather was pleasant was from "Her Favourite Pasttime" by British artist George Dunlop Leslie, RA (1864), which was posted by @WikiVictorian as well.

Jessica DeMarco-Jacobson (@Jessicadmj) read this novel and earlier recommended *Agnes Grey* by Anne Brontë to me, which is the book in Róisín's hands on that fateful day when Elizabeth returned. The loneliness of a governess attributed to Deidre O'Sullivan here is from that book and a memo comparing her to Jane Eyre by Jessica.

The Dermody House logo was produced by my sister-in-law, Beth Lin Garland, and her children's names are among those in the Campbell family. And, of course, I could not do this without the constant support of my wife, Bernice Garland.

It has been said that "Campbell" is a Scottish name. Indeed it is, the Campbells being a major clan. It is also the surname for many Irish and while my grandmother's birth surname was Dermody—hence the name of the publishing house—her widowed mother married John Campbell, though while I know my Campbells came from Ireland, I do not know from what part. A bit of that story, a mixture of fact and fiction, is in *Bridget & Joseph in 1918*, quite a short novella available in both ebook and paperback.